Esteban's Quest

by

Nick Iuppa & John Pesqueira

ESTEBAN'S QUEST

Cover designed by David Pettigrew
Cover photo: © 2016 Blend Images/Shutterstock

Published by Dos Milagros Press

Visit the author website: http://www.nickiuppawrites.com

ISBN 13: 978-0-9863241-6-1
ISBN 10: 0-9863241-6-7

10 9 8 7 6 5 4 3 2 1

Novels by Nick Iuppa & John Pesqueira

THE CARLOS MANN TRILOGY
Alicia's Ghost
Alicia's Sin
Alicia Bewitched

Avenging Adelita

Novels by Nick Iuppa

Taken by Witches
Bloody Bess and the Doomsday Games

Praise for Alicia's Ghost

"Irresistible characters in a wicked tale of suspense"
— Suzanna B. Stinnett, Author of *Starship Interlude*

"Who could have guessed that ghost sex would be so hot?!?! This page-turner had so many twists and turns that my head was spinning." — Janey Baker, Actress

"Ghostly fun."
— Marc Wade, Executive Producer, Digital Media

"Funny & fun to read! Kept me wondering what would happen next."
— Eric Dueker, Filmmaker

"Incredibly imaginative!" — Chuck Reedy, Author

"The storytelling is excellent. Can't wait for the sequel."
— Elke Hitto, Writer/Journalist

"I love the characters, and Alicia... these guys have the Latina in her down to a science."
— Becky Escamilla, Constant Reader

"So intriguing... demands attention."
— Rick Emond, Graphic Novelist

"These guys certainly spin a great tale. Hope they keep cranking out stories for readers to enjoy."
— Dave Couzins, Author of *Domers*

"If you think you'd like a world where ghosts whip up dim sum and enjoy making love with the living, then this book is for you."
— Terry Borst, Screenwriter

Dedication

For Lauren Ayer –
for all her good advice, her trust, and her sense of poetry.

.

Acknowledgments

We'd like to thank the friends who offered valuable advice during the creation of this book, especially: Natalia Manelska, David Pettigrew, Bram Druckman, Kimberly Behl, Maria Johnson, and Norma Cervantes. We appreciate the fast, professional, and very competent services we received from our graphic designer, Laurie Douglas. And, again, thanks to Janet Grady, for her honest, dependable, and courageous story advice and editorial work.

"A horrible judgment seemed to fall on La Sentencia, our town. I could smell evil in the air. It was everywhere. Soon came the terrible dust storms that brought sickness, death, and mysterious events. Then came incredible poverty. We could only fight with prayer and hope. We needed a miracle."

—Luís Romo, Proprietor, Tres Flores Restaurant
La Sentencia, Arizona

"I sing of arms and the man."

—Virgil, The Aeneid

Table of Contents

The Characters

Searchers for Cíbola
In the 16th Century:
Estebanico Dorantes – Moor from North Africa, and original
    guide on the first Spanish expedition to find The Seven
    Cities of Gold

In the 21st Century:
Esteban (Stevie) Dorantes – dreamer and leader of a modern
    quest to find The Seven Cities of Gold, 20th generation
    great grandson of the original Estebanico Dorantes

The Extended Romo Family
Luís Romo – El Patron, also called Papa, aging owner of Tres
    Flores Restaurant
Carmen Romo – his wife
Mario Romo – age 7, Luís and Carmen's grandson
Vanessa Romo – Mario's divorced mother

Gabriel (Gabe) Romo – Luís and Carmen's nephew, COO at
    the Blackmore Mining Company
Cecilia (Ceci, Cess) Moreno – Head of Human Resources at
    the Blackmore Mining Company, Gabe's girlfriend
Richard (Rich) Romo – Gabe's cousin

Lorena Torres – age 17, Luís and Carmen's granddaughter
Yolanda Torres – Lorena's mother, Vanessa's sister
Kenny McLaughlin – age 18, Lorena Torres's boyfriend

Sophia Gianello – age 5, mysterious visitor to La Sentencia

At the Blackmore Mine

Charles Augustus Blackmore — age 75, owner of the
   Blackmore Mining Company
Devlin Lucero – CFO of Blackmore Mining
Donny Hainer – VP of Marketing at Blackmore Mining

Other Citizens of La Sentencia

Jessica Amado – junior high school substitute teacher
VL Johnson DVM – town veterinarian, reporter for the town
   newspaper – El Milagro
Melinda (Mel) Johnson DVM – partner with her husband in
   the veterinary clinic
Bruce McLaughlin – President, CFO and founder of
   McCarwash chain – Kenny's brother
Waldo Mortimer MA – Principal of La Sentencia Junior High
   School

On the Quest

Dido – owner of Dido's Casino (and hotel) somewhere in the
   deserts of Arizona
San Pablo of the Cars – prophet who lives alone in the desert
Chucho (Chuck) Johnson – age 19, San Pablo's disciple
Father Samson – pastor of the Mission of Our Lady of
   Ominous Foreboding

Dwayne Rowdy – Native American movie star
Donald Vito – famous Hollywood producer/director

Acalon – desert chieftain
Liliana – his daughter
Coyotl – a warrior

Esteban's Quest

Prologue

The Haboob, a raging wall of wind a mile high and a hundred miles wide, roared across the Arabian Desert. It flattened tall trees, tore smaller ones up by the roots, slashed and bloodied every creature in its path with knife-blades of swirling sand.

Hamud Ansari spotted it coming, felt the stillness before the storm. It was almost as if the little oasis where they had pitched their tents was holding its breath waiting for the deadly onslaught.

In an instant he knew that this was no ordinary Haboob but a hideous beast from some Hollywood sci-fi epic, a monster that tore down homes, swept up humans and animals, and carried them off tangled amid the wreckage it had wrenched from the desert floor.

"Guarda il vento ... il muro di vento sporco," cried little Sophia.

The five-year-old girl stood behind Ansari looking at the oncoming storm. Then, she turned and rushed into the tent that stood behind her. It too seemed to be waiting in horrified anticipation for the winds to come and plunder it.

"Papà! Guarda il vento ... il muro di vento sporco," she repeated to her father who sat in a chair at the far end of the tent. She grabbed him by his hands, pulled him to his feet, and led him out to see the vision that had so terrified her.

"A wall of dirty wind," said her father, Giancarlo. He was repeating the little girl's words in English as they made their way outside. Behind them, Claudia, the girl's mother, followed.

"Is there no place safe?" she asked when she saw the maelstrom swirling toward them.

Ansari heard her and gestured to another tent that his men had just set up across the little oasis. They had lashed it firmly between three tall palm trees whose trunks stood like the pillars of some great cathedral.

"In there," Ansari called, "Quick."

Claudia followed Ansari to the fortified structure, as did little Sophia, but not Giancarlo. Instead, he raced back to the first tent to grab the greatest discovery he had ever made. It was a silvery object shaped like a shallow bowl. It had a wide rim etched with strange runic figures, and, inside it, a helicoid pattern spiraled hypnotically to a point that somehow seemed to sing to anyone who stared at it for more than a brief moment.

This was the kind of object that had led Dr. Giancarlo Gianello and his family to this desolate spot. Nine thousand years earlier it had been the home of the ancient Elamites. The noted archaeologist was not about to leave his treasure to the punishing fury of the wind. And so he clutched it to him as he raced out into the storm, which at that moment seemed to pause and gather all its fury just as it was about to descend upon the little encampment.

And then it hit.

Gianello had just reached the fortified tent, had just opened its door, but in doing so, he let in the wildness of the wind. It swirled its razorblade sand through the tent, tore it from the trees, and then swept away the mighty trees as well. It tossed the occupants into the open and tangled them into the flailing fabric of the tent. Then it lifted them all, carrying them away screaming: Ansari, Giancarlo, Claudia, and all the workers... everyone that is except little Sophia.

She lay amid the swirling sands, somehow sheltered by the one massive palm that had not been swept away. She raised her eyes and watched as the killer storm dragged her parents and all that supported them up into the skies and out of sight.

"Mamma... Papà," she called, "non potete lasciarmi! Vi prego di tornare, per favore!"

But, in spite of her pleas, they did leave her behind, and they would not come back.

It was then that the little girl heard something that sounded even more powerful than the wind, louder than the voice of the Haboob... a harsh mechanical drone.

"Dio aiutami," Sophia called as she looked up and saw what it was, and her eyes grew wide in spite of the wind.

"Dio aiutami," she repeated.

God help me.

Part One
La Sentencia

Chapter 1
Once Upon A Time

For Esteban Dorantes, the feeling that he must lead a search into the unknown had grown stronger and stronger. It was a search, he told himself, that must reach out across time, across oceans, across treacherous mountains, and burning deserts... all to be accomplished by a man who would not fear death.

Today on his 31st birthday it rained, soaking the desert floor and dry mountains with something that tasted of new beginnings. The smell of the Sonoran desert's wet creosote bushes filled Esteban's whole body, reminding him of the first moment he understood that there was a great journey he was destined to take. He was ten years old at the time, and his father (a high school history teacher) sat in their small living room with a book in his hand. He was pointing to the picture of a black man, an African, who led the Spanish expedition in search of the Seven Cities of Gold. The black man's name was Esteban, the same name given to the boy by his father. The black man was also the boy's great, great grandfather... 20 generations removed.

Esteban understood that the original search for the Golden Cities took place in 1539. Nearly five hundred years earlier. But great searches and great journeys of discovery were still possible in the modern age, he thought ... by the descendant of a fabled explorer, who knew in his heart that adventure was his destiny.

Esteban had never made a secret of these ideas, and perhaps that had not been wise. When he first expressed them in high school history class, most of the girls just giggled, but the boys began to make fun of him, to mock him and call him "Stevie the Great," "Stevie the Conquistador," and eventually, "Stevie the Weird."

Esteban took a sip from the large mug of coffee that he'd made for his short drive to work. He was an actuary now... someone who studies and analyzes the possibilities of risk for big insurance companies. He was very good at it too: at spotting trends and predicting what was to come... scientifically. The problem now was that he could clearly see the future of his hometown, La Sentencia, even if no one else seemed able to. And that future was bleak.

"How can you be so practical one minute and such a dreamer the next?" Ceci Moreno had asked him. She had been his girl for almost all of their senior year in high school. She was lovely, Esteban thought: intelligent, reserved, but with dark fiery eyes that hinted at so much that was hidden away.

Once, when the bullies had cornered him and forced him to answer a barrage of questions about the Golden Cities and how he intended to find them, ready at any moment to smash his face in, Ceci had come along with her prim and proper attitude. She had driven the bullies back with cruel, icy stares that seemed to melt even the toughest of them. In the end, she and Esteban laughed about it, and she let him kiss her, fall in love with her, and take her to the senior ball where her smoldering glances kept all the bad guys away.

Esteban was happy then; he really loved Ceci and enjoyed every moment they were together. He felt his affection for her starting to rise almost above his sense of destiny until he began to think that his dreams might not be anywhere near as important as he once thought they were, and there was something else too.

"Sometimes it frightens me... this feeling that there's something I have to accomplish," he once told Ceci in one of his moments of doubt. "It's not an easy thing to live with."

"Poor you," she said with a sympathetic smile and kissed him lightly on the cheek. Then she frowned. "Poor me."

"I'm sorry," was his response. But in the end, it didn't matter. When he went away to college, Ceci found a new guy, one more practical and sensible than Esteban. His name was Gabriel Romo. That's how the first and only real love of Esteban's life slipped away, leaving him with nothing but his crazy dreams and his love of numbers and patterns.

Oh, there were other girls who found him attractive, in a quirky way. He had, after all, nice features, especially those piercing, dreamer's eyes. And there was his well-groomed appearance and those neat, well-tailored clothes that he liked so much to wear. The shadow of an occasional mustache came and went with varying degrees of success, and seemed to give him an added sense of interest and even mystery.

The real problem with Esteban's romantic life was that the other girls just didn't understand him. Only Ceci had. And now she'd found someone else.

Memories of Ceci made Esteban sigh as he carried his mug of coffee out to the car. He opened the door, slid the mug into the cup-holder, got in, and drove off toward work. He was struggling with himself suddenly, torn between the promise of adventure and the frightening dangers such a journey might bring. The answer he decided as he drove along the familiar stretch of road was preparation. Yes. No matter how daring and brave the adventurer might be, there was so much to do before starting, wasn't there?

After all, he would have to talk to his employer. This was a very busy time of year. And he didn't want to burn any bridges just in case things didn't work out. Maybe October would be a better time to begin his quest or early next year?

"Perhaps we should talk about this," said a voice that was toned with a rich, North African accent.

Esteban glanced at the passenger seat and then he smiled nervously. The spirit of his great, great grandfather sat there looking at him expectantly. He wore a loose-fitting, earth-colored robe decorated with geometric patterns. The apparition had visited Esteban before, in his dreams, and now, apparently he was showing up in broad daylight.

Esteban said, "I don't think I'm quite ready, Great Grandfather."

The old man nodded and smiled as he always did. "Of course," he said. "Life is good. The sun rises and warms us every day."

Esteban nodded. Even in his dreams, his great, great grandfather had always started with something positive. The Conquistadors had called him Estebanico. It was a diminutive name that might be given to a little boy, or to a slave, which is exactly what Estebanico had been. But everyone also knew that Estebanico had been an expert negotiator, skilled at communicating even with people whose culture and ways he did not completely understand. Much of it might have been simply because he started out positively, agreed with those with whom he spoke, and listened very well.

"Warmth is comforting," Estebanico said to his great, great grandson. "Home is comforting. Adventure on the other hand is a challenge, and challenges are, by their very nature, uncomfortable."

"I have no map," Esteban said, "no method of transportation through the desert, no companions to travel with me."

"So very true," said the old man. "And getting started is far more frightening than dreaming."

"Yes, exactly."

"But challenges and opportunities do not wait. They must be answered before they pass."

"I think I have time. Don't you?"

Estebanico smiled. "The world is ready now, grandson. All things have moved into position, the universe sings in harmony. This is the moment."

Esteban slammed on his brakes as he barely missed hitting an elderly woman with a shopping cart who had tried to cross the broad boulevard against the light. She looked at him angrily.

"Watch where you're going, crazy man," she yelled. Esteban cringed; everyone in La Sentencia knew about him and his dreams... his crazy dreams.

"Did you see that?" Esteban asked. "Did you hear what she called me?"

"A prophet is without honor in his own country," said the old man. "That's from your holy book, not mine."

"Maybe so, but there's so much preparation that's necessary. I need to make lists, gather supplies and provisions. And then there are the other members of my expedition. No one has ever taken me seriously and now I have to recruit a group of followers... and probably pay them."

Estebanico chuckled. "Where's that enthusiastic little boy who was ready to head off on his quest the first time I told him about it? In fact, where's the excited man who walked out of your house this morning?"

"He's on his way to work?"

"And what is it that you do?" Estebanico was smiling as he asked the question. He seemed to be honestly interested.

"I study the probability that certain things will happen... or they will not."

"In that case," said the old man with a chuckle, "you are right to want to take your time in preparation. Because the journey of which we speak is very improbable. Some in fact might call it impossible."

Esteban shook his head. "So now you're telling me that the quest I've been dreaming of all my life is impossible."

"But why let that stop you? It is important... it must be done."

Esteban pulled into a parking space and then looked up. He wasn't at work at all. He was four blocks away at the local branch of the Bank of America.

"What are we doing here?" he asked.

"You need money," said Estebanico, "to help you on your quest."

In spite of all his dreams, in spite of a lifetime of bragging about his destiny, the fact that he must suddenly act, must soon actually set off on his quest began to panic Esteban even more. His great, great grandfather heard it in his voice.

"I need more time," said Esteban. "What about transportation, what about provisions? What about a map?"

Estebanico smiled that knowing smile. "God will provide," he said. "You do believe in God, don't you?"

"I did," Esteban answered. "Once upon a time."

"Exactly," said the old man. "Once upon a time. And that, grandson, is how all great adventures begin."

11

Chapter 2
Kenny & Lorena

Lorena Torres stared at her date barely blinking, waiting, not saying anything, just realizing that she'd never really been kissed before... not the way she hoped that she would be kissed tonight. And now here they were in the perfect place for it... and at the perfect time.

Kenny McLaughlin, short, broad, with a square jaw, a shock of red hair and a wide crazy smile, was maybe seventeen at the most. He lived over on the west side of La Sentencia, Arizona USA... the high-rent district as Lorena's grandfather liked to call it.

Still, here they were, sitting alone in the back seat of his sparkly new Dodge Challenger with the big blue strip down the center of the hood, an interior of all white leather upholstery, and a seductive new car smell. They sat close together, knowing that the only way they were going to kiss was if one of them actually did something about it.

Lorena batted those famously long eyelashes of hers – the ones her mother said would get her into all kinds of trouble someday – and Kenny moved his lips closer.

"Guess we should, huh?" he whispered as he placed one hand on the girl's shoulder.

Lorena loved his touch. She simply nodded. "Yeah, we should," and she swallowed hard.

Kenny closed his eyes; he was smiling a little, she thought, and he was moving very slowly toward her.

"Mmmmm," Lorena sighed and jumped forward to kiss her date before he could change his mind. Their teeth bumped unceremoniously, they both jerked backward... and at that moment, the car suddenly began shaking violently. In fact, everything was in frantic motion: the road, the hills, and the mountains. Rocks and huge mounds of earth came loose and slid down the mountainsides and out across the deserted highway.

The car's convulsions jarred the teens apart. Lorena opened her eyes just as Kenny's expression changed from sheer terror to absolute awe. His face turned bright red... then orange, then yellow-green... and then an unearthly shade of blue.

"Kenny, what's going on?" Lorena gasped. But the boy could only murmur, "Jeez, look at that," as he pointed out the front windshield.

Lorena turned and saw that the entire left side of the Challenger was pulsing with the same colors that kept flashing across Kenny's face. She turned the other way and could see the mountainsides and the sky glowing with the same ever-changing light. It seemed to be coming from just beyond a ridge of earth that Lorena was sure hadn't even been there a few seconds before.

"It has a beat," Kenny said with a sudden smile. And he began pounding the back of the car seat to the pulsing rhythm of the light. "How cool is this?"

Lorena was about to smile when another shockwave rocked the Challenger violently. It tore more rocks and debris from the mountainside and sent them spilling out across the roadway.

"Must be an earthquake?" Lorena said as the violent shaking continued.

"Psychedelic earthquake," Kenny added, and, for a moment, the two kids could do little more than hang on as the new car seemed to be trying to tear itself apart.

Then, a loud unearthly screech, like the call of some prehistoric raptor, fractured the air and filled them both with panic. The teens both turned quickly toward the sound and saw something that looked like a massive fireball begin to wrench itself free from the earth. There was another horrible screech, and then the fireball launched itself into the sky above them... still color-shifting as it went.

Gradually, the Challenger stopped rocking. Gradually, Kenny released his grip on the back of the car seat. Gradually, Lorena slumped against her boyfriend, pulled his arms around her for protection, closed her eyes, and quickly whispered an entire decade of the rosary before either she or Kenny could begin to process what had really happened. There was the dead silence that seemed to stretch out all around them. And then another sound, a sound that should have been familiar, but really wasn't, began to penetrate the black silence.

Clomp, clomp... clomp, clomp, clomp.

A shape was moving toward them through the dust that swirled up in the wake of the vanishing fireball.

Clomp, clomp...

"Damn," Kenny said as an unearthly countenance moved slowly toward the dust-shrouded side window of the car. "It looks like some kind of alien... something right out of Star Wars."

Lorena stared in terror at the face that now peered in at them. And then she giggled nervously.

"It looks more like... a camel," she said.

Kenny squinted, wiped his eyes, and looked out through the glass. "Oh yeah. It is a camel, nothing strange about that," but he found he was shaking. And he began shaking even more as another camel head, and then a third moved closer... until all three of them were there, bobbing and stretching outside the window as they looked into the sterile whiteness of the car's interior.

The head of the first camel slammed against the window, probably by accident, because it let out a nasty bellow before it jerked back quickly and turned away.

"That's enough for me," Kenny said as he twisted himself over the console and into the front seat. He turned the key in the ignition, put the car in gear, and urged it ahead. They rolled right by the camels, right through the dust that still hung in the air like some mottled curtain.

"What's that?" Lorena asked as the little car rumbled on down the road.

Some chrome and neon thing sat on top of a ridge where the departing fireball had pushed up a giant mound of earth. The thing pulsed with the same kind of light that had flooded the car when the fireball took off.

"Looks like a jukebox," Kenny answered as he guided the muscle car forward. And, almost as if in response to Kenny's comment, the jukebox flashed on full bright and began pounding out the words to an old heavy metal song that neither Kenny nor Lorena had ever heard before.

THINGS ARE STRANGE
THINGS ARE SO DAMN STRANGE!
GONNA CHANGE
THINGS ARE GONNA CHANGE!

Lorena's eyes widened, and she mouthed the words along with the song... even though she didn't really know them: "Things are gonna change!"

The Challenger was barely crawling now as it approached the pulsing light of the jukebox. Kenny put his foot on the brake, stopped the car, shut off the engine, and began to open the door.

"Gonna check it out, babe," he said.

"No, you're not," Lorena answered sharply, as she grabbed him by the collar and pulled him back into his seat. "And neither am I. Because we're both going to get the hell out of here... right now!"

Chapter 3
Esteban and the Camels

Esteban had prepared and eaten another gourmet breakfast. He did like to cook. And now he sipped his coffee as he rinsed the dishes thoroughly and slid them (almost completely clean) into the dishwasher. He would turn on the machine and let it run while he was at work. For Esteban perfect cooking and clean up was something of a ritual, as was eating healthy, as was keeping his house, car, clothing, and everything else around him spotless at all times.

Such a man would plan very carefully for a great adventure, he had decided, and would not set off until everything was in place. And regardless of what his great, great grandfather had said, he would not allow himself to consider the fact that all these plans, all these tasks that must be performed before setting out were in any way an excuse for delay. His grandfather had been right. Adventure was difficult, dangerous, and perhaps even impossible. But this damn trip was his, wasn't it? And he was going to do it his way.

Esteban dumped the contents of his coffee cup into his travel mug without spilling a drop. Then he rinsed the cup and put it into the dishwasher. He slung his suit coat over his arm and stepped out through the kitchen door and into the bright Arizona sunshine.

17

And there, right in front of him, stood a camel. In fact, there were three of them. They walked into his front yard and approached him. Each looked at Esteban with a friendly gaze and seemed to nod.

Esteban didn't run back into the house or reach for his cell phone and call the local newspaper to ask about these strange, clumsy creatures that had almost never been seen in this part of the world. Instead, he began to feel more and more distracted, hypnotized almost. As though he were in a trance, he stumbled out beyond the house, squeezed open the door to his immaculate, late model BMW, laid his briefcase on the front seat, his suit coat on top of it, deposited his travel mug in the cup holder, then closed and locked the car door without getting in, and turned to follow the camels up the road on foot.

#

The strange procession – three camels and a slight young man with neatly groomed hair and dreamer's eyes – strode slowly past Mr. Jordan's Grocery store with its racks of produce set out in the cool morning air. They passed Gloria's Bakery where the windows were already filled with empanadas, marranitos and other forms of pan dulce. At last, Esteban found himself outside the Tres Flores Restaurant. The camels had led him there. They spoke to him somehow, he thought. They understood that he was a dreamer and an adventurer, just as they must be. Now the animals stood nodding their heads, and eating the flowers that grew in the little boxes that flanked the restaurant's doorway.

After a few moments, Luís Romo and his wife Carmen, the owners of Tres Flores, came running out through the front door drying their hands on their aprons.

"Camels?" Luís moaned as he saw what was happening, "Vámonos!" and he charged at the beasts waving his arms in an attempt to drive them away from the flower boxes.

The nearest camel reared up on its hind legs, pivoted and galloped away from the restaurant. The others turned and followed... galloping, for a few yards, that is... before they again assumed the heavy gait that Esteban had been tracking. Now, however, the young man just stood in front of the restaurant looking at Luís and Carmen with a confused expression on his face and a faraway look in his eyes.

"The camels brought you here, Stevie?" Luís asked.

He nodded.

Carmen studied the young man and then asked," "Esteban, is everything okay with you, or are you dreaming again?"

Even she knew.

"I'm fine," he answered." "Fine." Though he didn't seem fine to Carmen, who had known Esteban since he was a child.

"If the camels brought you here," Luís asked, "shouldn't you be following them?"

Esteban looked over his shoulders at the camels. They were just standing across the street, eating the long grass in front of the Santa Maria Mortuary.

"I don't think so."

Luís smiled with some compassion, "Then how about some chorizo and eggs?"

Esteban shook his head distractedly. "No, thanks, I've already eaten."

"And aren't you going to be late for work?" Carmen asked.

"I am. Yes, I am."

"Then maybe you'd better get going?"

Esteban just stood there, still looking very confused. Luís put his arm around the young man's shoulder. "Maybe we should be talking about an insurance policy for our restaurant," he said with a smile, "from your company, of course."

"Insurance?"

"Business insurance, Steve."

"But I don't sell insurance. I'm an actuary."

"But you do work for an insurance company," Luís chuckled. "Remember? Come on in; let's talk. You can call your boss and tell him that you're on a sales call at the business of Mr. Romo, who might want to take out a substantial insurance policy on his restaurant."

"Yes, of course. Good idea." But Esteban still looked a bit distracted. "Do you really need insurance?"

"Well, I need help with something. Let's just put it that way."

Esteban followed Carmen and Luís into the restaurant where their young grandson, Mario, was at one of the tables doing his homework.

Without even saying a word, Luís went to the back of the restaurant and brought out a big mug of coffee and placed it in front of the young actuary.

"Compliments of the house," he said. "Cream and sugar?"

Esteban nodded.

Little Mario looked up from his homework. The kid was round-faced, big-eyed, sweet looking... short for his age, and introverted. He reminded Esteban of himself when he was seven years old.

"You see the light show last night, Stevie?" Carmen asked as she handed him a napkin.

"Light show? No. What happened?"

"The morning paper said it was aurora borealis," Carmen said.

"This far south?"

"Our niece knows better," Luís answered. "Lorena said she saw it happen first hand, said a fireball caused it out on Los Reales Road."

Mario's eyes brightened. He was usually a kid of very few words, but still he had something to add, "Flying saucer."

20

"Lorena said that it was buried in the earth, and then it just ripped right out, flew up into the sky and blasted away, putting on an amazing light show as it went."

"About what time was that?" Esteban asked.

"Two A.M., maybe."

"She said there was an old jukebox left out there where it happened," Carmen said.

"A jukebox just sitting out in the desert?"

Luís shook his head. "I wouldn't have believed her either if it wasn't for the damn light show... and the camels."

"She said the camels came from the flying saucer too?" Esteban asked.

"She didn't say it was a flying saucer."

"That was me," Mario corrected.

"They don't look like alien camels," Esteban said.

Luís chuckled. "Do you know what alien camels are supposed to look like, hijo?"

Esteban took a big swallow of his coffee and, for a moment, wondered why it didn't taste good as the coffee he made himself. Must be that ultra expensive coffee maker he'd bought himself for Christmas.

"Seems to me," Luís suggested, "that any camels you see wandering around here in Arizona have to be some kind of aliens... magical even. Breakfast burrito?"

"No, thanks." The conversation was giving Esteban a headache. "What about that insurance policy you wanted to talk about?"

"We can discuss that as we drive out to get it," said Luís.

Esteban looked even more confused than ever. "Drive out to get what?"

Little Mario giggled. "My jukebox."

Chapter 4
The Jukebox

They'd come to the site of the fireball, most of the town maybe: old prospectors with Geiger counters, little kids in shorts and flip-flops, teens in jeans and t-shirts, pasty-skinned sightseers, and sun-soaked adventurers. All the barrios had curious representatives... the upscale neighborhoods too. They knew they'd have to work fast. The police and military hadn't been able to cordon off the whole area yet... not the back way, which Luís (and apparently half of La Sentencia) knew.

Papa Luís (as Mario liked to call him) rumbled his old Ford F-150 pickup to the edge of the crater and got out. The dirt road he had taken ended abruptly at the ridge that Lorena and Kenny had told him about.

The old man was amazed. "Never seen nothin' like this," he said.

"Like what, Papa?" Mario asked.

"Like a crater caused by something that looks like it just blasted right up out of the earth... like it had been buried there for centuries... like the whole thing was part of some master plan."

Mario wasn't exactly sure what he grandfather meant, but he still managed to ask the most important question anyone could ask.

"Who would have planned it, Papa?"

Papa Luís eyed his grandson with an expression of awe.

"Who indeed?" Papa answered. "Who indeed?"

The old man walked all the way around the truck, slammed his fist against the door, which was the only way anyone could open it, and let Esteban out. Then he lifted his grandson down onto the rough gravel that formed the edge of the crater. The F-150 sat amid the dozen or so trucks, SUVs, and minivans that had taken this least-known route. The highway patrol had either forgotten about it or just decided to ignore it for the time being. In any event, through this one forgotten artery, the ants had found their way into the cookie jar.

"Gonna bring your Geiger counter, Papa?" Mario asked.

"No need," the old man answered, "what we've come for is right up there." He turned, and pointed up the steep face of the ridge, to the spot where a crowd had already gathered around the jukebox. In spite of the debris and dust that had buried everything else in a thick layer of grit, the machine was spectacularly clean and shiny. At that exact moment, a group of five teenagers in tight black jeans and white t-shirts, cigarette packs rolled up in their sleeves as if they were refugees from the fifties, were pounding on the jukebox, trying to get it to play. Their girls stood in a little group a short distance behind them, smirking at the boys, wearing equally tight jeans, and much tighter t-shirts, arms crossed, bright kerchiefs pulled over their uniformly bleach-blond hair.

"Come-on bitch," Tony, the biggest boy, shouted as he leveled a punch right into the grill of the machine.

Then, "Jeeezzzuuusss!!" his hand came away bloodied as though the jukebox had somehow found teeth and taken a bite out of him.

Tony fell away clutching his fist while Marla, his girl, rushed up to him grabbing his arm, ripping off her kerchief, and wrapping it around his mangled fingers.

"Come-on, Tone," she said. "Let's just leave the damn thing alone; let's just get out of here."

"All I wanted was to hear some music, babe," Tony growled, but he followed Marla away from the glowing machine. His actions, at least, had kept other interested parties at a distance... people who might have tried to take the jukebox home with them before Luís had his chance.

By now, he, Esteban, and Mario had made the rather hellish climb up the face of the rim to where the crowd had gathered. The recently fire-blasted earth was still giving off uncomfortable waves of heat. The fine particles on the slope were at such a steep angle that walking up its face felt like walking up a mountain on a distant planet whose gravity was five times that of Earth. Luís fell back several times until Esteban caught him and helped guide him and the boy up to the box.

A scholarly-looking couple in their late 60s, dressed in starched khaki shorts and shirts and wearing backpacks, was now studying the bright chrome and glass machine. So were several little kids, and several groups of workers who had just decided to do a little investigating before heading into work that morning.

Little Mario dropped his grandfather's hand and zigzagged through the crowd until he was right up beside the jukebox.

He didn't say a word, but his bright eyes showed his enthusiasm as he ran his fingers over the delicate filigree on the front of the box. Somehow it was tough enough to take Tony's best punch and repel it without showing a scratch.

Luís and Esteban now made their way through the crowd so that they were standing right behind Mario.

"My niece told me it played something last night," the old man said to Esteban.

"Impossible," said the 60-something guy with the backpack. He wore wire-rimmed glasses, had neatly trimmed hair, and carried some kind of guidebook.

"Guy's probably a professor over at AUT," Esteban whispered to Luís.

"There's no power source," the prof said. "The cord just trails off into the rubble."

"Lorena said it played," Mario said without looking back at the man, and then the little boy hit a combination of letters and numbers on the jukebox keypad, somehow sensing the ones that would make the jukebox play.

AA17.

The professorial guy looked at the woman beside him and smirked. "Son, I don't think...." He began. And then the jukebox answered all of them in the screaming voice of Clinton Max:

GET YOUR RIGHTS – YEAH – GET YOUR RIGHTS!
START THE JOURNEY AND BEGIN TONIGHT
SEE THE LIGHT– YEAH – SEE THE LIGHT
COME ON NOW AND
JOIN – THE – FIGHT

The old song by the Max-man began to blare out of the jukebox speakers.

As the song ended, everyone could hear distant police sirens suddenly calling out through the desert stillness.

"Damn," Luís said. "They're coming this way; they'll probably shut down the whole area. Let's get the box out of here."

Esteban ran to the side of the machine and did his best to tip it back so that he and the others could lift it. Luís joined him.

"Don't think you should be doing that," said the woman in the shorts.

"Sure they should," the prof answered. "If the feds take control of the area we'll probably never see the thing again."

He ran up to the group trying to lift the jukebox, and then three workers added their support. This muscular bunch looked like a group who did gardening and lawn care for the high-end homeowners on the Upper East Side (Kenny McLaughlin's neighborhood).

"Let us help you, Luís," the biggest guy in the bunch said.

Luís looked at him for a moment as though he'd never seen the man before in his life.

"We're good customers of yours," said another member of the crew.

"Hell man, you make the best chile rellenos in the valley."

Luís smiled his welcome.

Within minutes (and a very tricky descent down the face of the ridge) the group had the jukebox lying in the back of Luís's truck, and the old man was back in the cab with his passengers heading down the dirt road to La Sentencia. The gardeners and Mr. Professor and his wife followed right behind them in their cars, swerving along the winding, dust-clouded way just as a convoy of state troopers closed in on the site, ready to shut down this last access to the fireball's caldera. But they barely even noticed Luís and his band as they headed back to town.

Chapter 5
The Johnsons

Melinda Johnson, DVM, sat on the front porch of the La Sentencia Veterinary Clinic drinking a cup of coffee and studying the large animals that ambled down the street. She'd only seen camels in zoos and none of them here in the Great Sonoran Desert. But hey, they were moving right along, not really seeming to know where they were going. Dr. Mel expected that the camels would stop at the clinic anyway... if only to eat the bright orange poppies that she and her husband had planted along the front of the parking lot.

Dr. Mel's husband hadn't been in all morning. VL (as everyone in La Sentencia called him) was a vet too and a good one. But he also thought of himself as a musician... a holdover from the wicked sixties... more in love with that old-school guitarist, Rocker Jim, than with her, she felt sometimes... especially when he'd keep her awake until two in the morning trying to master some riff that he'd found in the middle of Midnight Blue.

VL's banged-up Harmony guitar just didn't sound right to either of them, but VL never tried to make Mel feel guilty for taking all the money he'd saved for a really great guitar and spending it to upgrade the clinic's treatment room last year. All in all, it wasn't a bad trade for either of them, Mel had said. VL had to keep his old guitar but she'd agree to be more tolerant of rock music played all hours of the day and night.

The camels were at the edge of the parking lot now, and Dr. Melinda slowly set down her coffee and walked up to them with the kind of patient calm that all good veterinarians have. She touched their flanks, took a look in their eyes, and judged them to be in very good health... for animals that had just appeared out of nowhere.

Mel reached up under the head of one camel and guided it, the way she was so skilled at guiding horses, toward the corral at the back of the clinic. She'd already decided that she and VL would have to run an ad in the local newspaper, El Milagro, to find the camel's owners... whoever they were... if the owners didn't show up at the clinic first, that is. After all, this was the most logical place for the camels to be, wasn't it?

Mel sighed as she steered the camels through the gate and into the corral. The animals didn't give her any trouble at all really, not as much trouble as her husband had given her this morning. It wasn't just that he had musical aspirations... he had photographic and literary aspirations too. The problem was Jessica Amado, the part-time teacher at the local junior high school. She was also a freelance reporter for the local newspaper: The La Sentencia Miracle (El Milagro), and after meeting her at one town hall session a few months ago VL had signed on to work with her as both a reporter and a photographer for the paper. Dr. Mel didn't care for Jessica and wasn't exactly sure that the part-time teacher's intentions were entirely honorable when it came to VL. Still, Mel didn't complain when her husband stopped by Jessica's house occasionally to work on a newspaper article or two. But she had gotten good and angry this morning when Jessica called at

4:30 AM and asked VL to hop into the clinic's Jeep and drive out to the site of the fireball, which all the big city Arizona papers were already covering.

Dr. Mel tightened her fist and stepped back from the camels. She watched for a moment as the animals clomped around the corral, found some old hay that was in the trough, and started munching. Mel had no real proof that there was anything illicit going on between her husband and Jessica. And he certainly was loving and affectionate enough with her, when he wasn't hammering Rocker Jim into the wee small hours of the morning or taking pictures for Jessica's articles. So these ideas of marital infidelity and secret trysts between the two were all in her head, Mel tried to convince herself. She'd just have to calm down and focus on the animals until her husband got home.

#

VL had arrived at the site of the fireball by 5:15 AM, before most of the prospectors and sightseers had come and well before Luís, Mario, and Esteban. He had climbed the side of the caldera and taken plenty of pictures. The area looked as much like the result of an impact as it did the remains of something that had launched itself from underground and then blasted up into the skies.

VL cranked through about twenty shots on his Sony RX10. They were digital photographs saved to a little card he could download to his PC and then email to Jessica. The problem he was having now was that there just wasn't anything unusual left to photograph... just ripples of heat rising above the cooling rubble left in the wake of the launch (or impact... or whatever it was).

VL turned his back on the caldera for a moment and looked desperately around for anything newsworthy to shoot. His eyes followed the gravel road that came from the parking

29

area where soon a dozen cars and trucks, including Luís's pickup, would be parked. And then he spotted something that made no sense to him at all.

There, in the dried desert earth, were the barefoot prints of a child, a little girl maybe. She couldn't have been more than five or six, he thought. The footprints barely made any impact in the surface of the road at all, and yet they were as clearly visible as if they'd been painted there. The steps came directly up the middle of the gravel road, and then, far more amazingly, they proceeded up the rise, over the lip of the caldera, and then around the entire area. The little girl's footprints were clearly visible where no other human footprints could be seen; not even those VL had made himself only a few seconds earlier.

VL stepped down hard next to the nearest barefoot print and then drew his foot carefully away. The rubble fell back into place leaving no sign of where he had stepped. But the girl's little prints remained, clearly visible in the steaming material… about a quarter the size of his own massive heel and sole.

VL snapped a few photos of the little girls footprints and then followed them forward, across the rim of the caldera, and toward some hulking metal object in the distance. VL struggled toward it wondering if it was easier for the little girl to make the trek than it was for him… somehow he was sure it was.

Twenty minutes later he was standing in front of the metal object, the jukebox, the same one that Papa Luís, Mario, and Esteban would be removing from the premises in a few hours. VL tracked the little girl's steps around the object. The jukebox sparkled in the morning light as if it had just arrived from the factory.

VL saw where the little girl's toes dug deep into the cinders at one point, as though she had stood up on them… up on her tiptoes. He reached forward and ran his hand over the chrome grill and the bright red letters that spelled out the word WURLITZER. He punched a few numbers and letters into the selection keyboard more out of curiosity than anything else. And suddenly the first wicked chords of the Rocker Jim classic blasted out at him.

"Midnight Blue comin down
"Stealin' round this old town."

The music almost knocked V. L. over backward. It was the real thing, better than ever. He stood there in awe, his mouth hanging open, his lips curled into a curious smile, his fingers unconsciously moving through the chord progressions. Then the music stopped abruptly. VL reached forward, tried other combinations of letter keys and numbers, but the box sat there mute. It was a full twenty minutes later when VL's phone rang. He was still standing there.

"Yeah?"

"Hi... it's Jessica. Did you get any shots?"

"Some interesting ones... and there's this jukebox out here."

"A jukebox."

"And footprints of a little girl... barefoot."

"But isn't the ground still hot?"

"Steaming. But she's walked all over the place."

"Did you get her picture?"

"No sign of her."

VL looked across the area again, but he knew that the girl was gone.

"Nope – don't even know exactly when she was here, but I can email you the pictures I have as soon as I get back to the clinic." He raised the camera to his eye and grabbed four quick shots of the jukebox.

Jessica said, "Why not bring them by my house right now?"

"Don't you have to teach today?"

"I'm taking a personal day."

31

That seemed odd to VL. But then, what did a veterinarian know about teachers' work hours.

"Okay, I'll stop by, but just for a second. I need to be getting back to the clinic. Mel's there all alone."

"She can deal. You know she can, and I really want to see those pictures."

VL laughed. They were something, some of those shots; even he wanted to take a longer look at them.

VL knew he drove right by Jessica's home on his way back to the clinic: her little bungalow at the edge of the barrio. It was only a few blocks from the junior high where she taught part-time. VL was worried about her safety. After all, he told her repeatedly; she was far too pretty to go anywhere in that neighborhood alone. Jessica simply reminded him that she knew practically everyone who lived there, had friends everywhere… some of them were big guys who would gladly beat the shit out of anyone who dared to get fresh with her.

#

The first thing VL noticed as he pulled into Jessica's little driveway was that she had drawn the blinds at the front of the house. And it looked like the front door was open a bit too. What was going on?

VL stomped hard on the Jeep's emergency brake, turned off the engine, grabbed his trusty Sony camera, and marched to the front door. It was part way open, but he knocked anyway.

After a moment, Jessica ducked her head around the corner of the door. Her lips were curled into an inviting smile. Her dark eyes sparkled behind black-rimmed glasses that VL thought made her look especially sexy.

"Oh, hi," she said sounding rather breathless.

"You okay."

"More than okay." Her smile widened. "Oh, good; you brought your camera."

Jessica opened the door slowly, still hiding behind it, letting VL in and then - when he was fully into the room - she took the camera from him and pushed the door forward letting it slam shut in back of him. She stood there in her usual teacher's outfit: a white cotton blouse, short black skirt, and high heels. VL didn't even notice her... because right beside her was something he had never seen before... not up close and personal anyway.

"Are you shitting me?" he whispered.

"Just something I thought you might like," Jessica answered. "Go ahead and touch it if you want... play it. It belongs to my brother Sammy. He's leaving for a gig in Vegas tomorrow, so he's going to let me borrow it for a few weeks."

"I didn't know he had anything like this."

"Oh yeah," Jessica answered, "and I wanted to surprise you with it."

VL didn't know if his eyes were playing tricks on him or not; this was the thing he wanted most in all the world... cared more about than the part-time teacher, the newspaper, his dedicated wife, his veterinary practice, or even his camera full of photos. It was an authentic Fender Stratocaster guitar, one that VL knew was a throwback to the sixties. Hell, it might have even belonged to Rocker Jim himself.

Chapter 6
Breakfast at Tres Flores

Three days later, on a Sunday morning, all the members of the extended Romo family made their way back to the Tres Flores Restaurant for their weekly after-church breakfast. They would spend the hours between 11 and 3 PM eating, telling stories, and relaxing before opening the place for dinner at five.

Carmen, Luís, and his aging father Manuel all rode together in the old F-150. It was the same truck that Luís, Esteban, and the others used to bring the magical jukebox down from the crater. The machine still sat in the back room of the restaurant. For some reason, it was no longer willing to play any music no matter who pushed the buttons. Little Mario didn't even try. He said the jukebox wasn't ready to sing again, and that was that.

Mario rode with his cousin Lorena and her boyfriend Kenny in Kenny's always sparkling Challenger. Mario's mother, Vanessa, and Lorena's mother, Yolanda, rode together with Mario in the back seat. Mario didn't say a word as always, but he grinned from ear to ear, thrilled with the power of this 21st-century muscle car. Lorena rode shotgun.

Mario's uncle Gabriel and Gabe's main squeeze, Ceci Moreno, pulled up in a little Toyota Prius. The whole rest of the family seemed to arrive crammed into a couple of aging minivans.

"So, when are we going to hear that jukebox of yours?" Gabriel asked Mario as they all got out of their respective vehicles at the same time. Mario, of course, didn't answer. But Papa Luís did.

"You'll hear it when you hear it," he grumbled. He was growing very tired of the question.

"But hey," Gabe said, "Ceci and I want to dance right now," and he turned to his girl, "Right, babe?"

Ceci moved primly in front of him. "Si Señor," she said with a grin, and she lifted her long Sunday skirt up slightly so that she could curtsy toward Gabe. He bowed, swept her into his arms, and began waltzing around the parking lot.

Lorena's mother Yolanda eyed Gabe and Ceci with disapproval. "Don't go getting any romantic ideas from those damn fools," she told Kenny. She disliked her daughter's boyfriend, especially because of his family's wealth and their Protestant religion.

"Oh, Ma..." Lorena sighed, "They're only dancing... what can be so wrong with that?"

"It's an occasion of sin for hot-blooded teenagers," said Yolanda as she shooed her daughter and the girl's boyfriend into Tres Flores.

Inside the restaurant, the rest of the workers and their children had already arrived, prepared breakfast, and set up a great table that stretched across the main dining area. They set all the places, positioned all the chairs, and began playing music through the speaker system.

Manuel Gomes, the gigantic chef, bulled his way proudly out of the kitchen as the family entered through the main door. He grabbed Luís in a big bear hug, kissed Carmen on the cheek, ruffled Mario's hair and joked, laughed with, and squeezed every single person in the family as they made their way in.

"He's just doing that so that he can hug the girls," said Gabriel as he pointed accusingly at the older man and then slapped him on the back.

"Why not, he's very good at it," said Ceci, and she squeezed the cook tightly.

"Better not hug him for too long, Ceci," Luís responded. "He has to get back into the kitchen, or we'll never eat."

He needn't have said it because almost on cue Manuel's nine children began funneling out of the kitchen carrying plates filled with huevos rancheros, chorizo, tortillas, rice, and beans... enough to feed an army.

"It amazes me how the place quiets down when the food appears," said Gabe with a big grin. And it was true. They had all scrambled into their seats for the saying of the grace, and now they were sitting quietly in anticipation.

Luís stood at the head of the table and spread his arms as if he were Jesus himself about to deliver the Sermon on the Mount. Mama Carmen, who sat beside Yolanda, couldn't help but laugh.

"He wanted to be a Padre, you know... but then I got pregnant, and my Papa insisted that we get married. Luís was never able to fulfill his true vocation."

"Rubbish," answered Yolanda. "His true vocation is running a restaurant. He would have made a terrible priest."

Gabriel, who couldn't help but overhear added, "a long-winded priest anyway. Let's hope that at least today Uncle Luís graces us with a few brief words, not like the twenty-minute prayer he offered last Sunday."

Luís heard all this, and so he stood up even taller. He arched his eyebrows as a menacing smile curled his lips; then he pushed himself up on his tiptoes in front of his extended family.

"Dear Lord," he began, "we thank you for this food...."

Luís paused as he stared everyone down, forcing them into absolute silence and rapt attention.

"AMEN!" he concluded and sat down.

Everyone was stunned.

"AMEN," shouted Gabriel, as a cheer went up. Last week's twenty-minute prayer had been shortened to less than 60 seconds!

From that moment on it was a free-for-all. Plates full of eggs, rice, and beans circled the table, often being completely empty before they reached the final guest. But just as quickly new platefuls found their way into the hands of the hungry family members who kept ladling out the food and eating nonstop.

"How's business?" Gabriel asked Kenny.

"Our car wash is doing just great," the teen answered. "The coming Haboobs will cover everyone's cars with dust. So we'll have plenty of customers... In fact, we're even thinking about opening a new location in this part of town."

"I love the name: McCarwash!" Ceci said. "I drive twenty minutes every week just to get to the one in the city center."

"We love repeat customers," said Kenny with a broad smile.

"But who's actually running the place?" Gabriel asked.

"We all run it together," Kenny said with a slight blush as though it may not be the complete truth.

Lorena smiled at her boyfriend, and – as secretively as possible – she slid her hand under the table and began running it up and down Kenny's thigh. The action wasn't lost on her mother, who glowered at Lorena from across the way.

"Hands on the table, Miss," Yolanda said. "I won't have you behaving badly in my brother's restaurant."

Luís looked from mother to daughter and back again. "She's all right. She loves the boy," he said. "Who knows maybe they'll get married. I've always thought we could use a wee bit o' Scotch in the family."

"Both hands above the table, Lorena!" Yolanda repeated.

37

"I don't know if you should discourage this relationship," Luís said turning to his sister. "These McKenzie kids seem to have turned their car wash into a gold mine."

The older woman gave her brother a stern look. "Stay out of this, old man."

"But Loretta could be marrying into a very successful family with a very bright future."

"But they're all Protestants, mijo," Yolanda whispered so that no one but her brother could hear her, or so she thought.

"MOM!" Lorena moaned, "He plans to convert, you know."

"I do," Kenny said. And everyone but Yolanda smiled and nodded as though it was very good news.

At that exact moment, Mario suddenly stood. Everyone thought that he was about to say how much he supported the budding romance. But instead, he turned first to Gabriel, then to Luís, and then to his mother and spoke very softly.

"Someone's coming!"

"Someone?" his mother asked arching an eyebrow.

"Sophia," Mario whispered. And just like that, the jukebox in the back room came to life and started playing a very melancholy tune. It was all mandolins and strings.

"Your machine is working again," Gabe said.

"But the tune is so sad," sighed Luís.

"Theme from the Godfather," Gabe responded, and everyone nodded in recognition.

Chapter 7
The Girl and the Haboob

There was a heavy knocking at the restaurant door. It sounded like two or three large men pounding at the same time.

Mario's mother, Vanessa, got to her feet, went to the door, and opened it. As soon as she did she covered her mouth with her hand and gasped, "Oh, no!"

In response, a sudden gust of wind sailed through the doorway and sent her hair swirling wildly around her face.

"Haboob!" she called frantically.

All the guests rose from their chairs at once. "Get down the storm-boards," Luís shouted. "Batten down the hatches!"

"It's too late, can't you see that..." Kenny called. "We were so caught up in our party that we didn't see it coming."

It was only then, as Vanessa was about to close the door against the wind that she felt a hard pull on the pleat of her skirt. It almost ripped the fabric. She looked down and there, in front of her, coming up maybe to no more than her hips, stood a little girl of five or six. Sand and sweat had plastered her long, black hair to her head. It almost covered her wide dark eyes. She wore a short, pink, ruffled dress that was almost buried under a heavy layer of grit from the storm. The little girl's feet were bare and coated almost to her thighs with the same grit that made up the mile-high wall of dust that Vanessa saw roaring toward them from the distance. She yanked the little girl inside, then slammed and bolted the door against the wind and the apocalyptic vision.

The girl stood in the doorway shivering for a moment, and then she began to speak in a low singsongy voice.

"Vorrei qualcosa da mangiare," she began, "Qualcosa da bere, e prego, dicami, dove è il bagno."

"She has to go to the bathroom, Mama," Mario called from across the room.

"I understood that much," Vanessa said.

"And she wants something to eat and drink."

Vanessa took the little girl by the hand and rushed her toward the back of the restaurant as Kenny moved to the doorway.

"We'd better cover our cars before the Haboob hits," he said. "Otherwise, we'll have sandblasted paint jobs and shattered windshields."

Gabe and several others got to their feet quickly and followed Kenny out into the swirling wind.

When they had all left, Ceci said, "You know, that little girl was speaking perfect Italian, at least as far as I could tell from the courses I took at the university."

Mario looked confused for just a moment, but then he grabbed a fresh plate from the sideboard. "Let's get her something to eat," he said. "She's starving." And soon almost everyone left in the restaurant was hurriedly passing the plate around the table, adding eggs and tortillas, and rice and beans. When the plate finally got back to Mario, he put it down in front of the empty chair next to him just as his mother brought the little girl to the table. She was now much cleaner and wearing an official Tres Flores t-shirt: size, extra small. It looked like a full-length gown on her.

The girl scrambled onto the seat, turned to Mario and said, "Il vento micidiale viene."

The boy nodded, but Ceci had to translate for the others.

"She says that a terrible wind is coming." Then she turned back to the little girl and told her in Italian that she'd better eat fast.

The girl nodded and started shoveling food into her mouth. In between bites, while she was still chewing she told Mario, "Io sono Sophia, ragazzino. Ed il vostro nome è Mario?

Ceci translated. "She says her name is Sophia, and she's asking if Mario's name is Mario."

"Sí, niña," the little boy answered and broke into a broad grin.

Sophia scowled and began wagging her finger at him as if she was a schoolteacher scolding a misbehaving student.

"C'è una terribile Haboob che sta colpirci in questo momento, lo sai."

The little girl said it so sternly that Ceci didn't react for a long moment while everyone leaned in awaiting her translation.

"Oh, sorry," Ceci answered as her eyes grew wide. "She says the terrible Haboob is about to hit us…

"RIGHT NOW!"

The crash of the wind was instantaneous and overwhelming. It shook the entire building and nearly battered in the door. Sand pelted the windows pulverizing the glass; then it reached inside and striped off the curtains and scattered them across the floor where they writhed like snakes.

"Damn it!" Gabe called as he forced his way back in through the front door, "we just didn't think something like this would hit this early in the season… we should have had the shutters ready."

"The damn storm-boards are still in the warehouse," Luís said as Kenny and the others made their way back into the shelter of the restaurant. A searing blast of dust accompanied them, swimming over the tables and food, dropping a thick layer of yellow-brown that fell into the eggs and the beans making them totally inedible.

"Clear this all away," called Luís as he began gesturing wildly to family and crew alike. "Then, into the back storeroom... all of you. This is going to be a real bad one."

Workers rushed to the back of the restaurant and came out with large plastic trays to hold the dirty dishes. The plates were cleared quickly including all the now ruined, uneaten food. Sophia grabbed a handful of tortillas as they were snatched off the table. She took a large bite of one and pulled all the others down through one sleeve of her t-shirt for safekeeping.

"There's more where those came from," Mario told the little girl.

"Ma io sono così affamato," Sophia sighed.

"She's so hungry, she says," Ceci said to Mario.

"I know what she said," the boy answered. "I understand her perfectly."

Just then the front window of the restaurant blasted in, destroying the delicately painted lacework lettering that spelled out the name Tres Flores.

Pebbles of glass imbedded themselves in the back, arms, and hands of Luís, who was the only one standing on that side of the table at the time. He was still working to clear the pitchers of juice and pots of coffee.

Gabriel rushed to his uncle, wrapped his arm around the older man, steered him away from the ongoing blast through the open window, and directed him to the back of the building.

The entire dining room was now wide open and at the mercy of the sandstorm. The Haboob swept through the place, rattling the pictures that hung on the walls above the small booths, jerking at the large papier-mâché parrot that sat on a chain above the doorway to the kitchen. It swirled the long, black, beautiful hair of a dozen women who still fought to clear and save all the silverware and salt and pepper shakers and bottles of hot sauce that had been set out in the booths.

The dusty breath of the Haboob lifted tablecloths and napkins and sent them twisting through the dirty air, directing them to catch and strangle anyone who wasn't quick enough to be able to duck out of their way.

As so many of the family members made their way into the back storeroom, Kenny called to Gabriel. "We can barricade the window. We can save some of the dining room."

"Good thinking," called Gabe as he plowed his way back against the wind. Lorena was right behind him. Together the three of them lifted the largest table onto its side and pushed it up against the window. The wind fought back, blasting sand around the edges of the table and into their already dirt-caked faces.

While Kenny held one end of the table and Gabriel the other, cousin Richard came running out of the kitchen pushing a massive rack of trays. He slammed it hard against one end of the table and locked the legs into place. The wind directed all its fury to the opposite end of the table then, but Rich found an enormous potted palm tree and dragged it up against that end, forcing the huge flat surface over the rest of the shattered window. The table now covered the lower two-thirds of the opening. But the Haboob wasn't done yet. It threw fistfuls of thick brown grit through the space above the table, blinding the workers for a moment as Kenny gestured to another large table.

He and Gabe lifted it and propped it up on top of the outstretched legs of the first table pressing it toward the opening caused by the broken front window glass. But the wind wanted none of it. With all its force focused on the narrow opening, the wind drove against the second table letting Kenny and Gabe know that two mere mortals were no match for the power of this Haboob.

The wind drove them back. The table seemed to take on the weight of a hundred such tables. Kenny slipped in the gritty sand, fell away backward, but before he could drop the table, Rich was in his place, lifting it up, struggling to push it into place. Then suddenly three workers jumped forward from the back room. They helped Gabe and Rich push the second table into the narrow space. Then they brought more indoor plants, tall racks of utensils, anything with the weight that they could use to barricade out the swirling fury of the Haboob.

Kenny was down on his back, tossed aside by the wind like the tablecloths that were now tangled everywhere across the floors and fixtures of the dining room. The wind seemed to single him out for punishment because all this boarding up had been his idea.

Kenny opened his eyes to see a pair of hands reaching for him through the still dust-laden air; it was Luís.

"Good boy! Good, good boy," the old man said to him. "You may just have saved my restaurant."

Kenny blinked away a faceful of dust and looked around the dining room. Grit caked the walls. Sand was piled almost ankle deep on the floor. But none of the tables were really damaged; none of the other windows were broken. The paintings still hung on the walls. Granted, the huge papier-mâché parrot had slammed into the far wall, its beak pushed in and destroyed. But it still looked like it could be repaired.

Kenny felt another hand grasping his shoulder then, steadying him, lifting him up. "You did good, Kenny," It was his girlfriend's mother, Yolanda. "I'm very proud and surprised," she said. "So come into the back of the kitchen, where we can get you all cleaned up," and, as she said the next few words, Yolanda smiled: "and I can teach you how to pray... properly... the Ave Maria... in Spanish."

Kenny turned and smiled back at the older woman who led him to the rear of the restaurant, where she allowed her daughter free reign to help clean him up... while the Haboob pounded at the little restaurant and all of La Sentencia, Arizona...

For the next four hours.

Chapter 8
The Package

Esteban was late getting home from work that Sunday. He had been working on Sundays for as long as he could remember. The truth was that he loved his job, loved considering the numbers, thinking about the future, plotting the risk involved in anything and everything that was going on. His car had been in the underground garage in central La Sentencia, at the only building that could possibly be considered a high-rise... five stories tall.

The winds had raged behind him as he sat with his back to the big picture window that revealed the worst of it. He was immersed in his numbers, glancing over his shoulder only once or twice when the Haboob had completely engulfed the building. Finally, when the winds had died down, he turned, saw the ghastly results of the monster sandstorm, and plotted a way to get home while avoiding most of the debris.

Twenty minutes later he pulled into his driveway.

Esteban was fastidious enough to keep the palm trees surrounding his home at a good distance from the building. That usually meant that his long driveway was clear, but not this evening. There were half a dozen huge palm branches strewn across the open space, blown in from God only knows were. Esteban parked his Beemer at the very end of the drive, got out and began lugging the palm branches down to the road.

He was wearing casual clothes... if pressed jeans and a starched chambray shirt could be considered casual. Half an hour later the driveway was clear, the car was parked up close to the porch, and Esteban was making his way toward the front door. That's when he saw it, a huge package from Amazon. The big brown box with the funny grin printed on the side sat right in front of his door and had weathered the storm amazingly well. Esteban found it hard to believe that it had been delivered in the midst of the worst Haboob of the year... and on a Sunday too. But even stranger than the delivery was the message attached to the top of the box. Right below his name and address, in very big letters it said:

DO NOT OPEN UNTIL TOMORROW.

Esteban's mind spun through the possibilities that the message implied as he unlocked the front door and went back to get the box. It must weigh sixty pounds, he thought, as he carried it into the living room and set it on the big sturdy coffee table. If he let the box just sit there the way it was, Esteban reasoned, he would never open it.

"Tomorrow never comes," he murmured as he yanked off the tag and stuffed it into his pocket. Still, he felt that he had to at least honor the note's request for the rest of today. And so he walked into the kitchen, opened a drawer, took out a book of matches, grabbed the note and set it on fire. It flamed up quickly, burned for a few moments as he held it, and then fell, still flaming, into the sink drain. Esteban turned on the water so that the flames wouldn't scorch the sink, and as a result one word was left almost intact as the message was washed into the garbage disposal.

"TOMORROW."

Esteban went to the refrigerator and took out the leftovers from last night's chicken Marsala. He put them on a new plate, stuck them into the microwave, and poured himself a glass of wine while the food cooked. Then, gathering up the meal, he carted it into the living room, put it down on a TV tray and ate, all the while staring at the package.

Five hours later, after he cleaned up, he returned to his chair and continued to stare at the box until almost midnight. He seemed more and more hypnotized by the image of the brown cardboard box itself, which seemed to multiply into double and then triple images as his eyes grew tired. And all through that time he replayed a movie of his life: his father telling him about his great, great grandfather, Estebanico; his love for Ceci; the high school bullies; his successful career at college; landing the actuary job after taking a series of written tests designed to uncover just the kind of mindset that had been Esteban's stock in trade: logical, detailed, numbers-oriented, fastidious, dedicated. And then of course, there was this latest directive from his great, great grandfather... it was time to begin his quest, and his response... there was so much preparation needed.

"Fuck it," Esteban said aloud as he suddenly shook himself from his reverie. "I have to know now!" And he rushed at the package, pulled a knife from his pocket, and was just about to slice open the package when the alarm he had set struck midnight. He smiled. Now it *was* tomorrow.

Esteban slit open the big box, tore away the plastic pillows that were used to protect the item inside, and then he lifted it from the box. Damn, it was heavy. The item was actually another package wrapped in paper with a bright red and white spiraling design. Attached to the outside of the paper was a small white envelope. Esteban set the package down outside the box and opened the envelope. There was a note written in an amazingly neat hand. It said:

> *You're like a young Aeneas about to flee the*
> *falling city of Troy. You will experience many*

adventures and find at last the greatest city in
the world. Come see me first.

Love,

Dido

Esteban studied the note for a moment. "What kind of crackpot sent this?" he wondered.

Oh, he had read *The Aeneid* in some Great Books Seminar in college, remembered how the ancient hero, Aeneas, escaped Troy as the Greeks, hiding within their Trojan horse, rushed from it at midnight and sacked the once great city. How Aeneas had then set off on a quest to find a great new home, which would someday become Imperial Rome.

On his journey, Esteban remembered, Aeneas met Dido, a queen who fell in love with him, who made him tell the story of the fall of Troy, who eventually tried to seduce and keep him with her. There was something else about the Aeneid Esteban remembered too, a famous line from the book that became a cliché for a terrible warning. What was it?

"Beware Greeks bearing gifts," said a voice from behind Esteban, and the young man turned at once to see the vision of his great, great grandfather standing behind him.

"So, I guess I should beware of this gift," said Esteban.

His grandfather shrugged but that same knowing smile was still there. "Every day brings new discoveries," he began, "and this is a new day. So open it."

And so, Esteban tore through the bright red and white paper, and then fell back in surprise. No wonder the package was so damn heavy. It was a pair of enormous saddlebags, strangely shaped ones, clearly not for a horse, but for some other beast of burden, made of what appeared to be a middle eastern tapestry with a pattern of red, black, brown and white diamond shapes across it. A piece of very strong leather with a slit in the center connected the two bags.

"I could wear it over my head to carry things," said Esteban.

"Things you will need on your journey to Cíbola!" Estebanico added. "Cíbola is the great, undiscovered land of this millennium."

Esteban opened the pockets of the saddlebags and found that they were already packed with items: a pair of Bausch and Lomb binoculars of the very highest quality, a compass, cooking equipment, matches, a first aid kit, several flashlights, a heavy parka, hiking boots, sturdy clothing for desert travel.

"Exactly my size," said Esteban as he unfolded a light blue linen shirt and held it up in front of him. "And my style too. This Dido must want to meet me very badly."

"I'm sure she does," said his grandfather. "But you'd better be wary. I don't think this investment is entirely unselfish."

"Then I shouldn't accept this."

"If it will limit all the preparation you keep talking about and get you on you way sooner, then you *should* accept it. Visit Dido; talk to her, make her happy for a little while... then be on your way. She will tempt you, I'm sure. But no great quest has ever been completed without temptation."

"Do you think she'll let me go? I mean she's just made an enormous investment in my journey."

The old man smiled. "It's part of the adventure, isn't it? And really it all depends on your ability to negotiate, to read people... your talents, your wiles, your skill at escape."

Esteban knew that he had no real talent for negotiation or really any sense of guile or trickery.

"I'm always very direct," he said.

"Sometimes direct is the best way to be," answered Estebanico. "It can be very disarming. Remember that when you really don't know what to say next."

"Maybe I should find someone to go with me," Esteban whispered, "someone who really understands people."

"That would be wise," said Estebanico with a knowing smile. "If you can find the right person... it would be very wise."

Chapter 9
The Old Man Arrives

"Charles Augustus Blackmore."

Ceci savored the name as she pronounced it. "So the old man is finally coming out to see the operation and you," she told Gabriel.

"Don't sound so damn cheerful," Gabe answered as he steered his little Toyota Prius toward the offices of the Blackmore Copper Mine. "I haven't told you all the details, but that new deposit we've been looking at doesn't hold much promise."

"What do you mean?"

"Beto Santos…."

"Your mine expert?"

"Yeah. He took me down to check out the latest test areas and frankly…."

Gabe didn't want to have to explain the details to Ceci, but Santos had led him into the mine for an inspection, had taken him deep into the exploratory tunnels, had knelt and run his hand over the far wall of the dig.

"No big deposit here," Santos had said.

"So the deposit's not as big as we thought it was," Gabe had answered.

"Should be, according to all the science we have. But it's not."

Beto smiled at that moment, and it had seemed so inappropriate to Gabe.

"Don't tell me that there's no deposit," Gabe had said in disbelief.

"That's what I'm telling you, boss. No deposit, no more work, no more mine."

The report Santos wrote was pretty black and white. Gabe had forwarded it to Blackmore. Who knew what the old guy might do? He did have other mining operations that he could leverage to fund further exploration in the vicinity. But Santos's report had addressed those possibilities too and didn't offer much hope.

"I'll be honest with you, Cess," Gabe said. "I don't think Blackman's coming here is a good sign."

"I think it's a very good sign," Ceci answered with a smile that seemed to light up the whole interior of the car. "He knows a lot, has a lot of options, and he's aware of what a great job you've been doing. I think he's finally going to give you the recognition you deserve… oh, he'll give you more responsibility, but also a Vice Presidency, I'll bet."

Gabe glanced over at Ceci. She was dressed in her best navy business suit; her black hair pulled primly back behind her head. She also wore nylons, high heels, and a conservative pink blouse complimented by a strand of pearls.

"For someone as beautiful and intelligent as you are," he said, "you just don't seem to understand what's really happening."

"What's not to understand? We're still making money, aren't we?"

"Yes, but profits are way down, and with Santos's report on the new explorations, Blackmore might just decide to shut down the whole operation."

Ceci smiled. But it looked rather forced to Gabe.

"He won't shut things down," she said. "You'll turn things around… you always have. You've been keeping Blackmore

Copper profitable for as long as I can remember... cost cutting, creative hiring. The old man may lean on you to streamline things a little more, look for new opportunities, but there still should be a big promotion in it for you... and a bonus."

"I love you," Gabe said honestly, almost gratefully. "Thanks for the confidence." He pulled the car into his private parking spot, shut off the engine and leaned over to kiss Ceci. "Let's hope you're right."

"I usually am, aren't I?" she asked as she gave him an almost businesslike kiss. They were, after all, at work.

#

Charles Augustus Blackmore stood at the head of the large conference table and surveyed the members of his senior staff. Ceci Moreno, Head of HR; Donny Hainer, Director of Public Relations and Marketing; Gabriel Romo, Plant Manager and, of course, Devlin Lucero, Chief Financial Officer.

Wait/what?

Did he know this guy, Lucero? Blackmore asked himself. There was a moment of doubt. The young man leaned back in his chair as though he belonged there, and Blackmore had the feeling that he'd been part of the executive staff for as long as the rest of them. But had he? Blackmore had the creepy feeling that the guy had just shown up that morning, come out of nowhere.

The kid, because that's what he was, no more than twenty-two or twenty-three at the most, was handsome in a hungry kind of way. His eyes were dark, his body well toned from what must be hours in the gym. His choice of clothing was conservative: a well-tailored suit, starched pastel shirt, an open collar showing just a wisp of chest hair.

Anyway, he must have been here all along, right? Blackmore thought. Then he shook his head, sighed, lit a cigar, studied the flame at the end of it for a moment, took a deep puff, and smiled. This was a non-smoking room of course; the whole plant was "non-smoking." But Blackmore was the owner of the mine. It was once the biggest, most profitable in the state… now one of the few copper mines still operating. The old man felt he had the right to light up regardless of the rules.

"Anyone care to join me in a good smoke," he asked as he threw a handful of expensive Cuban cigars into the center of the table. "Ceci?" he teased.

"No thank you, Mr. Blackmore," the prim young woman answered with a slight smile.

Blackmore grinned, "Course not. How about you, Gabe?"

Gabriel reached forward, took a cigar, but didn't light it. Hainer did, though, so did Lucero.

"Come on Gabe boy, light up," Blackmore said. "I've got good news for you…."

"Are you going to make Gabe a VP?" Ceci asked with a big grin.

"Better'n at," Blackmore said. "I'm makin' him President."

They all stopped and just stared at the old Texan.

"President of Blackmore Copper?" Hainer asked.

"Fuck no," the old man answered and then looked concerned and whispered, "Pardon my French, Ceci."

She had shuddered a little but then gestured (uncomfortably) that she wasn't offended.

"President of the new CleanSweep Mining Corporation," Blackmore said. "He'll be chief shareholder too."

"What are you talking about?" Hainer asked. "What happens to Blackmore Copper?"

"What Blackmore Copper, son? The business is dead."

"We're still making a profit," Lucero said. "Gabe's done a great job with cost control."

Again that creepy feeling started to tingle around the edges of Blackmore's consciousness. "Do I know you, son? How long have you been here?" he asked.

"You promoted me last year, don't you remember?"

Blackmore felt a sudden wave of nausea roll through his stomach. He turned to Ceci for confirmation. She seemed more focused on the conversation about the Presidency of the new mine, and the fate of the old. The old man cleared his throat and addressed this strange, unknown young man again.

"What's the point of cost control," Blackmore said looking down at the meeting roster his administrative assistant had prepared for him in Dallas.

Devlin Lucero, the page said. The name was tucked right in there with the rest of the staff as though he'd been with the company forever.

"Devlin, boy," Blackmore said, somehow really enjoying the sound of the name as he said it, "You cut costs to hold on till better times, to survive until things start working out. That doesn't happen in a mine; when the deposit runs out, the mine is dead. And let's face it, muchachos; our mine es muerta. I read the report from Beto Santos, so did you, Gabe. Did you read it, Hainer?"

Donny nodded.

"Did you, Lucero?"

"Of course."

"Then I rest my case. No more copper ore, simple as that."

"So what's this new CleanSweep Mining Company then?" Gabe asked.

"It's your golden opportunity; that's what it is. Think about it, son. What happens when a mine goes dry?"

"The Department of the Interior shuts it down."

"Yeah, shuts it down, but what else?"

"Well, there has to be a big clean-up, of course."

"Bingo!" Blackmore said, but then he shuddered. "Those clean-ups are damn expensive, son. Too expensive for my old bones."

"But you have to clean up the site," Hainer said. "The EPA insists on it."

"Well yes, someone has to clean it up," Lucero added, "unless the mine keeps running."

Blackmore liked that, liked the sound of the kid's voice, and his ideas.

"Right," he said, "the mine keeps running on a very limited basis, with limited staff, limited operation, just getting by… limited investments too."

Gabriel stared down at his hands and began to shake his head. But Ceci was smiling.

"It really could be your golden opportunity, Gabe," she whispered.

"I doubt it," he whispered back. "And where will I get the money to run it anyway?"

"You and Mr. Lucero, here, set up a corporation," said Blackmore warming up to the new guy and the confident look in his eyes. He and the kid seemed to be really simpatico. "Of course, I'll make a sizeable investment myself, no ownership position of any kind, mind you, but somethin' significant enough to get you all started."

"Operating capital?" Gabe asked.

"It'll be a small operation, few employees, just enough to keep the mine going."

"Not really making any money, though," Gabe pointed out.

"I didn't say that. There'll be enough investment to keep the place running at a very modest pace. You set the proper goals; it'll look great on paper. Hainer here explains and sells the concept to the locals… gets 'em to buy into it."

Gabe turned to Ceci, and he looked very troubled indeed. The young woman finally seemed to understand what was troubling him. "Mr. Blackmore," she said, " the mine has over five hundred employees right now. This new company can't afford to keep that many on board, can it?"

Blackmore shook his head. "I wouldn't think so. You'll have to downsize, girl. Surely they must have taught you something about downsizing in that fancy university you went to."

"Downsize from over five hundred… to how many?"

"That's up to the new president, isn't it and the CFO? They're the ones who'll have to make the decision. Of course, they'll also have to answer to the shareholders, and I know we'll have certain requirements."

"If you want a good guess based on our current numbers and the investments you'll be making, boss," Lucero said. (How'd he have any idea of the kind of investment Blackmore intended to make?) "I think we'll be able to afford a staff of maybe fourteen or fifteen people, including the four of us of course."

Blackmore nodded heartily. It was like the kid had somehow read his mind.

"That's ten actual laborers," Ceci said, "… maybe eleven. You can't run a mine with ten laborers."

Blackmore stuck the unlighted end of the cigar into his mouth and pulled it out slowly to moisten it. Ceci shuddered. The act was somehow obscene, sexual, repulsive, disgusting, meant to be so, to put her in her place, she thought.

"Hell in the old days, Ceci," Blackmore said, "Two hardy and ambitious boys could operate a good paying claim and become millionaires. I know. I did it."

Gabe suddenly rose to his feet. He turned his back on the others and looked out the window at the heavy equipment that Blackmore Copper used in its day-to-day operations. No more of that he thought.

"I don't get it." Ceci said finally throwing up her hands. "I don't think it'll work."

Gabe suddenly turned and looked at her. His face was filled with a dozen different emotions. There was sorrow there, certainly disappointment, and no small amount of anger.

"Whether or not it works depends on our goals," he said to Ceci. "If you want to make money, this new mining company can't possibly succeed."

Lucero nodded with every word.

"But if you want to save a fortune, it's a great idea."

"It is?"

"Sure," Lucero said. "We just keep a little dummy operation going here, very little cost, almost no profit, but it still runs. Do that, and we can write off the whole mine; more importantly we won't have to pay for the multi-million dollar clean-up that the EPA requires."

"You'll have to do it eventually," Ceci said.

Lucero's smile was broad and somehow almost devilish. "When's eventually, Cess? How far into the future is that?"

Ceci's mouth hung open for a long moment.

"But what about the laid off workers? What about the town?"

Chapter 10
Sweet Sunny Girl

As Charles Augustus Blackmore was explaining his plan to avoid the costs of cleaning up after the shutdown of his mining operation and wondering just who this brilliant new kid was, VL Johnson sat in Jessica Amado's living room. He was tuning up that miraculous Fender Stratocaster guitar that she had shown him. He'd been over to her place a few times in the last week, and she'd been sweet, pleasant, and very attentive, just as she was now, sitting across from him, eyes all moist and eager behind those sexy glasses. But the outfit she was wearing, VL thought. That look was killer.

"Feelin' just like Rocker Jim," VL said as his fingers caressed the guitar strings. He strummed the Stratocaster, felt the electronic wail of the full-throated E chord.

"Perfectly tuned."

Jessica glided toward him across the center of the living room. She was wearing a variation on her tight teacher's outfit... one of the few that she could afford, she always said, though any woman would know that was a lie. Her starched white cotton blouse had small ivory buttons down the front... buttons that were barely able to hold the blouse closed and keep the woman's ample figure in check. Her black pencil skirt squeezed her hips excitingly. She also wore nylons and heels so high that they would certainly violate the dress code of any high school in Arizona.

"How's your G-string?" she whispered with a smirk.

VL did a double take. Jessica had always pretended to be so innocent in his presence... the question was such a set-up.

"How's my G-string?"

He twanged loudly on the open G. "How's yours."

Jessica smiled a sexy smile. She wanted him, and he'd finally figured it out. Some guys are just that dumb.

"Wanna see?" she asked, all pretense of innocence now gone.

VL blushed bright red, and then without a further word, he began blaring out the dirty base line of Rocker Jim's class: Sweet Sunny Girl. The rhythm was hard, driving, and obscene... especially when VL intoned that Rocker growl,

"SWEET SUNNY GIRL!"
"HOT SUMMER LAAAAADY!"

"HOT!" Jessica smiled and began writhing seductively to the music. She began unbuttoning her blouse. VL's eyes grew wide. He was panting as he watched Jessica's lacy bra pushing aside the confining fabric. VL slammed out another progression.

"Hot Summer Girl," he rasped, and Jessica turned her back on him, lowered the blouse over her shoulders, and then spun, tearing it off and throwing it at him.

"Missed me," VL giggled in nervous excitement as he ducked the flying blouse without losing a single sensuous beat. Jessica smiled, turned her back on him again, and let her fingers glide over her hips... all the way to the zipper on the back of her skirt.

VL pounded harder on the guitar; Jessica's hips swayed as the zipper slowly opened.

"Sweet Sunny Lady," V. L. called, and Jessica began sliding the tight skirt down over her hips, over her thighs, over her knees. She bent forward, and then she dropped the skirt around her ankles and deftly stepped out of it.

VL slapped out a series of nasty chords and watched.

"Like the show?" Jessica breathed.

"HELLO IN THERE!" A woman was shouting, and then she began pounding hard on Jessica's front door. "WHAT'S GOING ON?"

"It's my wife," VL whispered as he froze for a moment stopping his performance and Jessica's. She frantically pulled up her skirt, gathered up her blouse and began rushing toward the bathroom.

"I'll get the door," VL said as he stood and set the magical guitar aside.

"I'll be right back," Jessica answered.

"Change," he told her as she ran.

"Huh?"

"Your clothes."

"Oh, yeah."

"Something less... hot."

The word made Jessica stop in her tracks. Then she turned back to VL and repeated the word as a question, "hot?" Suddenly she seemed to change her mind completely... and her direction. She just smirked at him.

"Get outta here," VL ordered. But Jessica didn't. Instead, she put on her too-tight blouse, buttoned it up, and walked to the front door, straightening herself as she went.

She answered the door herself.

Chapter 11
Mario And Sophia

Just a few moments earlier, Mario sat at the counter of his grandfather's newly cleaned and brightly shining restaurant. Tres Flores hadn't opened yet, and so Mario was able to finish the homework he was supposed to do the night before. Beside him sat Sophia, his constant companion since she moved in with the family two days before. She had a big box of Crayola Crayons and was busy sketching images... the same sweet kinds of images over and over again: couples, men and women, boys and girls all facing each other, all in profile, all smiling happily. Some of her drawings were set under the sea where divers and fish were swimming up to each other and smiling in a similar fashion. Some were set in the forest where happy bears smiled benevolently at squirrels and deer.

"What a cheerful outlook you have, Sophia," Veronica said as she came up and peered over the girl's shoulder.

"Non vi è alcun motivo di essere triste," the little girl answered as though she understood Mario's mother's English perfectly.

"What'd she say?" Veronica whispered to her son.

Mario turned to his mother with a slight smile. He still hadn't gotten used to the fact that he could understand Sophia's Italian completely when no one else but Ceci could...

even though he never spoke Italian or even heard it before Sophia had arrived.

"She says, 'What's the use of being sad?'" Mario answered.

Sophia turned and smiled at Veronica, who smiled back and patted the little girl on the top of her head.

Papa Luís made his way up to the trio. He had just finished rechecking the power to the jukebox, which now stood in the very center of the dining area. Gabriel and his brother had moved the box into the restaurant after it had started playing at Sophia's arrival. Ceci had identified the tune it played as *The Theme from The Godfather*. But now the box stood silent again. Luís had thought it might be the lack of power in the small outlet at the back of the restaurant. So he'd run an extra-strength extension in from the storage area. No luck.

"Whatcha up to, kids?" Luís asked Mario and Sophia.

"Homework," Mario answered gloomily.

"Famiglie felici," Sophia said, holding up one of her pages filled with images of happy families, smiling girls and boys, fathers and mothers.

Luís thought he understood the girl's words, and yet he still turned to Mario for reassurance.

"Happy families?" the boy said. But before Luís could comment further, Sophia spoke up.

"Sì nonno, sto disegnando la famiglia e mio padre e mia madre prima che l'uragano li ha portati via."

"She says, 'Yes, grandpa,'" Mario translated. "'I'm drawing your family and my own father and mother before the whirlwind took them away.'"

"Missing your parents must make you feel very sad." Luís responded, and he suddenly frowned.

The little girl nodded, shrugged, and sighed heavily. Luís went to the child and kissed her on the forehead.

"I sure wish you could speak English, honey," he said. And at that very moment the jukebox came to life, blaring out a series of wild chords, which happened to be the very same chords that VL was playing on the magical Stratocaster some five miles from the restaurant.

"SWEET SUNNY GIRL!

Rocker Jim sang from the jukebox, and suddenly Sophia jumped down from her stool and began dancing crazily to the music. It was a funny, innocent, but very energetic dance, featuring a double-step and a silly spin-around that made Mario afraid that she was going to lose her balance and plow right into him. She didn't.

"You go, girl," called Veronica, and she began dancing too. Her eyes sparkling, her lips formed a tight smile of concentration, and then she reached for her father's hand and pulled him out onto the dance floor.

It took Luís a moment to get into it, and then he was the man with the moves! This, after all, was music from his generation, and so he did a little frug, a little stroll, even a bit of clumsy mashed potatoes.

"Papa Luís can dance," said Sophia happily, and suddenly everyone stopped and looked at her.

"Hey, what?" the girl asked without stopping her dance for even a moment.

"You spoke English," Veronica said.

"Yeah, cool, huh?"

"Could you do it all along?"

Sophia shrugged, "I don't think so."

Veronica turned to Mario with a look of confusion, but the boy shrugged too. "Don't ask," he said, and then he was on the floor adding some break dancing to the festivities.

Suddenly, the front door to the restaurant slammed shut, and Mamá Carmen stood in the doorway with her hands on her hips. "What's going on?" she called in perfect unison with the words of Melinda Johnson those five miles away.

"Fiesta!" Luís answered as he danced over to his wife. "Come join us, my sweet summer girl." But at the moment, the music came to an abrupt end, and silence filled the restaurant.

"That was so great," cheered Sophia.

"She speaks English, now?" Mama asked.

"Shhhh," Luís whispered, as thought talking about it might end the miracle.

Mario smiled as he made his way up to the jukebox. He peered in through the thick front window glass and after a moment called out to everyone, "Hey, look at this."

The others all gathered around. Mario pointed to the row of titles listed on the box's menu.

"Was that there before?" he asked.

Luís shrugged. And then his eyes brightened. "Great, more Rocker Jim."

"And the Beatles," added Carmen. "And Dylan, and Elvis."

"So cool," whispered Mario.

"I love it," squealed Sophia.

Chapter 12
The Decision

"I can't do it," Gabriel told Charles Blackmore. "I won't preside over the dismantling of the mine and the ruination of our town."

"Ruination?" Lucero laughed.

"You can't be serious. Ruination?" Blackmore chimed in.

"You know what he means, you nasty old viper," Ceci answered angrily. "He's not going to be your henchman as you strangle our town until it wastes away to nothing."

"Ceci," Blackmore said without losing what was now clearly a very evil smile, "I thought we were friends."

"So did I," the woman answered. Now she was up on her feet, her arms crossed defensively, her eyebrows arched, lips almost sneering at the old man.

"I don't think you should call your friends vipers," Lucero said.

"I don't think Mr. Blackmore should make his friends betray their families and drive their whole community into poverty."

"Sit down, Ceci, I can handle my own fights," Gabe whispered to her. Ceci turned to him as though she were angry with him too. Then she steadied herself and slowly sat down in her chair. But her expression still burned with anger and a sense of betrayal.

Old man Blackmore turned to his CFO, Devlin Lucero. "Luce," he began, "I don't remember you as well as I should, I'm so damn old."

Lucero nodded. His grin widened.

"But I certainly like the way you think."

"Learned it all from you, Boss," the kid answered.

"Yes. Well anyway," Blackmore continued, "Do you think doing your job is the same as betraying your friends?"

"No, sir," Lucero answered quickly.

"So, what do you think of this little outburst by Ms. Moreno here."

Lucero eyed the angry woman, and then he smiled. "I think she's just sticking up for her..." he weighed his words carefully and then finished, "...lover."

"She and Gabe are lovers?" Blackmore's tone was pure mock disbelief.

Gabe rolled his eyes, but Lucero answered immediately, "Of course they are. You know it, everyone does."

Blackmore closed his eyes for a moment and enjoyed this new direction in which Lucero was steering them. Man, he thought, the kid was brilliant.

"Isn't that against company policy, Luce?" Blackmore asked.

"Seems like it should be... but I'm not sure about the exact rules."

"Then let's find out from our representative from Human Resources, here. Cecilia, how does the company feel about intimate relationships between executive employees?"

"I...." she began.

"This is all bullshit," Gabe said getting to his feet and walking up to Blackmore.

"No, it's not," the old man answered. "When you have your own company you can make whatever rules you want. But in my company, a relationship between unmarried executives is forbidden!

"Now as for you, Gabe, do you want to be the President of the new CleanSweep Mining Company or not?"

"I can't accept, sir," Gabe said lowering his eyes.

Blackmore grunted in disappointment; then a brand new idea seemed to take possession of him. He turned to his Chief Financial Officer.

"You want it, Luce?"

"The Presidency?"

"CEO. That's what we're talking about."

"Hell yes."

"Then it's yours."

Ceci groaned.

"With one stipulation," the old man continued.

"Anything."

"You keep these two lovebirds on in a diminished capacity. And, out of respect for company policy, keep them apart."

Lucero stood, walked slowly up to Ceci, and studied her… studied her entire body carefully.

"I think I have the perfect assignment for you, Miss Moreno," he began. "You'd make a fine personal secretary.

"Don't you think so, Gabe?"

Gabe felt like rushing the kid and beating him senseless… whoever the hell he was. But in the end, Gabe just stood there looking at the floor and saying nothing.

"What do you say, Ms. Moreno," Lucero asked, "you and I, together… in charge of Clean Sweep?"

Ceci jerked herself away from Lucero and marched toward the door. "I'm finished with all of you," she said. Then she turned toward Gabe and flashed her angry eyes at him. "You too, you… you damn coward." And she was gone.

"Why, Cecilia…" Blackmore said shaking his head and laughing. "Such language."

Gabe started to go after her.

"Wait, Mr. Romo," Lucero called. "If I actually get the presidency, I'll need your expertise around here. I suggest you stay; you may end up being the only person in your family who's employed."

"My family runs a very successful restaurant," Gabe said.

"We'll see how successful it is if the economy of the town begins to fail," Blackmore responded. "You can have a hand in preventing that failure, you know."

Gabe sank into a chair. He studied his big hands for a moment. "So, what's the deal?" he asked. "The presidency?"

"That ship has sailed, boy," Blackmore said. "You turned me down, remember?"

Lucero grinned then. "Just so happens I have an opening for a Foreman. It doesn't pay anywhere near what your current Plant Manager position pays, and, of course, nothing like the presidency of the new company. But if you're willing to advise me on day-to-day operations... you know, from the Foreman's point of view... I think we can arrange for some cash incentives."

Gabe just sat there staring at his hands, and nodding sadly.

"And Ceci?" he asked at last.

"If she's willing to come in and serve as my private secretary," Lucero began, "I'm sure she'll find me rather... generous."

Gabe looked up at Devlin Lucero. "I'll talk to her," he said, "but I don't think I'll get anywhere. Remember I'm on the outs with her too now."

Lucero shook his head sadly. "So then where am I going to find a bright, sexy, hard working young woman to work with me?"

Chapter 13
Confrontation?

Jessica Amado flung the door open and stared out at the wife of the man she had been so close to seducing.

"Oh, hi, Mel," she said with a wide-eyed innocence that made Mel want to scratch her eyes out. "What's up?"

"Is my husband here?" Melinda Johnson asked. There was no way of hiding the anger she was feeling. "And just what the hell have you two been up to this morning anyway?" she felt like asking it… but she didn't.

"Actually…" Jessica began with that same tone of innocence, but before she could finish VL popped up right behind her.

"Hi Mel, just working on that new Rocker Jim riff I told you about. Want to come in and give a listen?"

Jessica turned to VL, flashed a quick look back at his wife and then shook her head. "Not today, guys," she said. "I'm afraid I have to go out. I was just about to tell you that when Mel here…."

"It's okay;" Mel answered. "We can't stay anyway. I need you back at the clinic, VL."

"What's wrong?"

"It's one of the camels," she answered. "He's disappeared."

Chapter 14
The Prayer

Ceci walked down the road from the mine and ducked into the little church that stood across the main drag from the operation's outer parking lot. The place was dead quiet inside. Rows of pews faced an ornate altar decked out with buckets full of lilies. A very peaceful Jesus looked down from his cross at the front of the church. He seemed to be smiling benevolently.

Ceci slid into the back pew, knelt for a moment, and then closed her eyes to squeeze out the tears that had been forming ever since she left the meeting.

"Assholes," she prayed and then, realizing that the word was far from appropriate, she thought, "Forgive me. And deliver me from those... what? Assholes."

She didn't like what they were doing at all, and old Blackmore, whom she had expected to be so very generous, was in reality as greedy as everyone said he was. She and he had only met a couple of times, she thought, in a few meetings, at a few company parties. And here he was pretending that he knew her well and that she shared his point of view about the fate of the mine and the town.

She pictured the last day for their 500 workers, all of them laid off... by whom? She and Gabe would have to do it, according to Blackmore.

Bitterness. Resentment. Hell, workers at other companies had been known to kill people who were conducting layoffs. And these were mine workers... big tough people, used to working in difficult conditions, who weren't afraid of anything... including violence. She and Gabe would still be employed through it all, and would surely be seen as traitors to their own town.

Would she do it... would Gabe? It was their job supposedly.

"Like some shit," she murmured, and then, stunned at her latest obscenities, she put her fingertips to her lips and giggled. What was she doing talking like this... she never did... and in a church?

It was all Gabe's fault, she decided. He had been such a disappointment. Instead of making an impassioned plea on behalf of the town, convincing old man Blackmore to keep the mine open and keep its workers fully employed, he had taken the coward's way out.

"No sir," she mimicked him under her breath. "I can't take the evil job you're offering me, but don't worry; I won't stand in your way. I'll let you and Lucero strangle the town while I go wait on tables in my uncle's restaurant."

Ceci shivered a little; she had been sweating, and the AC in the little church was up very high. "Asshole!" there was that word again. She'd said it out loud too this time. But you know what? Gabe really was one... wasn't he?

"Excuse me," said someone directly behind her. Ceci jumped at the sound and then turned quickly. Esteban Dorantes was standing there. He had a good job, a much safer one than hers or Gabe's... or so it seemed this morning. Of course, half the people in the town still thought he was crazy.

"You okay, Cess?" he asked.

"Me?"

"Yeah, you seem to be shivering."

"Well, it is a little chilly in here."

Esteban leaned in closer to study her face. "And aren't those tears in your eyes?"

Ceci's eyes were watery. She fluttered her lashes, but it only seemed to make things worse. Now tears were rolling down her cheeks.

"It's been a rough day at the mine."

"But things are okay with you and Gabriel, right?"

What made him ask that? Ceci wondered. Might as well be honest, though. "Actually," she had to admit, "they aren't."

Esteban walked around the end of he pew and moved in beside her.

"But your job is okay, isn't it?"

Ceci shook her head. "Not really."

Esteban rested his hand on her shoulder and looked into her eyes. His expression was so sympathetic, so kind that it made Ceci remember how sweet he had always been to her. It also made her think of the great difference between his attitude and that of everyone in the meeting she had just come from.

"Assholes," she murmured again.

Esteban broke out laughing when he heard the word, and that made Ceci start laughing too, and then she was crying again.

"So, are you happy or sad?"

"Both," she answered. "Actually no, just sad."

Esteban pulled Ceci to him and gave her a hug.

"The latest study says the mine is drying up, and they want to shut it down," she told him. "They want Gabe and me to lay off all the workers. Everyone will be out of a job. The whole town will be impoverished."

"Won't that happen anyway," Esteban asked, as he pulled back so he could look at her. "If the mine dries up, that is?"

"I guess so," Ceci sobbed. "But they could keep it open for a couple more years; I know they could. Gabe could figure out a way."

Ceci started sniffling, then coughing. "I'm making a mess of myself, aren't I?"

"I think you look beautiful," Esteban said, "as always. And it's nice to be close to you again."

Ceci couldn't help but smile.

"Besides the town is going to be rich very soon anyway," Esteban added. "I'm sure of it."

"Yeah right," Ceci said as she gathered herself and tried to smile back at Esteban. "How?"

His eyes suddenly lit up. "Cíbola!" He whispered the word as though it were a prayer.

"Not that again?" Ceci said suddenly feeling just as disappointed in Esteban as in everyone else.

"The Seven Cities of Gold! I know where they are, and when I find them I'll use their treasure to restore the wealth of La Sentencia."

Ceci's face twisted with disappointment. "The Seven Cities of Gold? You know that's nonsense... an old legend made up by a bunch of crazy survivors from a failed expedition."

Esteban's eyes were as bright as ever. "One of the crazy survivors you're talking about was my great, great, great, great whatever... grandfather Estebanico Dorantes. He visits me in my dreams. He's tells me that I have to undertake a great quest, to find Cíbola. And I want to use its treasure to restore our city."

"But our city doesn't need to be restored. It's fine, and it can stay fine if old man Blackmore will just let Gabe manage the mine the way he has been."

Esteban smiled as though Ceci was the one hearing ghostly predictions about the town.

"Won't happen."

"Who told you that?"

"You did, Ceci. The mine has dried up."

The girl melted, lowered her shoulders and her eyes. "Yeah."

Esteban put his arms around her, held her for a moment, and then she put her arms around his neck and burst into tears once again.

They sat like that for a long time, Ceci sobbing, Esteban consoling her and then, when she seemed to be all cried out, he pulled away from her, eyes brighter than ever, and said, "Hey, why don't you come with me?"

"Where?"

"On the quest."

"Are you nuts?"

"Why not. You said you're about to lose your job, Gabe has let you down, and the town is going to hell. Why not a change of pace? Why not a whole new adventure? Come with me."

"To Cíbola? The place doesn't exist, Stevie, and how are you going to get there anyway... wherever it is?"

"New Mexico."

"How do you know that?"

"Dreams remember... as for transportation...."

Before Esteban could even finish the sentence, the back door to the church swung wide open and a camel clip-clopped its way down the main aisle of the church. It didn't look at either Esteban or Ceci, just went up to the altar and stood there nodding.

Ceci looked wide-eyed at the man she was still holding on to.

"Was that camel in your dreams too?" she asked.

He just smiled.

"GIT! Get outta here!"

Father Riley came scurrying out from the sacristy arms flailing. He raced up to the camel and tried to shoo it away.

The camel studied the wild-eyed priest with the same peaceful expression that Jesus seemed to have as he hung so benevolently on his cross.

The priest grabbed the beast by the neck and tried to turn it around. He propped his feet against the steps of the altar and heaved. The camel didn't move. It wasn't acting stubbornly, it seemed to Ceci. It didn't make a sound. It just wouldn't obey the priest.

Ceci looked over at Esteban and smiled.

"Transportation," he said. Then he pulled away from the young woman, went up to the front of the church, took the camel by the neck, turned it around, and led it easily from the church as Father Riley looked on in grateful exasperation.

Ceci watched the proceedings. She caught the eye of the priest and just smiled shyly and shrugged. Then she murmured one word,

"Cíbola."

Chapter 15
The Deal

Hours had gone by. Blackmore, Lucero and eventually even Hainer had really worked Gabe over, trying to get him to stay with the firm in a diminished capacity.

"So now, Gabriel," said the old man, "I want you to think very hard, think about the one thing that you really want... one thing that is so important to you that you'll be willing to join our new operation if we give it to you. We can keep you on at your current salary even as a foreman... but we'll also..." and here Blackmore's eyes lit up as though he were about to perform some amazing magic trick, "give you something in exchange for your enthusiastic participation."

"Anything you want," added Lucero.

"How about a bio-break," Gabe asked. "I mean, we've been here for hours."

Lucero eyed Blackmore. This kind of organizational torture (endless meetings with no bathroom breaks) was very much to his liking. But Blackmore smiled.

"Sure Gabe. We want to work with you, and we certainly don't want to turn this into a pissing contest."

Lucero laughed at that. "Ten-minute break then," he added.

"But be ready to give us your answer when you get back," Blackmore said. "What will it take to keep you here... the one thing that will make you accept the foreman job?"

Ten minutes later Gabriel Romo was back in his chair at the conference room table. Blackmore had yet to make his way back into the room, but Lucero was there. So was Hainer.

"The old man's on a call," Lucero said. "Be back here in a minute. In the meantime, have you got any recommendations for a personal assistant."

"Ceci'll never do it," Gabe said.

"Guess not," Lucero sighed. Then he took out his iPhone, pressed his thumb on the button and called up the home screen. He selected his photo album, found the image he was looking for, then turned the phone around and held it up to Gabe.

"Here's a pretty good alternate candidate, don't you think?"

Gabe looked. "Isn't that the substitute junior high school teacher?" he asked, "the one who works on the newspaper."

"Jessica Amado," Lucero said. "I've had my eye on her for quite a while."

"I like the glasses," Hainer added, as he looked at the image over Gabe's shoulder, "very sexy."

"Wonder what the school administration thinks of her strutting around in an outfit like that?" Lucero added. "I hear she's already been censured by the school board."

Gabe didn't say anything. This wasn't his kind of conversation.

Just then Blackmore came into the room.

He took his seat at the head of the table and turned to Gabe. There was that bone-chilling smile again.

"Have you come up with something, Gabe," he asked, "something you really want... maybe a hot new car, time at my place in Cancun?"

"Not that, but I do have something in mind."

"Well, don't keep us waiting, boy," Blackmore insisted. "What the hell is it?"

"Jobs."

Blackmore and Lucero looked at each other for a long moment.

"For all the workers you lay off," Gabe added.

Hainer laughed. "Are you nuts?"

"He's not," Blackmore said immediately, holding up his hand to Hainer. "Maybe it can be arranged."

"Jobs for five hundred workers?"

"Doesn't have to be that exactly, does it, Gabe?"

The young man stared at the older one for some time. "No, I guess not, just reasonable job opportunities for them."

"We'll need to have strict rules for proper performance, then," Lucero added.

"How about this," Blackmore said. "We'll set up an alternate operation, one we think will offer opportunities for the laid-off mine workers. It won't be a mine but something that matches their skill level. There won't be jobs for everyone, but there will be fair openings for those who qualify. If their performance is acceptable, they'll do well. If not, they'll be replaced by any other mine worker who's interested in a new career."

Gabe stared at the old man for a long moment and then smiled, a more genuine smile than Hainer had seen all day long. "I think I can live with that," Gabe said.

"But no meddling in the operations or the policies of the new business, whatever it turns out to be."

Gabe thought for another minute and then nodded. "Seems reasonable. As long as your business practices are legal."

Lucero laughed. "Oh, we know the law, believe me."

"We may bend it a little from time to time," Blackmore added, "but we never actually break it."

Again there was that evil smile; it seemed to add a thousand new lines to the old man's wrinkled face.

Gabe looked from Blackmore to Lucero. He didn't like either of them at all. They both made him feel creepy as though he were dealing with the devil himself. Still, their proposal did seem reasonable.

"Okay," Gabe said quickly, and he slammed the palms of his hands onto the table as if to reassert his conviction.

"Got a contract right here," said Lucero. He pulled a set of papers out of one of the folders in front of him. "Sign on the dotted line, and we'll put all these plans into motion."

Gabe signed without even reading the contract, as though all he wanted to do was get it all over with and get the hell out of there.

"Can I tell Ceci about this?" he asked.

"Sure, go ahead," said Blackmore. "And you know, I'm damn glad that you're going to be part of our team."

Gabe nodded curtly, then stood and left the room without even looking back. Hainer started to go too, but then he turned to the old man.

"So tell me. Just what kind of business are you planning to start anyway?" he asked.

Lucero eyed Blackmore and then the two said it together.

"CARWASH!"

"But there's a chain of successful carwashes already in town," Hainer said.

"Yeah," Blackmore answered. "But they're not very efficient."

"And," Lucero added, "With all the foul weather we've been having lately, it does seem like a perfect opportunity."

"But the McCarwash chain is run by some pretty good guys, you know," Hainer said.

Blackmore sneered. "Good guys don't make it. You should know that by now, boy. Business is business. Let the best man and the best car wash win."

And then Blackmore pulled himself to his feet and hobbled from the room.

Chapter 16
Good Times

"Grandpa Luís," Sophia called from across the room in her little girl's foghorn voice, "Just what are you doing with that jukebox?"

The old man was bending over the machine studying the selections.

"This crazy thing seems to be updating itself," he said.

"Got some new tunes?" Mario asked. Once again he sat in one of the booths doing his endlessly overdue homework.

"Not exactly new," Luís said.

"Oldies but goodies?" Sophia said putting her hands on her hips, and the old man eyed her wondering how she ever picked up all these words and phrases so quickly.

"Even older than oldies," he said. "Listen."

Luís pushed three selection keys; a mechanical arm moved within the jukebox, selected a 45 RPM record, pulled it from its slot, placed it on a turntable, and then pulled back as a record needle moved into position and lowered itself onto the disk.

Suddenly, the heavy brass flare of that old swing number, *In the Mood*, filled the room.

Luís clapped his hands and did a few jitterbug steps.

"Oh grandpa, I like it!" Sophia cried as she ran up to the old man. "Teach me, teach me," and she took his hands in hers and began swaying her hips and shuffling her feet to match the movements of the man she had already come to think of as her adopted grandfather.

Luís swayed with the girl, pulled her close than pushed her back, spun her around and then twirled her under his arm.

"Am I doin' good, grandpa?" Sophia squealed with delight.

"You're a regular bobbysoxer," he said.

"Bobbysoxer," the little girl repeated trying on the word and deciding she liked it.

"Pretty soon we'll have to get her some penny loafers and a big hoop skirt." These words came from Mama Carmen, who had once again snuck in to wonder at the crazy things that her husband was doing with the kids.

"I like your choice of music," she said.

"Before your time, Mama," Luís answered.

"Before yours too."

"Just barely. My Aunt Minnie taught me these steps when I was just a kid. Said they would help me impress the girls."

"Well, I'm impressed," said Carmen. "Are you, Sophia?"

"I'm impressed, and I can dance good too," the little girl said. "I love this music."

"I thought you would," said Luís, and then a loud bray of approval came from the open window at the side of the restaurant. Everyone stopped and turned toward the sound, only to see one of the camels standing there. It seemed to be nodding to the music.

Sophia laughed and ran up to the beast and put her arms around it. "I thought you'd like it, Jasmine," she said.

"Jasmine?"

Mario got up from behind his mountain of homework and walked up to the camel. "Sophia and I named the camels the last time they came through town. We even told Dr. Johnson, and she likes the names too."

"We named the camels Aladdin and Jaffar," said Sophia.

"And this is Jasmine,"

"She's the girl."

The music ended, and Luís swept Sophia up off her feet and carried her over to the counter at the front of the restaurant.

"Soda, Señorita Sophia?" he asked.

"Sí, Señor," the little girl answered and curtsied.

"She speaks Spanish too?" asked Carmen.

"Solo un poco," said the little girl.

Luís sighed happily as he scooped ice cream into a tall glass and poured strawberry soda on top of it. He felt wonderful. Things were going so well.

"Sold out again tonight," Carmen told her husband as she checked the reservation list at the front of the restaurant.

Things couldn't be any better, could they?" he said.

"There hasn't even been a dust storm in weeks," Mario added.

"We're in the good times," said his grandfather. "I think they started when the camels first came to town, don't you?'

Carmen nodded her head, so did Sophia.

"I think it was when Sophia showed up," said Mario.

"Or maybe the jukebox," added Luís. "Let's have another tune shall we?"

Mario went over to the box and picked another song, *That Good Times Rock & Roll.*

#

Across town at the veterinary clinic, Esteban was talking to VL, negotiating to take the camel with him for a few months.

"Let me get this straight," VL said. "You want to borrow Aladdin to accompany you on a trek into New Mexico... and you're going on foot?"

"That's the way it has to be," Esteban answered.

"You and Ceci Moreno?"

"Yep."

"Impossible!"

Esteban stepped back as though he'd been punched; then he shook his head emphatically. "She understands my vision."

Dr. Melinda joined them. She had treated her husband with ice-cold indifference since she had confronted him at Jessica's place. Mel hadn't accused VL of anything exactly, just spoke very curtly, even when they got back to the clinic and found Esteban already there.

Mel didn't even look at her husband now. She simply smiled sadly at Crazy Stevie (as she often called Esteban) and asked him to repeat the story he had just told VL, which he did, in clipped phrases:

"Goin' to New Mexico on a quest.

"Idea came to me in a dream.

"Told Ceci about it. She got all excited.

"She's coming too. So's the camel."

"Are you asking if you can rent the camel?" Mel asked.

"Why would I do that? You don't own him."

"We're taking care of them all... looking out for their well-being."

"They don't need your caretaking. They came here all by themselves didn't they? Got here in one piece."

"I know, but there were three of them."

"So now there can be two of them... it's for the good of the community, Doc."

Mel squinted the way she often did when she was unsure of something. "How can it help the community?" she asked.

"I promised Ceci that I wouldn't tell."

"Oh great!" Mel said. "Have her call me."

Then she gave her husband another cruel, icy stare and walked away.

"Ouch," said Esteban, "what'd you do?"

VL shook his head. "Just take the camel."

"But Mel said...."

"I'll deal with her. I'm the one who owns the damn clinic. You want the camel for your adventure or not?"

"Absolutely."

"Then take it and get the hell out of here before Mel comes back with more rules and regulations."

Chapter 17
The Argument

Gabriel was exhausted when he finally made his way up the walk to Ceci's home later that same evening. She lived in a small garden apartment on the ground floor right off the street. Gabe used the key Ceci had given him and walked right in. The place was dark; the shades were drawn against the late afternoon heat, so the entryway and living room were deep in shadows. Still, Gabe could see a light in the bedroom and knew that Ceci must be in there. He started down the hallway toward her, but before he could get there, he heard Ceci calling to him.

"Gabe?"

"Yeah, it's me."

"You still with the mine?"

The young man smiled as he made his way into the room, then stopped short. Ceci had her backpack out, the big one she used when they went on those long treks into the mountains. She had different outfits lying on the bed, and she was selecting clothes to put into it.

"Going somewhere?" he asked.

"Answer my question."

"Are you running out on me?"

"Are you still working for the mine?"

Gabe moved all the way into the room and sat down in the old wicker rocking chair in the corner. "Well, yes I am," he said. "But it's going to work out okay, Cess. I made a hell of a deal with Blackmore."

"I think the operative word in that sentence is 'hell,'" Ceci answered. "The guy's some kind of devil, don't you think?"

Gabe shrugged. He couldn't disagree with her.

"He must have come here right from Hades."

"But he did make me a great offer."

Ceci turned and faced her boyfriend at last. She put her hands on her hips. "In exchange for what?"

"Staying on as the foreman of the new mine at my full salary... but there are some really positive aspects to it."

"There'd better be?"

Gabe stood, walked up to Ceci and put his arms around her. He pulled her to him and stared into her eyes.

"He promised to find jobs for all the workers we have to lay off."

"Jobs for five hundred workers? How's he going to do that?"

"Well we haven't worked out the details yet, but I'm sure you and I can...."

Ceci pushed Gabe away in anger. "No way. I'm done with Blackmore... and I'm done with his mine."

"But we can save the town."

"By finding non-existent jobs for five hundred people in a place where there are no jobs?"

"Okay so it will take some work on our part, Cess, but together...."

"Un uh, Mister, there's no together anymore."

Gabe raked his hand through his hair in frustration.

"But we have to save the town."

"You save it your way, I'll save it mine."

Gabe felt a sudden sense of panic. He stepped back and studied the whole scene: the clothes on the bed, the half filled backpack, and the anger in Ceci's eyes. "Where the hell are you going anyway?"

Ceci was starting to cry now. She tried to sniff back tears, but it didn't work. "On a quest," she managed to say. "So what?"

"A quest? Ceci, who the hell have you been talking to?"

"Esteban."

"Esteban? Dorantes? Crazy Stevie?"

"He's not crazy, and we ARE going on a quest... together."

Gabe rolled his eyes. "Great! Just what kind of quest has he talked you into?"

Ceci turned back to the bed and began shoveling clothing into her backpack with a greater sense of urgency. "Cíbola," she whispered the word under her breath as though she was embarrassed to admit it.

"What was that? Cíbola?"

"Yes, Cíbola... the Seven Cities of Gold. He knows where they are, and we're going to find them together and bring back a treasure that will save this town from the evil bastard that you just agreed to keep working for."

Gabe just looked at Ceci in disbelief. She had always been a little romantic, maybe a little impulsive too, but this? Agreeing to go on a quest with a certified lunatic? Finally, he calmed down enough to ask another question.

"And just where are these Golden Cities supposed to be, according to Stevie, that is, on Fantasy Island?"

"No," Ceci answered. Her nose was turned up proudly now, but tears still covered her cheeks. "They're in New Mexico."

"New Mexico? Where in New Mexico?"

"Esteban knows."

"People have been searching for those damn cities for centuries, Cess. Everyone knows they're not real. How the hell can he claim to know where they are?"

"His great, great... whatever grandfather came to him in a dream and told him exactly where to find them."

Gabe just shook his head. "Damn, Cess... you're going on a quest into New Mexico to find a place the whole world knows doesn't exist." He sighed, moved back to the rocker, sat back down again, and placed his face in his hands. Finally, he looked up.

"So, how are you going to get there? Walk?"

"Yes!"

"Carrying all your belongings for hundreds of miles."

"We'll have help."

"Well thank God for that... a minivan?"

"A camel."

"You're walking across Arizona and who knows how far into New Mexico with a madman and one of VL's camels."

Ceci turned toward Gabe then, her nose still in the air, wounded pride oozing from every pore, tears still streaming down her face. Gabe stared at her for a moment, wanted to jump up and put his arms around her and protect her from these crazy ideas and the madman who created them. He stood finally, moved toward her; she backed away.

"Don't you come near me," she called. "You're the one who's making deals with the devil."

"Ceci, I won't let you go."

"Try and stop me, Mr. Romo!"

"I'll have that nutcase Stevie arrested."

"On what grounds?"

Gabe thought for a moment, "for contributing to the delinquency of a minor."

"I'm almost thirty years old, Gabe," she said. "And the only delinquent *miners* I know of are planning to close down the one source of employment in this part of the state."

"But I worked out a deal; I told you that."

"You wish," she answered bitterly.

Gabe went to her and tried to put his arms around her. She shrugged him off, stared him in the eyes, and then began shaking all over in anger.

"GET OUT OF MY HOUSE!" she shouted.

"But Cess I need your help, I need your HR skills."

"My skills aren't available to devils, Gabe. Have Black-more find you some sorceress to conjure up five hundred jobs out of nothing. And while she's at it maybe she can conjure up a backbone for YOU! Now get out of here! I need to pack."

Gabe stared at her for a very long moment. She returned his gaze defiantly. Finally, shaking his head, he pushed past her into the hallway and out the front door. What else was there to do?

When Ceci heard Gabe leave she threw herself onto the bed, right on top of all those clothes and began to sob loudly.

"Oh Gabe," she cried, "What am I doing? What the hell am I doing? Where am I going? I'm so fed up with this town, so disappointed in you and those monsters at the mine....

"But why, for God sakes, didn't you stop me?"

Chapter 18
The Gift

The fire-engine-red Mercedes convertible pulled up in front of Jessica Amado's little home. The car's white leather upholstery and chrome trim gleamed golden in the sunset. Then a tall, handsome young man in an expensive suit got out of the car. He touched the car's door handle and heard the Mercedes honk three times as it locked itself.

The young man reached into the passenger seat and lifted out a basket that had an overwrap of pink tissue paper. There was a big red bow on top. Something was alive inside the wrapping. Jessica saw it moving around in there.

She watched the handsome stranger and his squirming package uneasily through the front window of her home.

She'd been so damn angry after Mel had interrupted her seduction of VL that she brewed up a batch of strong black tea, drew a bath, stripped naked, and got into the steamy tub. Then she just sat there through most of the afternoon, sipping tea and adding hot water until she was thoroughly soaked... as clean as a newborn baby, she decided. And that made her feel very sexy.

The visitor was a handsome bastard, anyway, she told herself. But there was something frightening about him too. Maybe it was the way he carried that package away from his body as if he didn't want it to get too close to him. Maybe it was the strikingly confident air about him. He was so purposeful that he seemed… what? Dangerous!

Jessica felt a cold shiver begin to tingle through her. "Wonder who he is and what he wants."

The young man knocked at her front door and Jessica, who had just slipped into a comfortable but bulky sweater and a pare of cut-off jeans, waited for a few nervous moments before she opened it.

"Evening, Ms. Amado," he said in a silky voice. His smile broadened. There was something very sensual about it. "I was asked to deliver a present."

Jessica couldn't speak for a moment. "Are you sure it's for me? Who's it from?"

He didn't answer but simply pushed the basket, cover and all, toward her. She could see something tearing at the wrapping from the inside. Sharp claws cut the tissue paper, and suddenly the face of a small black kitten peered out through the wrapping. Its golden eyes looked up at her, and it began to purr.

Feeling relieved, Jessica took the basket, tore away the rest of the wrapping, pulled out the kitten, and pressed it to her cheek.

"It's so soft and sweet," she sighed.

"We thought you'd like it."

"We?"

"Yes."

The young man smiled, but the look in his eyes hardly matched the gift he had presented to her. He looked her up and down, undressed her with his eyes. She understood the look at once, and not too surprisingly, it thrilled her.

"It's been a pleasure," he said at last, and then turned to go.

"Wait," Jessica called as she nervously pushed her glasses up on the bridge of her nose. "Isn't there a card or a message or something? You have to tell me who's responsible for such a sweet gift."

The young man turned back; his smile seemed absolutely evil now and so damn hot! "An admirer," he said.

"And you are...."

"Devlin... Devlin Lucero."

It was a name she'd never heard before, she thought, but there was something familiar about it, something that hinted of sex and magic.

"Do I know you?"

"I work at the mine."

"An administrator?"

"Chief Financial Officer..."

His eyes held hers. She couldn't look away, even when the kitten began twisting to get out of her grasp.

"Can't you, at least, tell me who my admirer is?" she asked, and then grinned. "Doesn't he know that kittens can be a whole lot of trouble?"

Lucero's smile grew stronger and more seductive still. "We think you can manage. You'll enjoy the little tomcat." And then he turned away yet again and began walking to his car.

"Wait!" Jessica called once more. "I was only teasing about the kitten."

Lucero walked back to her, and he smiled what was becoming an unbearably sexy smile. "I'll bet you're exceptional at it."

"At what?"

"Teasing."

Jessica blushed. The last thing she knew she should do was invite this guy (dangerous eyes, obscene smile) into her home. And yet that's exactly what she did.

"Please... come in for a minute," she said. "I'd like to talk to you about my... benefactor."

Lucero let Jessica lead him into her home. He carried the basket, and she now had the squirmy little tomcat pressed tightly against her chest. Surprisingly the kittens claws were pulled in, not snagging the sweater the way he probably should have, feeling sexy against her breasts not playfully destructive, the way Mr. Lucero seemed to be. When she got inside the door, Jessica set the kitten down and watched him bound into the kitchen.

"I don't have anything for it to drink," she said.

"No problem," answered Lucero. He pulled a quart of pure cream from the basket and held it up. "I think there's a bowl in here somewhere too." And then he fished out a small silver bowl from under the wrapping.

She went into the kitchen to retrieve the kitten, and when she returned she found that Lucero had already filled the bowl half full of cream. She placed the kitten on the floor, watched him move curiously toward the bowl, and then he began lapping delicately at the cream.

"Is cream good for little tomcats?" She asked.

"It's a little rich," Lucero answered, "but it's okay for starters. I can bring something special for him tomorrow if you like."

"Only if you tell me who this mysterious admirer is."

Lucero's smile turned into a full grin that showed glistening white teeth. For a moment, Jessica thought how pleasant it would be if he took a nice big bite out of some delicate place on her squeaky clean body.

"Me," he said at last. "I'm the admirer."

"You said, 'we'."

"My personal secretary and I. She knew you'd enjoy the little tom."

Jessica's heart felt a sudden touch of disappointment.

"She was right," she said, the disappointment apparent in her voice.

"Too bad I had to dismiss her... my personal secretary."

"Really?" Jessica sounded happier now. "Why?"

"Poor performance."

Jessica scanned Lucero up and down. Their conversation was turning him on, she could tell. And she really liked that.

"Okay…" she said. "So what do we do now?"

Lucero walked up to her, reached up and touched her on the cheek for just a moment. She felt a tingle at the press of his fingers. His eyes gleamed hypnotically. "Trust me," they lied. She caught her breath. This guy was so fucking dangerous.

"We should talk," he said, "maybe tomorrow, or the next day."

That stopped her. Jessica didn't want him to leave, not when he had suddenly seemed to be suggesting so many exciting possibilities.

"Why not today… right now?"

"You should probably get to know the little tomcat first, don't you think? He has a lot to teach you."

The statement made perfect sense though she didn't know why. She bit her lip.

"Okay."

"I can pick you up tomorrow evening. We can go out to dinner."

"A date?"

"That depends on where we go for dinner, I guess."

His eyes had completely disrobed her. She felt that she was standing naked in front of him, and the feeling was tantalizing.

"Someplace fancy," she suggested.

"Chez Pierre?"

"The best restaurant in town?"

"I go there often… we could try it together."

"I'd like that."

Suddenly the whole idea of having an affair with VL the veterinarian seemed ludicrous to Jessica. Devlin Lucero was the caliber of man she should be going after.

He gave her a devilish smile. "Wear something sexy," he said.

Jessica looked down at the bulky sweater and cut-off jeans she currently wore. He was right; she could be far more inviting than this, and she wanted to be.

"I will," she murmured.

"Great." And before she could say another word, Lucero turned and was out the door so quickly that he seemed to vanish.

Jessica rushed to the window and watched him make his way to the sparkly convertible. She heard him get in, start the engine, and then drive off.

She turned toward the kitten. "How well do you know that guy?" she asked. The tomcat had finished all the cream in the bowl. Then he licked his paws, looked up and seemed, almost certainly, to grin at her.

Chapter 19
McCarwash Central

"This way," Kenny said to Lorena as he led her through an alley between two run-down buildings. He took her by the hand as they crossed a busy highway and then followed the battered sidewalk to a high wooden fence. Around the corner, on a deserted side street, he stopped.

"Should be right about here," Kenny said, and he slammed his fist hard against one of the boards and gave out with a yowl when the board refused to move.

"Damn!" he said. "I was sure that was the one."

The girl crossed her arms and just glared at him. "I thought we were going out for pizza and video games," she said.

Kenny smiled enthusiastically. "Yeah, I just got a great new game. We'll pick up the pizza and then head back to my house. My folks are out of town for the weekend, so we'll have the whole place to ourselves. But you gotta see this first."

"See what?" Lorena asked not at all happy about where they were or what they were doing. "I never ever want to be in this part of town, especially at night."

"You'll want to be here as soon as you see this," Kenny said, and he walked down a half block and slammed his fist into another fence board.

"Goddamn!"

It didn't budge.

Lorena hobbled after him in her high platform wedges. Her jeans were tight making it impossible for her to move very quickly. Her cotton blouse (worn for their big night out) was a little too thin for the evening air. She could see goosebumps rising on her arms in a very unattractive way.

"I'm cold, and I'm hungry. Is this some kind of joke, Ken? Let's get out of here before we get mugged."

"You'll be glad when you see this, Lore, honest."

"See what?"

Kenny gave her a stupid smile and just ignored her. He was studying the top of the fence boards, looking for the one with the big knothole just about six feet up. It was the loose one that he could pound open... and suddenly he found it.

"Here we are, babe!" he said, and he punched the knotted board right in its center. The board came loose, flew backward, and opened a space into the great, darkened area beyond.

"Right this way," he said as he held out his hand so that Lorena could take it and walk with him through the opening to whatever wonders were on the other side.

It turned out to be a large vacant lot: parched earth with a few low creosote bushes that were littered with scraps of paper, tin cans, and other debris.

"Very nice," said the girl, not meaning it at all. "I see it. So now can we get something to eat?"

"But what about all this?" Kenny asked as he spun around gesturing to the whole area.

"All what, a big, junked-up vacant lot? Why did you want to come here anyway?"

Kenny came up to his girl then and kissed her.

"Listen. I've got it all figured out. This is going to be McCarwash Central. The McLaughlin boys are going to make millions here."

Lorena didn't know quite what to say. She knew better than to second-guess Kenny and his lucrative family business. Still....

Kenny could see the confusion in her eyes.

"Don't you get it, Lore? With the booming economy and all the Haboobs that'll come blowing through here, people will need their cars washed three times a week maybe four. This town is ripe for a carwash explosion."

Lorena nodded. "Okay, now I understand. But I thought you were going to college next year."

"College? Oh yeah, maybe. But the opportunity is here and now, starting in this very lot."

"How many car washes are you planning on building, anyway?" Lorena wasn't sure she liked this new super-ambitious version of Kenny. Besides, she hadn't seen him for two days and nights; he'd been locked in meetings with his brothers... meetings he claimed to have called himself, and, when he'd finished and picked her up for a night of pizza and videogames, he'd bought her here.

"Come on Lore, share my dream." And then he walked away from her and started picking up the papers and the tin cans that were scattered around the vacant lot.

"More garbage is just going to blow in on the next Haboob," Lorena said.

"Yeah? Well, we're going to put an offer in on this place tomorrow morning. This'll be our first location... then we'll have five more by the time the rainy season starts."

"And where are you going to get the money to fund it all?"

Lorena adjusted the scoopy, white smock top that she was wearing; the one that Kenny said made her look so grown up. But he didn't seem to be thinking about that at all right now.

"We meet with old man Hotchkiss down at the bank tomorrow," Kenny said. "The loan will be a slam dunk."

"That's nice, and I'm excited for you. But I'm also getting hungry. Where's this pizza you've been promising."

"Down at José's."

"Great! It'll take an hour after we get there."

"No problem, babe. I phoned our order in 30 minutes ago."

"Lorena smiled and rocked back on her heels. This was more like it. This was what she liked about Kenny, besides his cute looks, and hot car. He was thoughtful. Who else would have interrupted his tour of the future McCarwashes of Southern Arizona, to call in a pizza order for his date?

"Hawaiian style, right?"

"Hawaiian Pizza with all the trimmings. Plus I've got something special for you in the back of my car."

"What's that?"

"Something you'll like."

"Something illegal?"

"For kids our age, anyway... A gallon of pre-mixed Margaritas."

"So cool."

"Plus the latest version of Playroom Maniacs."

"See your guts on the nursery room floor!" They both said in unison. It was the slogan of the million seller video game series.

"The one where you can pick your own toy character and go around slashing the hell out of the other toys?"

"That's it."

"Can I be Psycho Barbie?"

Kenny eyed her up and down. "If I can be Slasher Cowboy Joe!"

"Of course."

Lorena moved closer then and gave her boyfriend a big sloppy kiss.

Kenny smiled that silly grin and took her by the hand.

"Time to head back," he said.

They walked together to the fence, and as they did Lorena took one last look at the vacant lot. That's when she spotted a small sign in the far corner, almost covered over by creosote bushes... just a stake stuck in the ground with a small white card attached to it. How had Kenny missed it? She wondered.

"Future home of CLEAN SWEEPS INC.," the sign said.

Lorena paused for a moment, puzzled over it, and finally decided not to mention it to Kenny... at least not until after the pizza, the margaritas, the Playroom Maniacs, and whatever else might happen that night.

Chapter 20
All the Kingdoms of the Earth

Principal Mortimer eyed Jessica the way he always did… a way that made her skin crawl.

They were together in the Principal's office. Mortimer wore the same rumpled white shirt, brown striped tie, and gray slacks that he wore every day it seemed.

Jessica sat across from him. Her feet were tucked modestly under her chair though her posture couldn't hide the effects of her usual dress for substitute teaching: pencil skirt, white cotton blouse, and little gold chain around her neck.

The Principal got up and walked around to the front of his desk. He tried to sit on the edge, but he was much too short and chubby, and his leg kept slipping off. The act made him look so clumsy. He was sweating too… and he seemed almost aroused. Jessica tried to contain a sarcastic smile… tried to convert it into one that was more welcoming, one that said, 'I like you Principal Mortimer,' when in fact she loathed him.

"You're a very attractive woman, Ms. Amado."

"Thank you sir."

"Yes, a very attractive woman." He was sweating more heavily now. "And a job opening is coming up at our school this next semester. We need a full-time English teacher. Would you be interested in the position?"

"I'd like that, sir," Jessica answered as she pushed her glasses back up onto the bridge of her nose. A full-time position did offer a much higher salary, membership in the teachers' union, and lots of other benefits. But she would still have to work with creeps like Mortimer and a staff of mostly old and disgruntled men and women. Still, it would help her current financial situation greatly.

"You don't have a teaching credential," Mortimer said. "That does present a small problem."

Jessica frowned.

"Then there's the issue of your dress. It's very provocative. No wonder the young boys in your class talk about you behind your back."

"They talk about me? How do you know that?" she wanted to ask, but she didn't. Instead, she simply said, "I'm on a limited budget, sir, this is what I can afford."

"That's not what I hear from some of your colleagues," Mortimer answered. "They say an outfit like that would set them back well over a hundred dollars. And you have several such get-ups."

"It's just that I'm a very good shopper sir," Jessica answered, certain that almost no man would have any idea what women's clothing would cost, or what the effect of careful shopping might have on its price.

Mortimer studied her; he might have been about to question her, but then she took off her glasses and began to nibble on the end of the earpiece, a move that definitely distracted the Principal.

"Yes I see," said Mortimer. "Well anyway, what may be affordable for you may be an occasion of sin for your young male students."

Jessica's face was turning red, and she began to feel that she probably had a good case of sexual harassment against old man Mortimer if she wanted to. But it hardly seemed worth the effort especially with a new job hanging in the balance. So, she said nothing.

"In any event, there may be a way to help you financially, Ms. Amado," Mortimer said. "As Principal, I'm allowed to make an exception to some of the job requirements if the candidate is extraordinary. And you, Ms. Amado, are extraordinary." He was looking directly at her breasts now, and that infuriated Jessica, but she kept smiling as benignly as she could and only allowed herself to answer... "Thank you, sir," as she slipped her glasses back on.

"So I was thinking, if you and I could get together some evening this week, we could discuss how we might qualify you for the new position."

Jessica's stomach was churning. Still she nodded.

"Perhaps dinner tomorrow evening at Tres Flores?"

Jessica relaxed just a little. The old man certainly wouldn't try anything in a family restaurant. Not with the Romo family around. She'd always thought of them as rather stuffy, but at the moment that's just what she needed.

"I am free tomorrow evening," she said. She knew it was the necessary thing to say.

"Then it's a date?"

"Yes, Principal Mortimer."

"Great, we'll leave right after school. And, Ms. Amado..."

"Yes?"

"I'm certain we can find a way to qualify you for that teaching position."

Jessica forced a smile, yet she felt sick to her stomach as she made her way from Mortimer's office and out into the broiling Arizona afternoon.

It was a two-block walk to her home, and she longed for a nice cooling shower. Then she could take a break, maybe talk to her kitten. "Oh shit," she said aloud, "the tom kitten!" The man who'd given her the cat! Her date with Devlin Lucero...

this very evening, Somehow this conversation with Mortimer made her forget all about it.

A horn honked as she strode along. She looked toward the sound and saw Lucero's hot Mercedes pulling up next to her, top up, air-conditioning on. She stopped and turned toward the car as he rolled down the window.

"Want a ride home?"

Jessica wasn't sure, but it certainly looked cool inside that car. She lowered her glasses for a moment and stared at him.

"Why not," she answered, as she opened the door and started to climb in. Another kitten was sitting on the passenger-side… another black kitten.

"Who's this?" she asked, as she scooped up the cat while lowering herself onto the comfortable leather.

"Just Dick," said Lucero. "I thought Tom might be getting a bit lonely."

"So you brought me another tom kitten named Dick."

"Yep, you gotta admit he's cute."

"He is that."

Jessica pressed the little cat against her cheek and felt the softness of his fur.

"You're sure he's a he?" Jessica asked.

"Oh yeah. Take a closer look at Dick's…"

Jessica blushed but held the little kitten up. It was hard to tell, but she seemed pretty sure that the necessary male equipment was all there.

"See, no problem at all," said Lucero. "They'll be best buds."

Minutes later, the Mercedes rolled up in front of Jessica's condo.

"You're a little early for our date, you know," she said. "I'll need at least a half an hour to get ready."

"If you can do it that quickly, I'd say you really are a remarkable woman."

"Just a quick shower and change of clothes."

"I can drive around for a while if you'd like, or I can come in and help organize the kittens."

"Is that one of your administrative skills," Jessica giggled, "Cat wrangling?"

"Kitten wrangling. Yes, I'm actually extremely talented in that regard."

"All right, then. Why don't you come in and, while I'm upstairs changing, you can introduce Tom to Dick and see if they get along."

"Brought some kitten stuff too... cat beds, cat food, cat litter, the works."

"Sounds good, follow me," and with that Jessica got out of the Mercedes and marched up the steps to her little bungalow, carrying the cat, and hearing Lucero's footsteps as he followed her.

Half an hour, a complete shower, shampoo, and blow-dry later, Jessica slipped into her very best undies, then into a strapless cocktail dress that she had promised to return to one of her girlfriends weeks ago... same with the matching high heels.

There was something about Devlin Lucero that made her know that he was well worth the effort. Something special was going to happen between them tonight; she knew that it would. It had to.

Principal Mortimer's invitation was just too nasty... too disgusting; she didn't want him to take her to dinner so that he could explain how he could bend the rules for her. His bending the rules about credentials and requirements suggested that she would probably have to bend her rules about teacher/principal relations. No way did she want to be put in a position where she would have to do that.

What she was wearing now (the strapless) really was provocative, and she felt especially happy with it as she marched downstairs and into the kitchen. Lucero looked up at her and smiled. He had taken off his suit coat and tie and was down on his hands and knees arranging some plastic partitions that he must have brought with him. He'd constructed a little cat apartment right there in the kitchen. On one end was a big bed that could have slept three or four kittens. Across the way was a kitty litter tray filled with very sweet-smelling cedar chips. Sweet smelling for now at least, but still, how thoughtful. Near the bed were two large bowls one already filled with milk and the other with cat food.

The partitions that set off the little tomcat apartment were high enough that the kittens couldn't get out, but still there was enough room in that one little corner of the kitchen to see that they were very comfortable.

Lucero stood and looked at her.

"Wow! Stunning," he said, and he gave her an approving, if not entirely innocent, grin.

Jessica struck her Miss America pose and smiled back.

"And what's all this?" she asked.

"The best kitty corner money can buy. And that's raw goat's milk," said Lucero, "best thing for kittens to drink."

"You'll have to tell me how much I owe you for it."

"Nothing... nada. It's part of the package."

"Package?"

"The kitten package... sent by your admirer."

"But that's you."

"I know. He smiled again. "But the Mine will pay for it and tonight's dinner too because we need to have this very serious discussion. Shall we go?"

"Kind of early isn't it?"

"The Restaurant, Vivace, is all the way over in Tumac City, and it takes half an hour to drive there."

"Can't we talk on the way?"

"The ride is beautiful, the car is air conditioned, and I've selected some music to help you relax. Clear your mind; feel good. We're going to have fun tonight… it's not all about a serious discussion… it's about the whole experience."

Jessica's smile broadened. "But don't you think I should.…"

And before she could say any more, Lucero reached down, swept her off her feet and carried her out to his Mercedes. "Your chariot awaits," he said. "Let's not be prudish."

#

Vivace was not only the most exclusive restaurant in Tumac City; it was the best restaurant in that part of the state. Its décor looked as though every piece, every brick, every porcelain vase and tablecloth had been flown in directly from Florence. The walls were a dark royal red. The huge front window looked out onto the street, but lace curtains hung across its lower half limiting the view of passers-by.

The tables were small and rectangular. All had starched white linen table clothes, elegant silver place settings, and large crystal wine and water glasses. At the far end of the room, a high rosewood counter allowed the chef to set out the entrees as he prepared them. Behind him, a row of pots, pans, and kettles hung from the ceiling; assistant chefs in big white hats stirred and sautéed and fried while flames shot up from great skillets as the meals were cooked. The food preparation itself was quite a show.

Along the far wall, curtained booths offered almost private dining for anyone who had the connections. Above the booths, original, amazingly true-to-life pencil sketches showed famous Italian movie stars from bygone days: Gina Lollobrigida, Sophia Loren, Claudia Cardinale, Marcello Mastroianni.

All the waiters wore tuxedos, as did the busboys and the wine steward.

"Welcome, Mr. Lucero," said the maitre d' as they entered.

"Good evening, Giuseppe."

Giuseppe's eyes brightened when he saw Jessica. She was very glad that she had borrowed the cocktail dress; nothing that she owned would have been acceptable for such an elegant establishment.

He smiled, and Jessica, sensing his approval, smiled back.

"You're usual table, Signore?"

"Please."

Giuseppe led the couple to the private booth at the very back of the restaurant. The couple slid into it as Lucero turned to Giuseppe and whispered, "Cristal, please."

"Of course."

Jessica took in a deep breath and wished that old man Mortimer could see her now, in her hot party dress, with handsome Devlin Lucero, and Giuseppe smiling at her approvingly. She remembered that Lucero had mentioned that his personal secretary had just been fired, and she wondered if the job was open. Was this serious discussion possibly a job interview, or just a simple seduction? At the moment, she didn't really care.

Fabio, their waiter, now arrived with a big bottle of Cristal, an ice bucket, and two elegant champagne flutes. He made quite a ceremony of wrapping a towel around the bottle, popping the cork so slowly so that he merely lifted it from the bottle, and then pouring a quick splash for Lucero.

The handsome young man tasted it, closed his eyes and savored the flavor. He nodded. Moments later he was toasting her.

"To spectacular opportunities for both of us."

"Yes," said Jessica. She liked the idea.

Through the course of the dinner, they talked about the food, the surroundings, and her work as a teacher, which she made sound much better than it was because she didn't want Lucero to think that she even needed a job. In fact just to tease him a bit, she brought up the promotion that Mortimer had offered her. That came during the soufflé... after appetizers of oysters (which she had never tasted before but which she sampled with enthusiastic giggles because they just seemed so sexual), and after the Florentine steak (which was better than anything she had ever tasted in her life).

Lucero tasted grappa now while Jessica did her best to hang onto a small sense of sobriety as she sipped some very delicious Grand Marnier.

"Are you going to take the full-time teaching job?" Lucero asked her finally.

"Do you think I should?"

"Depends on how you feel about Principal Mortimer."

Jessica looked puzzled. She hadn't mentioned him by name. How could Lucero know that much about the old geezer?

"I think you should give it all up," Lucero said. "Give up your relationship with that stupid veterinarian too."

"Veterinarian?"

"VL."

How did he know about that?

Fabio brought the check. Lucero studied it for a moment, smiled, added a tip, a total, a signature, and then handed the check back to the waiter.

"No credit card?" she asked.

"The Mine has an account here," he said. "In spite of the fun we're having, this really is a business dinner. Time to go, okay? I want to show you something?"

Jessica felt her anticipation intensify. A flash of lightning and a crash of thunder added a sudden exclamation point.

The parking attendant pulled Lucero's Mercedes up in front of the restaurant, and she saw that he had lowered the convertible top. "I think we can outrun the rain, don't you?" Lucero asked as he opened the door. He touched her arm gently and kissed her on the cheek. Jessica blushed, thunder crashed.

Lucero walked to the other side of the car, opened the door, and slid in behind the wheel. Then he touched the circular dial in the center of the controls and music blared through all the speakers: Rocker Jim: Sweet Sunny Girl!

The car roared out of the circular driveway and into the desert night. It was very warm; even the wind was warm. It caressed Jessica's face and found its way up her skirt as if it wanted to touch her in very private places.

Twenty miles, and half a dozen Rocker Jim songs later, Lucero pulled suddenly off the main highway and onto a narrow side road. It cut sharply up the side of a mountain offering cooler air as it ascended. And there were more rumbles of thunder.

"The view from here is spectacular," Lucero called above the wind.

The road ended, and the Mercedes rolled effortlessly up a steep dirt embankment until it reached a lookout point far above the caldera where the ball of fire had launched itself into the sky so many months before.

"Come," Lucero said, as he moved quickly around the car. He opened Jessica's door, pulled her up, and walked her out to the edge of the point.

Jessica reached into her purse and took out her glasses. It was the first time she'd worn them this evening. She slipped them on and turned to Lucero.

"I like the look," he said. "Very sexy." She smiled and turned to take in the view.

"Oh my God," she sighed as the panorama opened in front of her.

"This is nothing," Lucero called, "let me show you what we can really see from here."

He stepped forward and raised his hands like some orchestra conductor and began gesturing dramatically.

Lightning flashed, thunder rumbled, and the clouds rushed suddenly toward them.

Jessica gasped.

"Fun, huh?"

"I guess so."

Now, the clouds parted, and beyond them, a great city seemed to rise where none had been before.

Jessica saw broad highways, lavish homes, and beyond them, sets of pyramids topped with golden temples, gilded walls, lush gardens, and the businesses of a vast metropolis.

"Like it?" Lucero asked.

"Of course, but there's no city out there, that I know of... what is it?"

"CÍBOLA!"

"The Seven Cities of Gold?"

"Absolutely."

"But they don't exist... they're a myth."

Lucero turned toward her. The reflection of the fabled cities shimmered in his eyes. His smile was unstoppable.

"I'll give it all to you."

Jessica turned toward him at once. "What are you talking about? Who are you?"

Jessica lowered her eyes, and where Lucero's feet should have been, she now saw him standing on cloven hooves. His head, with its gigantic smile, seemed to have sprouted horns.

"My God, are you the devil? Are you Lucifer?"

"Of course not." But his smile was devilish.

"Then who?"

"Never mind that, Jessica, will you partner with me. I can offer you such great power!"

"Power?"

"GREAT POWER!" Lucero's smile now bordered on megalomania.

Jessica almost fainted; she had never entertained the thought of power before, never in her entire life, but now the concept filled her mind: power to undo all the bullies and the assholes and Principal Mortimer of the world... those who thought so little of her... power to rise above all of them, to stick it to them, to fuck them over, power to join with this handsome devil (maybe not Satan himself but certainly a close relation) and have it all.

Jessica began to giggle. Lucero put his arm around her waist. He threw his head back and laughed wildly, crazily along with her.

After a moment the laughter fell away, and Jessica looked up at Lucero. His eyes were bright; there were no horns. She looked at his feet; there were no hooves. Across the horizon the thunder died, the lightening quieted. Sunset sifted the sky into gentle bands of gold and pink and blue. The fabled city had vanished, but it didn't matter. Lucero squeezed her.

"Anyway," he said in the most normal of voices, "I'd like to offer you a job at the Mine."

"Did we have to come all the way up here to talk about that?"

"No, actually. I just like sunsets. They help clear my mind... know what I mean?"

Jessica didn't think that what had just happened could actually be classified as clearing her mind... or could it?

"Are you interested in the position... as my personal secretary?"

Jessica was still too dazzled to think clearly. "I guess so."

"Actually, I may have a much more important job available. Seems we are about to lose our head of HR... know anything about human resources?"

"Not really."

"You don't have a teaching credential either, and that hasn't stopped you."

Jessica suddenly looked frightened. "I don't know. And then there's...."

113

"Yeah, you'll have to give up your part time job at a news-paper too. But that VL partner of yours isn't worth it anyway."

"Probably not, but...."

"Don't worry; I can coach you in HR. You look like a natural to me."

"I don't want to get in too deep."

"If the job is available, I'll be able to offer you three times your current salary."

"What?"

"That isn't enough?"

Jessica reached up and tried to straighten her glasses. She felt faint.

"Okay, if things work out, two hundred thousand dollars a year."

"Are you insane. I'm not even qualified."

"More objections? Okay, and a company car... how about a new Corvette?"

"But I...."

"You're right, not enough, I'll throw in a wardrobe allowance too."

Jessica's knees gave out. She would have fallen, but Lucero caught her, gathered her up and carried her back to his convertible.

"I'll let you know if the job is open tomorrow, okay? I'm almost certain that it will be, but our current HR head is such a tight-ass that she might decide not to let go of it after all."

"But my teaching job... Principal Mortimer?"

"Oh yeah, that guy... I'll take care of him," Lucero said as he deposited her into the passenger seat.

"Really?"

"Oh yeah!"

"Okay then," Jessica said. "If the job is open, I'll take it." And suddenly she was giggling again. "You really don't have to worry about old man Mortimer though."

"I said I'd take care of him," Lucero repeated, "and I will."

Part Two
The Quest
Begins

Chapter 21
The Departure

Ceci Moreno slung her backpack over one shoulder, heaved a heavy sigh, and grasped the handle of the door to her little apartment. She took a quick glance back over her shoulder at the warm, friendly rooms that she had come to love. She wondered if she would see them again.

"Anyway... here goes," she said as she flung the door open and was shocked at what she saw. There was quite a gathering out in front. She had hoped that she and Esteban could sneak out of town without catching anyone's attention. No such luck. It was a veritable circus. Esteban hadn't shown up yet, but Gabe was there. So were Devlin Lucero and Donny Hainer. So were Papa Luís, Mama Carmen, Mario and Sophia, Mario's mother, Vanessa, and even those horny teenagers, Kenny and Lorena... they had all come to put in an appearance.

Ceci stepped out of her front door, heard the buzz of the crowd, and tried to duck back in again.

"Oh no you don't," said Gabe as he rushed up to her, caught her by the arm and pulled her out onto the porch.

"We've come to talk some sense into you," Devlin Lucero said as he came up the steps. "You say you're concerned about La Sentencia? You say you're worried about the workers?"

"Do you think it's going to do them any good if you run away?" Donny Hainer added as he stepped up beside Lucero.

Ceci turned from one man to the other. She liked them, even though they had seemed to be nothing more than agents of that devil, Blackmore.

She gave them a polite nod and a smile that was friendly, if a little weak.

"Come on, Cess," Gabe said. "It took me hours to convince Blackmore to come up with a plan to get new jobs for the workers. Help us out. You can make it happen."

"The town needs you," added Papa Luís as he approached rather shyly.

Ceci turned to Gabe and narrowed her eyes in anger. "You had to resort to this? You had to bring half the town here to keep me from going on our quest?"

"It's for your own good," Gabe whispered back. "There is no Cíbola, there is no gold. What there is is hard work that has to be done here, and you're trying to run away from it."

Ceci came down the steps and looked around for Esteban. Maybe he could help her deal with the crowd. But he just wasn't there, and then a long black Lincoln Town Car came rolling up in front of her place. The engine revved for a moment and then died. A chauffeur got out of the car and walked around to the back; he opened the door and helped an impeccably dressed Mr. Blackmore get out.

"There you are, girly," the old man muttered as he strode toward her. He wore a suit so expensive that it was the only clothing that anyone would remember about the morning. He pushed Papa Luís aside rather rudely, then strode right up to the young woman just assuming that Gabe and Donny and Devlin would move out of his way... they did.

He scratched his head, then looked up into Ceci's eyes. She was a very intelligent woman, he realized, so he'd better choose his words wisely.

"Look, Miss Moreno," he began with an awe-shucks kind of smile, "maybe I didn't make myself clear in our last conversation."

Ceci was already shaking her head incredulously.

"I care as much about the mineworkers and this town as anyone," Blackmore said. "Why, a lot of our men and women look up to me as though I were their..." he glanced around and finally focused on Luís, "...as though I were their papa."

Ceci sighed, rolled her eyes, took a step forward, and tried to brush past him.

"What I mean to say," Blackmore continued as he caught her arm and spun her to him, "is that I want to take care of the workers and the town as much as you do. That's why I'm here... to convince you to stay with us and help us do the important work of...." Blackmore suddenly realized that not everyone present knew exactly what was going on at the mine, so he stepped closer and began to whisper.

"Redeployment," he said. "You're very good at HR. We all know that. So please help us find jobs for the men and women who are about to be laid off."

Ceci's eyes turned stone cold.

"It's impossible, you lying criminal!"

Blackmore's face darkened, and yet he forced himself to smile through clenched teeth. The resulting look was terrifying.

"Ceci, girly...." He opened his arms. "I've planned a big bonus for you, if you'll sign on for the redeployment project, I'll see that you get ten thousand dollars, cash... immediately!"

Ceci couldn't believe her ears. It made her even angrier. Why didn't the guy just apply the money to the business and keep the mine open for a few more days? She looked at Gabe accusingly, then at Donny and Dev.

"You can't buy me, old man," she spit at him. "I'm going on a quest!"

At that moment, Esteban made his way through the crowd. Following behind him came Aladdin, the camel. There was a saddle fastened on its back, put there almost certainly by V. L., who, although he had been among the bullies who picked on Esteban in high school, was now someone who wanted to help.

"Wow, this is great," said Esteban enthusiastically as he misunderstood the purpose of the crowd completely. He raised his arms above his head and shouted out, "To Cíbola!"

No one responded. No one said anything. Esteban didn't care. He just shuffled up to Ceci and asked, "Ready to go?"

"No, she's not," said Gabe.

Ceci turned from one to the other with a look of sudden confusion. Blackmore realized that the best thing he could do at this moment was shut up... and so he did.

"Your quest is a joke," Gabe said turning toward Esteban and shoving him so hard that he fell. The other onlookers gasped. Hainer, and Lucero and even Blackmore now moved up beside Gabe and formed an arc blocking Esteban from Ceci.

"Come on Cess, let's go," Esteban said as he got to his feet and tried to move toward her.

Ceci raised her head proudly and stepped forward almost forcing the men to part as she approached Esteban. But then she stopped, turned, looked toward Gabe, then back at Esteban, then at the camel, then at Hainer and Lucero. Tears were welling up in her eyes again. No one said anything, but somehow they didn't have to. The young woman realized that even now, she was torn.

"Bella Signora, Cecilia," said a voice that sounded like a foghorn. It was coming from the very back of the crowd, but it cut through the silence like music through a misty night. Everyone turned and saw little Sophia making her way forward through the crowd. For a moment, Blackmore stepped in front of the little girl to block her path. The girl smiled and simply said, "Mi scusi, signore."

Blackmore crossed his arms and planted his feet.

Sophia kicked the old man right in the shin and sent him hopping across the yard, screeching and grabbing at his ankle.

Sophia moved forward, then reached up and took Ceci's hand. She smiled.

"Non abbiate paura, signorina. Il viaggio è un buon compromesso. La ricerca vale la pena. Giusto?"

Because Ceci alone in the crowd spoke Italian, she was the only one beside Mario (through some kind of magic) who understood what the little girl had said:

"Don't be afraid, Miss. The journey is a good one. The quest is worthy. Right?"

Ceci smiled. "Yes," she answered and together she and Sophia walked back through the crowd to Esteban.

"Let's go," she whispered to him.

Mario cheered, but everyone else seemed stunned.

The couple walked off down the street with the camel plodding slowly behind them.

"Come back, you crazy bitch," Blackmore called as he tried to follow them. He found himself hobbling too badly.

His words silenced Gabe and the others and probably turned them all against him at that moment.

Maybe she's right, Gabe thought to himself.

"Of course, she is," Sophia answered. Gabe looked at the little girl. Was she reading his mind now?

"Vaya con dios!" Gabe suddenly shouted to the adventurers.

Ceci turned back and gave him an uncertain smile that moved slowly to appreciation.

"Thank you," she shouted back, and now there was cheering from the crowd, from Luís, from Mama Carmen, Mario's mother Vanessa, from Kenny, and Lorena, from Mario and Sophia, even from Donny Hainer, but not from Blackmore or

Lucero, of course. The old man limped to his limo where the chauffeur was waiting.

"Damn you all!" he called to everyone as he ducked into the car. "You'll pay for this." And then the door to the Town Car slammed, the chauffeur rushed around to the driver's side, got in, and soon the great car lurched forward and was out of sight.

There was stunned silence. Everyone looked at each other with concern and a little sadness.

"I'm hungry," Sophia whispered suddenly.

"Me too," added Mario.

"Well then, friends," said Luís with his usual fatherly grin, "free tacos for everyone at Tres Flores. What do you say, amigos? On the house! Let's go!

"Let's go."

Chapter 22
Into the Desert

Eight hours later, Ceci and Esteban had already trekked sixteen miles due west across the Arizona desert; the sky had been a dark almost-purple blue; the creosote bushes and scrub pines almost seemed to be running along beside them, keeping them company. Hawks raced across the sky spanning the wispy clouds, calling sharply, diving down after some distant prey and then soaring again with their catch in their talons.

Desert lizards and scorpions heard the pounding approach of the camel and scurried out of their way. Rattlesnakes looked on in annoyance, and the sun continued to bake down relentlessly.

Esteban was not an outdoor person, not used to traversing great distances over parched, thirsty earth. Yet, he didn't complain, tried to smile with every step, but in spite of his best efforts, Ceci could see that his beautiful eyes were turning hollow, his feet were dragging. She, of course, had taken so many long mountain hikes with Gabe that she felt just fine.

At last, they came to a rise in the desert, a small rock outcropping that offered a little shade. Aladdin pounded right to it, scattering the creatures that might have been hiding there.

"You okay?" Ceci asked Esteban as she pulled back into the shade and leaned up against the face of the outcropping.

"Great, just great."

"Really?"

"Actually, my feet are killing me," he sighed.

"Want to ride the camel?"

Ceci could see the idea bring eager anticipation to a face she'd thought very handsome when she was a teenager and in love with him. Now he seemed very dedicated and yet so... quirky.

Esteban quickly shook off the idea of riding the camel; his look turned playful, and then he grinned.

"After all, I'm a Conquistador!" he said.

Ceci giggled and curtsied to him. "Of course, you are Señor, but what does that make me?"

Esteban's brows twisted in thought. He puzzled over the question for a long moment and then his eyes brightened. "A highborn señorita from some vast rancho?"

"I think not," she said so primly that Esteban just rolled his eyes.

"Okay then... be whoever you want to be, Cess."

Ceci smiled; that was the perfect answer.

"A Conquistador as well?"

"A Conquistadora?"

"Why not?"

"Exactly. Why not."

Ceci took her canteen and pushed it into his hands. And at that moment, her memory flashed to the Christmas that Gabe had given her the canteen, along with the backpack she was carrying, and the sleeping bag, and the tent, and all the other gear that was now mounted on the camel; all presents from Gabe... and she had turned her back on him... but then at the very end of their departure, he wished her well, didn't he?

Suddenly she missed him badly. She bit her lip, but then smiled softly. It was the price all Conquistadors must pay, right... leaving behind their loved ones, trusting to God that they will understand? Still at that moment, at least, she wasn't sure how she could live without his love... or ever seeing him again. She touched the side of her neck gently... the very spot where he had kissed her so many times. Tears began to form in her eyes. And just then Esteban cried out in excitement:

"The Pacific. We've found it!"

And yes, there, only a short distance in front of them, just over a ridge of low hills, he did see the ocean or thought he did.

"We've found the Pacific, Ceci, just as the great Balboa did!" And he went racing in the direction of the sparkling waters.

Ceci just shook her head. "No, Esteban," she murmured. "It's a mirage. I've seen them all my life. I'm afraid your knowledge needs to be broadened..." and then she whispered to herself, "just like so many of us Conquistadors."

#

Three hours later, darkness had descended onto the desert and brought with it a great overarching ceiling of stars. A comet flashed. The pair had not yet stopped to eat supper or to make camp. They were about to do so now that they had made it all the way to the base of a butte that Ceci had set as their first day's destination. She had pointed to it from miles away and said that it would offer some shelter for their tents. But suddenly, strangely, there was a glow on the horizon, just beyond the butte... a colorful brightness that flared up then disappeared then flared again in cycles. It seemed so out of place in the desert.

It was very repetitive, not like the glow of a city or even a home or a store.

This was a garish glow that pulsed brightly as though calling to them.

"What kind of place is that?"

Esteban pulled his binoculars out of the camel's saddlebag and raised them to his eyes. The light was still too far away to make out clearly.

"Looks like a neon sign on a building," he said. "But it's so alone... so out of place."

"Can't be a motel, can it? There's no highway nearby," said Ceci.

"Do we camp or do we investigate?"

Ceci turned to Esteban and shrugged. "I guess it could offer a warm place to sleep ... might be nice on our first night out."

"Just one more look," Esteban said, as he raised the binoculars to his eyes once again. He zoomed in tighter, tried to make out the letters on the sign, and when he finally did, he gasped. They spelled out the word, 'Dido's.'

He hadn't told Ceci about Dido or the fact that she might step into their adventure and ask for payback for a very big favor. Still, Esteban was aware of the dangers, having been warned by his great, great grandfather. He knew that Ceci was very skilled at handling people, and, in spite of what might be dangerous demands, Dido was their benefactor, after all. They were using the saddlebags and the supplies that she had given him. So what could he do but get a grip on Aladdin's reigns and say, "Let's go then."

Chapter 23
Dido

It was a casino out in the middle of nowhere with only the sparsest of dirt roads leading to it, a couple of cars, a few old pick-ups parked in a dusty lot far away from the main building. Only two horses were tied to a hitching post on the back edge of the parking lot; there were very few other signs of customers of any kind.

The building was low slung, adobe, with a neon sign above a narrow entrance flashing the name DIDO'S from pink to purple to green and back again. Esteban walked up to the doorway and pushed inward. The door swung slowly open. He entered; Ceci followed… so did the camel.

Inside, the casino seemed much bigger than it appeared from the front; there was a long bar right across from the doorway. Behind the bar a pretty-faced, Native American woman was polishing glasses, smiling, and talking to two young men who sat nursing bottles of beer in front of her.

The whole place seemed sepia tone to Ceci: mahogany walls, mahogany bar, and stools, even the painting behind the bar had a sepia coloring to match the décor. It was faded but the subject of the painting was clear enough – a romantic vision of the Seven Cities of Gold. Esteban didn't hesitate for a moment. He walked up to the bar and studied the painting.

"Cíbola," he murmured. And the Native American woman nodded.

"You Dido?" he asked.

"I wish," she answered. "She'll be out at suppertime. My name's Rosa."

Esteban smiled.

Ceci turned to her left and saw racks of slot machines marching off into the depths of a room that was a few steps lower than the barroom floor. A grungy young woman in a striped tank top, tight jeans, and scuffed cowboy boots was pumping quarters into the nearest one-armed bandit. Beyond her, an elderly couple sat side by side each playing their own slots. The machines clinked and whirred and spat out an occasional small jackpot. Deeper into the room, other shadowy figures played blackjack while still others were gathered around a roulette wheel. There was the slight mumble of the crowd, the soft shuffle of the games, and, now and again, the harsh jangle and clank of the slots.

Ceci turned to the right and saw a big dining room with a buffet where great trays of roast beef and chicken steamed invitingly. She also spotted poached salmon and mashed potatoes, kettles of beans, corn, and carrots, and platters overflowing with desserts. She felt her mouth watering. It had been a long time since their last meal.

Further to the right, a long hallway extended almost to infinity. On either side of the hall, doors were spaced evenly apart, clearly the entrances to guest rooms.

"Do you have a room for us?" Esteban asked.

Rosa smiled. "You don't happen to be Esteban Dorantes?"

"I am."

"Wow, we've been waiting for you, weren't sure you'd make it tonight."

"Well, here we are. Do you have two rooms?"

"Together?"

"Could be," Ceci answered. At this point, she was willing to take anything she could get as long as it came with a ticket to the buffet.

"Adjoining rooms," Esteban insisted.

"We made arrangements for your camel to stay in the shed out back," Rosa told him. "And we'll feed Aladdin, of course."

"Of course."

"The mistress has also made arrangements for you to join us for dinner."

Ceci eyed Esteban. How did they know the camel's name, she wondered. Just how much of everything about them did they know?

"Maybe we should check out the rooms first," she said.

Rosa smiled and flipped two keys up onto the bar. "Sure, no problem," she said, "Rooms 101 and 103 right down the hall... adjoining. Stay away from the far end of the hallway, though. We have some guests back there who don't like to be disturbed."

Esteban nodded.

"I'll have the kid take your camel outside." Rosa hit a bell on the counter, yelled, "Sammy!" and a small Indian boy of about six, in jeans and a flannel shirt, came in from the buffet area. He walked right up to the camel as though he had been tending camels all his life. He patted the creature's nose. Aladdin didn't seem to mind. Esteban nodded, and so Sammy took the camel back out the front door.

Ceci and Esteban inspected the rooms together. They were very nice: dark wood furniture, clean sheets, tiled bathrooms, tubs, and showers. The towels were thick and fresh. The carpets were spotless. The view out of the window showed the desert night and a tapestry of stars. Whatever parking there was must have been on the other side because there was no headlight glare to spoil the view.

"Bathrooms are wonderful," Ceci commented. There were even little packets of soap beside the sinks.

"How can they afford to offer such beautiful rooms out here in the middle of nowhere?" Esteban asked, "and dinner too?"

Ceci shrugged, "Seems crazy, doesn't it? In fact, this whole place seems unreal. Makes me uncomfortable."

"Well, we do have a personal invitation from Dido herself," Esteban answered. "Who knows what she wants in return."

"I'm starved. I really need some of the food they have out there," Ceci said. "So let's go along with it. If you can't handle her, I'm sure I'll be able to."

Esteban remembered how Ceci had taken care of the tough kids who had bullied him in high school, and he knew she was right.

Returning to the front desk, Esteban smiled. "Great rooms," he said, "and we really want some of that delicious looking buffet."

"Of course," Rosa said. But she was no longer looking at Esteban. Her eyes were turned toward the dining area, where – from the very back of the room – the most beautiful woman Ceci had ever seen in her life slowly made her way toward them.

"Dido," Rosa whispered as she nodded in the woman's direction. She was not young, thought Ceci, but it didn't matter. She could be any age from twenty to one hundred. Her eyes were wide, her lashes long, her skin ebony... blacker even than that, if it were possible. Her lips were perfectly formed, soft pink. The shadows painted above her eyes were midnight blue, as was her dress. It was so simple that dress, almost a chemise; short, showing off the woman's long, perfectly formed legs. She walked like a model on flat shoes that did not add an inch to her height; she didn't need it; she was very tall, perhaps six foot three or four, Ceci thought. And then she whispered to Esteban, "Where the hell did she come from, and what does she want with us?"

Esteban didn't answer.

Dido made her way up to Ceci and smiled warmly. "Cecilia, it's a pleasure to meet you." She offered her hand. Ceci took it feeling somehow in awe of the much taller, far more beautiful woman.

Dido turned to Esteban. "Nice shirt," she said.

"Thanks, it's one from the saddlebags."

"I know. You look very handsome in it. I trust the bags are serviceable."

"Oh, yes," answered Esteban while Ceci looked on in confusion.

"She gave us the saddlebags?" she asked.

"I've been meaning to tell you."

"I've been waiting for you, Esteban, for a very long time, actually."

Esteban nodded.

"And I've read so much about your famous ancestor, Estebanico. He was from Africa, after all. Not a Spaniard."

"Morocco," Esteban said. "There are so many legends about him that it's hard to tell fact from fiction."

"But you know the truth, don't you, Esteban?"

"I think I do."

"Then you must tell us all about it after dinner." She turned to Ceci. "You will both join me as my guests, won't you?"

Ceci was getting more and more nervous. There was something so unreal about this woman, about her perfect diction that sounded like it was learned from expensive English tutors, about the whole place... a casino out in the middle of nowhere that looked so small and unimposing from the outside but was so enormous and wealthy within. And then there was this new revelation: that she had given Esteban the saddlebags that they were using on the trip, and apparently the clothing and supplies inside. Yet Dido's friendliness combined with her striking beauty was hard to resist.

"Of course, we'll join you," Ceci heard herself saying.

"Wonderful," Dido answered, and she took Esteban's arm and turned him toward the dining room. "Come, you must tell me all abut your legendary forefather and his search for the Seven Cities of Gold."

Even though the food was displayed buffet style, Dido directed her guests to take their seats at a great, round table. She sat at the farthest place from the doorway, Esteban beside her. The elderly couple from the back of the gambling area sat to his right, then several patrons, probably from the blackjack table beside them, then Ceci, then several other guests. The net effect of the arrangement was to move Ceci as far away from Esteban as she could possibly be.

"Not liking this," Ceci mumbled to herself until the young man sitting beside her looked over and smiled.

"Wow, you're beautiful," he said. Ceci blushed and lowered her eyes. The truth, she thought, was that she might be attractive, but this guy: lean, tanned, square-jawed, bright-eyed, could have been Mr. America... if there was such a title.

"My name's Joseph," he said. "My friends and I like to come to Dido's every Monday night. The food is so good."

Ceci sighed and nodded.

"So, tell me about yourself," Joseph said. "I hear you just quit your job at the copper mine."

Ceci flinched. How did these people know so much about her and about Stevie? She was about to ask Joseph, but then a waitress came up to her with a tray full of appetizers.

The dress of the entire wait staff was Southwestern: wide-sleeved cotton shirts, tight black jeans, and vests decorated in the colors of the desert.

Ceci selected a serving of shrimp as a young Indian girl poured water for her and another placed a carafe of wine at her end of the table.

"Can I pour you some?" Joseph asked.

Ceci was still on guard against the strangeness of the whole scene. But the first bite of shrimp had been so delectable that she felt herself weakening. Okay, so she would allow a small glass of wine. No more, though, she thought.

"How do you people know so much about us?" Ceci was finally able to ask. "I mean, I had barely decided to go on this journey last night and might have canceled the whole thing this morning."

"You never would have canceled it," Joseph insisted. He rolled himself a little taco from the ingredients he had selected from the appetizer tray. "You know you're not like that, Ceci."

Ceci did know. But how did this guy... handsome though he was? "You're probably right," Ceci said. But again there were those questions: Who were these people? How did they know so much? And what were they up to?

The conversation continued to be light and friendly through a meal of some of the most delicious food Ceci had ever tasted in her life. She looked across the table and found that Esteban was engrossed in conversation with Dido and the couple sitting next to him. The wine was delicious and definitely going straight to her head. So much for being careful, she thought as she made small talk with Joseph through the rest of the meal. Then, when the last of the coffee had been sipped, and the last bits of desserts were savored, when snifters of brandy were offered to everyone, and even Ceci decided to indulge, Dido stood.

"We welcome our guests from La Sentencia," the woman began. "We know that their quest is noble, and we are eager to help them on their way."

Everyone at the table nodded as they sat back in their chairs and sipped their brandy.

"Señor Esteban has consented to tell us a little about his renowned ancestor," Dido continued, "the Moor, who set off on the same journey he intends to make, only more than 400 years earlier. So, please, sit back, relax, and listen as he tells us the tale of his great, great, great, great grandfather, who journeyed to the new world with the Spaniards and led the search for Cíbola."

Chapter 24
The Tale of Estebanico

Silence descended on the great hall. Those in attendance barely breathed, they were so intent on listening. The silence grew even more oppressive, becoming at last uncomfortable. From across the table, Ceci saw Dido turn and arch an eyebrow at Esteban. That was all that was needed. In spite of what might have been considerable misgivings on his part, he smiled and spoke up from his place at the head of the table.

"You want me to tell you the story that my ancestor revealed in my dreams," he began. "It's not a pleasant one. But if you're so anxious to hear it, then listen."

Estebanico was born in the city of Azemmour in Morocco, North Africa. He was a dark skinned man, a Moor, of the same ethnicity as our own Saint Augustine, though of course not of the same faith. He was a believer in the teachings of Mohammed although some of his actions clearly went against the teachings of his faith, or so he told me. It was something for which he apologized again and again, even to me.

In my dreams, Estebanico said that he was captured by the Portuguese and sold as a slave. The man who bought him was a wealthy adventurer named Andreas Dorantes. Some years after my great grandfather's purchase, Dorantes brought him on an expedition heading to the new world, to colonize land that Captain Narváez had been granted in Mexico. The Expedition, with soldiers, women and children, horses and goods, sailed for Cuba, and from there headed toward Mexico. But they were blown off course on the last leg of their journey and ended up on the west coast of Florida.

As soon as he reached the first native villages, Captain Narváez began hearing of wealthy cities some distance off. The stories encouraged him to head farther north than he would otherwise have gone, and as they journeyed, he and his party encountered local tribes, many of whom had some gold in their possession, and all of them talked about great cities beyond where the gold was far more plentiful.

Both soldiers and settlers suffered greatly as Narváez led his party up the west coast of Florida. Many died on the trek, but my great grandfather learned a great deal on the march and had a chance to apply many of his innate skills. His talents as a negotiator made him especially good at dealing with the natives. He became the chief emissary of the dwindling group, establishing relations with the natives and arranging for their accommodations.

My great grandfather told me that he had learned many cures and potions as well as some basic medical practices from his friends and acquaintances back in Azemmour. And this knowledge, as well as his sensitivity to human need, helped him especially in one village where the daughter of the chieftain had fallen to a terrible illness. Almost everyone in the village felt that the girl was already dead. But Estebanico was able to awaken her from a death-like sleep and quickly bring her back to health. From that time on, he was viewed as a healer and treated with so much respect that, when at last the bedraggled remains of the Narváez expedition reached Mexico and told everyone stories about their encounters with the Indians, Estebanico was the natural choice to lead the search for the fabled Golden Cities to the north.

The governor of New Spain outfitted an expedition to be led by Marcos di Niza, a Missionary. Estebanico was to serve as their guide. Their mission: to explore the lands to the north and find out if there was any truth to the rumors of great Golden Cities. But as soon as the trek was underway Estebanico and Marcos began to disagree about almost everything: which direction to take, which goods to acquire, how best to deal with the Indian tribes that they encountered. Marcos began to question Estebanico's medical practices and even began to suggest that they hinted of witchcraft... an offense punishable by torture and death. Eventually, Estebanico started to separate himself more and more from the main body of the expedition. He headed off on his own, disobeying direct orders from Marcos. He gained a significant amount of personal freedom in the process and (at least according to Marcos's bitter reports) accumulated great stores of turquoise and other valuable minerals, and the accompaniment of several beautiful native women.

My great grandfather told me that these stories were pure fiction, created by the evil priest to discredit him and to disassociate him from the expedition. In fact, he soon found that he could no longer tolerate the insults and insinuations he received from Marcos and refused ever to meet with him again. Instead, Estebanico ranged ahead of the main party, communicating only through messages that he would leave tied to simple crosses he would erect along his trail. The notes allowed him, at least, to provide the minimum requirements of his job, advising the party of the best routes to take and warning of the dangers they might encounter.

It was with such a message that my grandfather made the great mistake of informing Marcos of ever increasing rumors of a vast civilization that had built seven cities with wide boulevards and multistoried buildings, where people wore fine garments and worshiped in temples of pure gold. He advised Marcos and his band that they must contain their enthusiasm about such news and proceed with great care... for they were coming to Cíbola a kingdom populated by extremely violent people.

My great grandfather smiled at me in that dream you know, and told me that he had - in fact - made up the name Cíbola from the name "Cibao," a failed Spanish gold mine that he had heard about in Hispaniola.

As he talked, his look became even more playful, and he told me that it was on that very day that he decided to sever his ties with the Spaniards forever and lose himself among the Indians. And so he had the Indians carry back stories that he had been murdered on first contact with the great tribe of the Zunis. But instead, he went on to lead a long and happy life among the Native American tribes."

Esteban turned to Dido, bowed and said, "Thank you, madam, for your hospitality. My story is complete."

The beautiful woman did not return his bow. She was shocked. She glanced around the room at the other guests nervously and only after several moments was she able to contain herself. Then she smiled and said, "But Esteban, we don't really know what finally happened to your great, great grandfather and whether or not he found the fabled cities. Do you know?"

"Of course. He told me."

"Well then, won't you please tell us?"

"It's of little consequence now."

Dido bit her lip. "Please, Esteban?"

"But it's already so late."

"Esteban!"

"Okay," he answered. "Tomorrow at breakfast after we've had a good night's sleep. Then I'll take the time to tell you everything."

"At least, whether or not your forefather found the Golden Cities, and if so where they are?"

Esteban smiled. "Tomorrow."

Now Ceci stood and began moving toward her companion. "Dido," she said. "I doubt that you or your friends will remember much of a story that's told to you as you're falling asleep anyway... not at so late an hour and after so much good food and wine. Let's all rest now and we will talk in the morning."

Dido hesitated. Ceci thought she saw a trace of terrible anger move slowly behind the woman's eyes before she forced a smile. But at that moment Ceci understood everything. Dido had come here to intercept Esteban because, through some unknown means, she'd found out about Esteban's dreams. She thought that his great, great grandfather had explained much about the location of the Seven Cities of Gold. She was motivated by simple greed, just as Blackmore was, just as the Conquistadors had been.

"Shall we reconvene at sunrise?" Dido asked Ceci and Esteban. "We can hear the last little part of your story, and then we can help you on your way."

"Excellent," said Esteban as he attempted to make his way past the tall woman. But she reached out, grabbed him by the shoulder, turned him toward her, lowered her head, and kissed him.

"You know," she whispered, "You could share my bed tonight."

Esteban stepped back and just looked at her for a moment. "It would be an honor," he was surprised to hear himself saying. "But I'm really not worthy."

"I think you are."

"No, ma'am, I am not."

And with that, he turned to Ceci, took her hand, and they left the banquet hall together. But no sooner had they made it into the barroom than he whispered, "Quick, run for it!"

As the couple rushed toward the front door, many of Dido's clients were already moving to block them. Some were suddenly sporting machetes, others carrying pistols, their faces twisted in anger, their lips mouthing strange unexpected words. But Esteban and Ceci moved more quickly than any of them.

They threw open the doors and charged out into the night, realizing at once that they had entered a whirlwind whose angry voice roared all around them. Great gales almost bent the trees in half. Dust swirled up from the surrounding desert and made a deadly gauntlet through which the couple had to run. Yet, beyond the darkness and the sandstorm, they could see Aladdin kneeling at the end of the driveway waiting for them. Little Sammy was with the camel, holding his reins, and beside the boy was an even smaller person, a little girl: Sophia!

"Sbrigare!" she shouted into the gale, "Hurry up!"

Esteban and Ceci rushed to the camel.

"Onto his back," Sophia called. "And take me with you."

Esteban gave Ceci a leg up, and she vaulted into the saddle, which twisted perilously. But when it jerked back in Esteban's direction, he jumped on board just as Dido and her retinue broke through the doorway. Sophia clambered onto the camel too, and at that very moment the wind grew in intensity. A two hundred foot tall Haboob, nearly invisible in the darkness, descended full force. It cut Dido and her followers off from the camel riders.

"Sammy, come with us," Sophia cried.

"No, I have to stay with Mama. They haven't seen me. I'll be all right."

The camel pushed himself up onto his feet and started running. "Arrivederci!" the little girl called back to the boy, and as they rode away, she saw that he was saluting them.

Dido's soldiers (for that's what they were) were nearly on them then, but the Haboob seemed intent on holding them off.

Sammy ducked behind a great tree and hoped no one had seen him helping Esteban and his friends. Meanwhile, the camel picked up speed and outpaced the wind.

"How did you get here?" Ceci asked the little girl who, in spite of the sand swirling everywhere around them, was smiling broadly.

"I travel with the wind," she answered. "And I like it."

"We do too," Esteban answered. "Thank you for saving us."

The little girl raised a chubby hand and blew him a kiss. "Prego," was all she said in reply.

"You're welcome."

Chapter 25
San Pablo of the Cars

Several hours later, just as the sun was starting to burn its way onto the horizon and heat devils began to ripple in the air above the desert floor, Sophia gave a cheer.

"There it is," she said though neither Ceci nor Esteban could recognize anything specific ahead of them.

"Right there." And she grabbed the reins away from Esteban, who had only been holding them loosely anyway, not actually steering the camel in any particular direction, and she turned the beast toward the south. She clicked her tongue as she had heard camel drivers do in what was almost another lifetime with her parents, and she urged Aladdin into a trot.

In less than twenty minutes Ceci and Esteban both recognized the small flat building they were approaching for what it was... a rest stop along a desolate stretch of desert highway.

The camel now pulled in front of the structure, tromped out into the empty parking lot, slowed, and then knelt: front legs first, then back. He waited for the riders to dismount. Sophia slipped off the front of the saddle first, then Ceci. Esteban used the saddle's one stirrup to step down from the camel. Once his riders were clear, Aladdin rose to his feet and ambled across the parched earth to where a few bushes had found moisture from a small underground stream. There was just enough water trickling to the surface to give Aladdin a much-needed drink.

"Are you coming with us on our quest?" Esteban asked Sophia.

"No, sorry. I can't," the little girl answered. "You can go on, though, I can wait right here... a ride's coming by to pick me up."

"They're on their way to meet you?"

Sophia nodded.

"But who, from where?"

"I don't know," the little girl answered, "my rides just show up when I need them."

Esteban looked at the girl for a moment with an expression that seemed to say, "and they think I'm crazy?" But finally, he smiled.

"So, how about some breakfast?" Sophia asked.

Ceci looked around the little rest area and saw that scrubs and bushes were everywhere. She walked slowly over to a prickly pear cactus and carefully pulled a small fruit from it, then grabbed a pocketknife, sliced the fruit open, and sucked out the sweet jelly from the inside. "Mmmmm," she sighed. "Just as good as anything at the banquet last night."

"It was quite a feast," said Esteban as he approached the cactus. The wary look in his eyes suggested that he had no idea how to pick the fruit.

"Carefully," Ceci responded to the look, and then she nudged him away from the cactus. She reached down, and neatly pulled off another prickly pear, then turned to Sophia.

"I don't feel safe leaving you alone out here in the desert."

"I'll be fine," the little girl answered as she too picked fruit from the cactus and handed it to Ceci.

"Want me to cut it open for you?"

"Yes, please."

Ceci worked her jackknife on the pear. "Can't we, at least, take you to the outskirts of the next town?"

"My ride's coming here," Sophia answered, "and pretty soon too. You can wait with me if you want. You're going to have to wait till Aladdin's had enough to drink anyway."

Ceci nodded.

"So, let's get some more fruit," the little girl continued, "and take it over to that picnic table in the shade. Then we can rest until he's ready for you."

And they did.

Within an hour, as the sun rose higher in the sky and the floor of the desert started to feel like the bottom of an oven. Ceci awoke to hear a soft zooming sound. She had fallen asleep sitting at the table with her head resting in her arms. Esteban was a short distance away from her, lying spread-eagled on top of another table. His mouth was wide open, and he was snoring with amazing power.

"Stevie, was that you?"

"Huh?"

"That sound?"

Zoom, zoom... the sound came again from the other side of the rest area. Ceci rushed around it, but any car or taxi or anything that might have zoomed in had also zoomed out by then... and Sophia was gone.

#

Esteban, Ceci, and Aladdin moved on slowly through the intense desert heat. Ceci hadn't realized just how twisted and sore she had become from the pitch and sway of the animal's movements. She tried to adjust her position, wondering why she had let Esteban talk her into riding again. Okay, she knew. He was just trying to be gallant. And she wanted to reward him for it by accepting his offer to let her ride. It was clear that Aladdin didn't care. He had carried her and Esteban and Sophia together with no problem whatsoever. Besides, if she were willing to put up with the muscle-churning ride, then Esteban would probably take a turn... and they could move along much more quickly when he did.

She scanned the horizon hoping for the sign of some kind of hill, a rise, someplace where they could rest and she could get back on her feet, hopefully with Esteban up on the camel. There was something that looked like a hill out there in the distance, she realized, but it didn't seem quite right. There was something very strange about it.

"Over there, Stevie," she called as she pointed.

Esteban reached for the binoculars in the camel's saddlebag. He raised them to his eyes... scanned the horizon for a moment. "No hill out there, Cess, just a bunch of junked cars piled up a mile high."

"I don't think so, Stevie," she answered.

"Hey," he said with a smile, "who's got the binoculars?" Then he passed them to her. Ceci took a brief glance and recognized the crushed, rusted frames of dozens of old cars that must have been baking for decades in the Arizona sun.

"Let's go over there anyway," she said. "Maybe there's a little shade, a place to rest and have a drink."

It still took them over an hour to get to the mountain of cars, and when they did Ceci noticed a beat-up old Buick Special convertible sitting with its top down just in front of what must have been a General Motors dumping ground. The cars were Oldsmobiles, Chevys, Pontiacs, and other GM brands, all piled into a rough circle some three hundred feet in circumference and maybe a hundred feet high.

As she lurched forward on the camel, Ceci was able to look down into the interior of the Buick, and then she gasped.

A man was sitting in there. He was on the passenger side, in what had once been a plush leather interior. Now, however, the leather was cracked and dry, and it looked like most of the top of the seat had been blasted away by the desert winds. The man's hands were folded, prayer beads dangling from his fingertips.

As the camel moved into the man's field of vision, he shaded his eyes from the sun so that he could look up, and what he saw surprised him: an attractive young woman riding on an enormous camel.

The man lowered his hand, and Ceci could see that he had a scruffy white beard, and wore white cotton robes, the kind some orders of priests might wear. The robes had full sleeves with purple ribbons sewn into them. The man gave Ceci a questioning look and, almost in answer to that look, Esteban popped up beside the car and smiled.

"You okay?" he asked the man.

The guy recoiled. "Hey, stranger! You scared the hell out of me. What do you want?"

Ceci answered for both of them (and the camel). "We were just trying to get out of the sun, maybe have a drink, and make sure that you're okay."

The man's face crinkled in annoyance. "Don't I look okay? Besides, what do you care?"

Ceci, not sure of what to do or say, just nodded. The man seemed to be well fed, muscular... as though whatever he was doing out here in the desert must be giving him quite a workout. He stood up in the convertible, then looked up at the blue, cloudless sky and raised his hands to heaven. When he did it, the broad sleeves of his robe fanned out making him look like a portrait of some preaching saint.

"I am San Pablo of the Cars," he announced. "And I have come to the desert to speak to God."

"San Pablo of the Cars," Ceci murmured as she rolled her eyes at Esteban, "I should have known. Let's get out of here."

145

Esteban shook his head. "Not yet. The guy's harmless, and who knows, he may have some wisdom to impart."

"Yeah, right, wisdom," Ceci answered. "Okay, talk to him if you like. I'm staying up here on Aladdin."

Esteban nodded and moved closer to the man. He checked out the rusty old Buick. "Nice car," he said.

"No, it's not," snapped San Pablo, and then his look became suspicious. "Just what are you up to, man?"

Esteban shook his head and held out his hands in protest. "Nothing, it's like she said, rest, a drink, and your welfare."

In response, San Pablo jumped out of the Buick and began to climb the mountain of cars as though he were a primate in his own, very familiar monkey cage. Within minutes, he was up at the very top looking down at the pair.

"You probably think I'm some kind of lunatic, right? Just out here to get a good suntan or something."

"Of course not."

"But you do have a nice tan," Ceci added kindly.

"Listen, Miss: I'm up here on top of Car Mountain, closer to God than you and your camel will ever be. I've come to live amid these rusty skeletons because they're symbols of greed. I'm praying that God will teach me a way to wipe away the love of money and earthly possessions from people's minds."

"Makes sense," said Esteban with a nod, and he approached the mountain of rusted cars and began climbing it. "Except that people have always been greedy... from day one, you know?"

"Yep," San Pablo answered. "All things bright, shiny, and electronic turn them on, make them feel good, but what about their souls, man?"

"I hear you," Esteban answered still climbing, trying to reach the summit of Car Mountain.

"Get back down here, Stevie," Ceci yelled. But her friend just kept going.

"Greed has gotten even worse in today's world," San Pablo continued. "It's poisoned the minds of our corporations, our politicians, and our heroes. It's destroying our planet."

"Absolutely!" Esteban shouted as he reached the very top of Car Mountain, and flung his arms wide in exaltation. Unfortunately, he lost his footing in the process and began to topple backward. Ceci let out a desperate scream.

"You gotta hold on, man!" San Pablo said, as he reached out and grabbed one of Esteban's flailing arms at the last minute, pulling him back safely onto Car Mountain.

"You gotta hold tight," San Pablo repeated, "but you must also let go." And he let go of Esteban then, and again the young man began to topple backward. When San Pablo grabbed Esteban this time, he dragged him along the tops of several wrecked cars until he was able to get him safely onto the wide, flat hood of a long Cadillac Eldorado. The self-proclaimed saint's eyes were blazing, and he continued to preach. "To hold on, you must let go. To gain, you must give up. To have, you must have not!"

Esteban was face to face with San Pablo now, almost eye to eye. The comments made no sense to him at all, but he was damn relieved that the holy man had saved his life.

Ceci watched the two of them standing at the very pinnacle of Car Mountain. In spite of his near fall, Esteban was so entranced and confused by San Pablo's words that he seemed to be unaware that they were hundreds of feet above the ground with nothing to keep them from falling if they should get too close to the edge and lose their balance.

Ceci wanted desperately to call Esteban down from up there but was afraid that it might distract him and cause him to stumble.

"What should we do, Aladdin?" she whispered to the camel.

Aladdin either wasn't concerned at all, or he simply had no sense of propriety because his response was, at first, a nasty belch... and then he took an enormous dump right there at the foot of the peak. The smell was immediate and alarming.

"Ahah!" cried San Pablo as he looked down. "Your camel has answered the call."

"I know," moaned Esteban as he fanned his face with his hand. "I can smell it all the way up here."

"Don't you recognize the sign, man?" asked San Pablo with a crooked grin. "It's great; it's wonderful!"

"Wonderful?"

"Of course, it is. Breathe deep, man. Fill your nostrils with that disgusting smell, because it's the best warning you're ever gonna get."

"Of what?"

San Pablo sat down cross-legged on the hood of the Eldorado, "Of how our whole world's gonna smell when greed finally takes over completely."

Esteban lowered himself onto the hood of the Cadillac and stared into San Pablo's wild eyes. "Greed," he repeated.

"GREED," reaffirmed San Pablo.

"Greed," echoed Ceci shaking her head in disbelief once again.

The camel dropped another load.

Chapter 26
Jessica's Last School Day

Greed was exactly what sparkled behind the Dolce & Gabbana sunglasses that Jessica Amado wore at that very moment. She was studying the sleek, brand new, candy-colored Corvette that Devlin Lucero had just driven to the curb in front of her home.

"Your chariot, milady," he said as he hopped out of the great machine and turned to her with a grin.

"Mine?"

Greed tightened every muscle of Jessica's body. Lucero could almost see it happening.

"Yours," he said as he handed her the keys. Then he walked slowly around to the passenger side and got in.

Jessica slid into the driver's side and saw that there was no place to put the key.

"Just push the button," Lucero told her, and she did. The car rumbled to life and brought something like six hundred horses to her command.

Jessica had spent the morning at the beauty parlor making herself fantastically beautiful, she thought... to match the fantastically beautiful wardrobe that Lucero had purchased for her in Phoenix the night before. They had flown to the big city, shopped at all the designer boutiques and returned to her home with boxes and boxes of expensive clothing. Jessica, already in

149

the grasp of near-paralyzing greed, wanted more and more. And, as he had placed a chaste kiss on her lips before he left that evening, Lucero promised that they would return to expand her wardrobe very soon.

Today, she had decided to wear the richest looking outfit of them all: a cord lace sheath dress, cut perhaps inappropriately short, accented with a very expensive golden necklace, matching earrings, and astonishingly high heels. Jessica looked like she was going to a grand cotillion, not to her very last day as a substitute teacher at La Sentencia Junior High.

She was already almost half a day late, of course. Her classroom might be wild by now... unless the administration was able to find someone else to teach her class before the kids tore the place apart. Jessica hoped that Principal Mortimer would have to do the job himself. In fact, she realized, if she could get there quickly enough, she might even be able to put in an appearance and see him in action before the last period ended.

"So, let me just hop back into my car," said Lucero, "and I'll follow you to school." She smiled and nodded. So Lucero opened the door of the Vette, slid effortlessly out of the car, jogged back to his Mercedes, and gave Jessica a thumbs-up just before getting into his own vehicle.

Jessica floored the accelerator, felt the car jolt forward, and felt a greedy rush of excitement as it blasted toward the school. A few minutes later, she swerved into the red zone just outside the front door and parked there illegally.

"Who gives a fuck," she cooed as she leaped from the car and ran up the front steps just in time to make it to the last minutes of her class.

The receptionist, a prudishly chubby Miss Melissa Millstone, gasped as this high fashion version of Jessica Amado rushed past her and clattered up the hall in those devilishly high heels.

Now, no more than a minute before the bell rang, Jessica tottered to a halt just outside her classroom door and peered in through the window. She was in luck; Mortimer did have to take over her class. She straightened her dress and her hair, pulled a compact from her tiny Gucci handbag and checked on her makeup. It was still perfect. Nodding in satisfaction, she closed the compact, put it back into her bag, and threw open the door.

She stepped through the doorway, cocked her hip, and stood there looking like a million dollar supermodel from the cover of Elle, Vogue, or even Cosmo.

Mortimer turned toward her at once. His eyes flew open, his jaw dropped. The kids in the class read his look and turned toward the doorway too. The girls gasped, the boys were speechless, almost all of them.

"Helloooooo, Mama," a fat kid hooted from the back of the room. No one else said a word. In fact, the embarrassing silence seemed to stretch on for minutes.   •

"M - Ms. Amado?" Mortimer stammered at last.

"Principal Mortimer," Jessica answered immediately. She arched an eyebrow and smirked.

"I think I'd better see you in my office right after class!" he said.

"Alone?" she asked, the arch in her eyebrow growing even more pronounced.

"Well yes!"

"I'd like to see her alone in your office too," the fat kid chimed in from the back of the room. The entire classroom burst out laughing, and at that moment, mercifully Principal Mortimer thought, the bell rang ending the period.

151

Chapter 27
The Disciple

Ceci had regained a little of her composure now that Esteban was sitting down on the hood of the rusty old Cadillac, which rested like a great eagle at the top of Car Mountain.

"Get down from there this instant, Stevie," she called.

"Hey, woman," San Pablo answered angrily, "Can't you see we're having a palaver up here?"

Ceci focused on her partner. "Don't listen to him, Stevie! He's out of his mind!"

San Pablo stood and walked to the very edge of the Eldorado's massive hood. He looked down at her haughtily.

"Our of my mind? It's been said of all the great prophets."

"You're no prophet," Ceci accused.

"Of course, I am. I prophesy the destruction of the world through GREED."

Ceci made some of the clicking sounds she had heard Sophia making, and Aladdin responded by slowly lowering himself to his knees. She dismounted from the camel then and walked purposefully toward Car Mountain.

"If you were a prophet you'd have disciples."

"Ah, yes. And I do."

Ceci put her hand over her eyes to shade them from the sun as she scanned the horizon. "I sure don't see any disciples coming this way."

But suddenly she could hear the rumble of an old truck in the distance. Ceci turned toward the bounding, bumbling noises as they drew nearer. It sounded as though the truck was bouncing up and down wildly on worn out springs... bottoming out with crash after crash and still it managed to keep coming.

San Pablo spread his arms again, letting the sleeves of his robe fall like those of the great prophet he claimed to be. "My disciple," he announced.

"Only one?"

"He's a start."

"Yessss!" bellowed the driver of an ancient, red Chevy pick-up as he roared into the area. He slammed on his brakes and, with a squeal of delight, did a wide, wild donut that spun him around until the truck came to rest right beside Ceci.

The rusted door of the truck exploded open with a clang of bent metal and a shower of red-brown rust, and a tall, thin kid of about nineteen stepped out. He had a big jutting jaw, baby blue eyes, and a narrow gangly frame. The only thing holding up his tattered jeans was a shank of rope. His black Metallica t-shirt clung to his scrawny chest and was so worn and shrunken that it barely covered his navel.

"Brought your provisions, oh wise one," said the kid.

San Pablo grinned as he turned to Ceci. "Meet my very dedicated disciple. This is Chucho Johnson."

"Call me Chuck," said the kid with a smile and a bow. "Or Chucho... whichever you prefer, ma'am." He bowed again, and then looked up to the top of Car Mountain.

"Came to make the quarterly delivery," he called. "Mind if I unload?"

"Go for it, son," San Pablo called, and he scrambled down the mountain so quickly that, once again, all Ceci could think of was some nimble zoo monkey scurrying around his habitat without even looking where he was going.

Up on the hood of the Eldorado, Esteban peered down, wondering just how he was ever going to descend.

"What ya got?" San Pablo asked Chucho.

"The usual provisions." And the boy immediately crunched opened the back of the pickup, which was loaded with fifty-pound bags of rice, beans; huge sacks of tomatoes and peppers, as well as an enormous bundle holding dozens of rolls of toilet paper made from 100% recycled material.

"No greed here," said Ceci with a smirk.

"All good, all biodegradable and recyclable. It'll last me for months. I match it up with the crops I grow out back, and I can be pretty self-sufficient."

For once Ceci didn't know quite how to respond.

"Lemme give ya a hand," San Pablo said to Chucho. But the kid motioned him away.

"Prophets aren't supposed ta work, your highness," he said as he jerked a thirty-pound bag of beans out of the pickup and pushed it into Ceci's arms. "But you can help, ma'am, if you're of a mind."

Ceci couldn't believe her eyes. She looked up at Esteban, and her expression was accusing and desperate. "Look what you've gotten us into," she muttered toward him. Esteban gave her an apologetic smile and then closed his eyes and leaned out over the edge of Car Mountain.

"No!" Ceci screamed dropping the massive bag of beans as she realized his intention. But it was too late; her partner had already thrown himself from the hood of the Eldorado. He grabbed and caught the Cadillac's big bumper as he did so. Then he swung wide, landed on the bashed-in roof of a Pontiac Firebird and then scrambled blindly on down the rest of the mountain of old rusted cars, swinging like an orangutan from bumper to door-handle to chrome trim to tire rim, but somehow managing finally to get to the base of the mountain.

"Halleluiah! Blind faith in action," grinned San Pablo as he patted Esteban on the back when he finally arrived.

"Absolute lunacy," screamed Ceci. "Don't you ever do that to me again, Stevie. What do you think would happen to me if I lost you out here in the desert? I'd be alone with no one but this stupid camel for company?"

The camel seemed to take exception to her remark, probably feeling that he would be excellent company indeed, and so he dropped yes another shit-load right beside the first piles that still smoldered on the desert floor.

"I love it!" called San Pablo. "Fill your lungs, boys and girls. Smell the stench of our coming decay."

"Yeah, right," said Ceci, then she picked up the thirty-pound bag of beans again, turned angrily to Chucho. "So, where do I put this, Mr. Disciple?"

"Oh, sorry ma'am," the kid replied. "Follow me."

Esteban stepped forward, grabbed a massive cellophane-wrapped bundle of toilet paper, and followed what was now a small procession heading around to the backside of Car Mountain.

Chapter 28
Jessica's Retribution

At that very same moment, Jessica Amado made her way into Principal Mortimer's office. She found him sitting behind his desk, waiting for her with a very satisfied smile on his fat face.

"Looks like you're ready for tonight's date, young lady," the Principal said in what he thought was a very seductive voice. Jessica found it disgusting.

"I still think your attire is a little provocative for the classroom," he continued, "but very appropriate for our negotiation later this evening."

"Thank you, Principal Mortimer," Jessica answered like an obedient schoolgirl. But she felt herself shuddering. Wasn't he drooling a bit as he spoke?

"If you have no objection," Principal Mortimer continued as he moved around the desk like a very awkward alley cat, "maybe we could stop by my place first. I have some very interesting etchings I'd like to show you."

Jessica giggled out loud. How could she not, the line was so trite. What a fool this man was.

"Is something funny?" the Principal asked.

"You are, you flaming asshole," she thought but didn't say it. Instead, trying to sound breathy and inviting, she cooed, "Oh, no, Principal Mortimer. I'd love to see your... etchings."

Mortimer leaned back against his big desk, tried to shift his weight onto it and slipped off, as he had in their last interview. He fell clumsily backward, regained his footing and, undaunted, smiled and hoisted himself up onto the desk with both hands, twisting on top of it, facing Jessica at last and crossing his legs awkwardly in the same motion.

"You know I can be very generous, Ms. Amado."

"I've heard that, Principal Mortimer."

"Especially with those who are willing to... play ball, so to speak."

Jessica giggled.

"Ms. Amado, you're laughing again?"

"Oh no, sir, don't misunderstand. It's just that you're so... so... charming, that it makes me nervous. Of course, I'll play ball with you."

Mortimer's erection was tiny but obvious. Jessica laughed out loud, and just then the door opened behind her.

"Well, what have we here?" the newcomer asked.

It was Devlin Lucero who came into the room and took a seat beside his protégée.

"See here," Mortimer responded. "This is a private session. And who the hell are you, anyway?"

"An interested third party," Lucero answered with a not-so-friendly smile. "I'm afraid that Ms. Amado won't be able to accept your ridiculous offer."

"Ridiculous?"

"What salary did you have in mind?"

"None of your business."

"I'll match it."

"I don't think so."

"I do. I'm the CFO of the Blackmore Copper Mine. I need a new Head of Human Resources, and Ms. Amado has all of the qualifications."

"What do you mean?" stammered Mortimer. "She barely has the qualifications to be a teacher's aide. How can she run an HR Department?"

"Let's just say that I see things in her that you must have missed."

"I know what you see in her," Mortimer fumed.

"My offer is two hundred thousand dollars a year," Lucero interrupted, "... plus a company car... and a wardrobe allowance."

"You can't be serious."

"But I am... and there are a couple more things too."

Mortimer jumped to his feet and pointed toward the doorway. "Get out of my office!"

Both Jessica and Lucero were grinning now.

"Number one," Lucero began as he moved toward Mortimer and not toward the door, "I will never ask Ms. Amado to check out my etchings...."

Jessica's eyes blazed at Lucero's words, and Mortimer finally understood the contempt she felt for him. He rushed Lucero, who deftly sidestepped and sent the Principal crashing into the wall. Half a dozen inconsequential diplomas jarred loose and landed right on his head.

"Number two," Lucero continued, as he spun Mortimer around and pulled his arm behind his back in a hammerlock, "I think Ms. Amado here, can easily charge you with sexual harassment, Mr. Mortimer.

"Or would you rather just kick the shit out of him, Jessica?"

The young woman's eyes brightened even more as she suddenly realized what a valuable weapon her uncomfortable high heels could be.

"Principal Mortimer," she said, "here's what I think of your offer!" and she blasted him with the pointed toe of one of those high heels... right in the knee. If Lucero had not been holding Mortimer up, he would have fallen to the floor.

Instead, he stood there totally exposed as Jessica adjusted her two thousand dollar glasses and then cried out, "and this is for all your impure thoughts, you dirty prick!" And she jabbed another sharp kick into the other knee.

No longer able to stand, Mortimer was now completely supported by Lucero's powerful hold.

"HELP!" shouted the Principal. "Someone help me, I'm being assaulted!"

Lucero tightened the hammerlock and whispered in the Principal's ear. "I took the liberty to ask your assistants to leave for the afternoon. So, no one can hear you scream."

Jessica nodded in understanding as she delivered a perfectly placed spike-heeled karate kick right into the Principal's groin.

Mortimer crossed his eyes, gave out with a strange inaudible squeak, and finally caught his breath enough to cry out, "you fucking bitch!"

The words brought an even harder spiked-heel to the balls... and then another, and another. Lucero threw Mortimer back against the wall and joined in the assault. He pounded the educator's face, delivering a blast to the gut while Jessica took her hot new Gucci handbag and used it to pummel Mortimer's head and shoulders. The bag's bright, golden clasp drew first blood, which poured from just above Mortimer's left eye. Then a right cross from Lucero tore open the Principal's lips and sent blood gushing all over his shirt.

Mortimer was nearly unconscious when Lucero grabbed him by the hair and lifted his head. Through bleary eyes, the Principal saw a small recorder surface from Jessica's Gucci purse. The young woman flipped it on, and he heard himself speaking:

"You know I can be very generous, Ms. Amado."

"I've heard that."

"Especially with those who agree to... play ball so to speak."

159

Lucero let go of Mortimer's head, and it lolled miserably between his hunched over shoulders.

"I'm going to drive you home now," Lucero hissed at Mortimer. "I'll have one of the medical staff from the mine's infirmary take care of your problems. But breathe a word about this little…" he looked at Jessica as though he couldn't quite think of the correct way to express it.

"Retribution," she said with accusation still glaring from her eyes.

"Right! See, I knew you'd make a great head of HR."

Then he turned back to Mortimer. "Any word of this 'retribution', and we'll see that you lose your job and your teaching credentials permanently… and maybe spend a few years in jail, too. Understand?"

Mortimer nodded weakly.

"Do you have anything to add, Ms. Amado?" Lucero asked.

"Only this," Jessica answered, and she swung her purse from behind her head and slammed it so hard into Mortimer that he fell to the floor.

"So there!" she said.

"You take the Vette," Lucero told Jessica, who was now gasping for breath from all that destructive exercise. "Go to the mine. You'll see the employment offices as soon as you enter the grounds. Just wait for me there. I'll drop this sack of shit back at his place and meet you in the office."

Jessica nodded. Then, though she was still trembling, she went to Lucero and gave him a long, sweet, grateful kiss. She could hear Mortimer groaning sadly as she did, and that made it all the better.

Chapter 29
Car Mountain Caverns

They were making their way to the far side of Car Mountain, San Pablo, Esteban, and Chuck, with Ceci now in the lead. Halfway through the trek, Ceci suddenly stopped cold. Instantly, sweat broke out on her forehead and she couldn't breathe. There, no more than a few feet in front of her, was an enormous rattlesnake, maybe five or six feet in length. The buzz of its furious rattle seemed to silence every other sound of the desert. The snake was poised to strike.

Ceci felt as though she was losing her balance... was sure that the snake would soon sink its fangs deep into her leg. Could she throw the thirty-pound bag at the monster before it struck her? A soft moan escaped her lips, and the rattler jerked backward at the sound, about to launch itself forward!

Just then there was a loud whistle and the snake froze.

Ceci felt herself tottering, about to faint. She closed her eyes as she heard San Pablo running past her. Her eyes blinked open, and she saw the scrawny man standing in front of her, his eyes fixed on the snake. Then he knelt in front of it.

"No, Beautiful," he soothed. "Not now." The snake jerked its head even further back, becoming even more ready to strike.

"This woman has no intention of hurting you. She's helping me. She's my friend; you're my friend. Let's work together. Let us pass, please."

An image suddenly blasted into Ceci's terrified mind: the snake, lunging at the crazy old man, striking him full in the face, jerking backward, rattler screaming as the prophet fell to the ground and the snake lashed out at her. Ceci had to do everything she could to stifle a scream. And then the monster settled back into its coils, paused for just a moment, and then slithered away toward the back of Car Mountain.

"Follow her now," San Pablo told Ceci. "She won't harm you; she's clearing the way."

Carefully Ceci hefted the heavy bag and continued on her way.

As they finally made their way around the mountain, Esteban could see what looked like a wildlife park filled with all kinds of animals: jackrabbits, roadrunners, a puma resting in the open sun, dozens of different sized lizards, and a noisy troop of javelina rumbling around right beside their most feared predator. Behind the animals, a deep ravine fell away into unimaginable depths, but all along its edge was a natural garden of food-bearing desert plants: prickly pear cacti, agave plants, saguaros with their edible flowers, aloe vera, and even ironwood trees.

"Welcome to my back yard," said San Pablo as he gestured to the animals and the rows of desert plants. "Most of the food I eat comes from here. Unfortunately, it's not enough for my friends and me... so I have to supplement our meager diet with a few supplies... as you see."

In the very center of San Pablo's back yard lay a low flat Chevy Nomad, it's top crushed in, its tires long gone, but its trunk fully intact. Chucho went to the car, opened the trunk, and dumped two large bags of rice into what served as a large storage area. He then took the sack of beans Ceci had been carrying and added it to the supply. Esteban approached with that massive pack of toilet paper, but there was clearly not enough room.

"Goes up front," San Pablo said, and he walked to the driver's side door and jerked it open. Although the front of the car had been crushed, the door itself had been jimmied away from the body so that it could be opened and closed, and so Esteban was able to toss in the large package and then hear a resounding slam as San Pablo pushed it closed.

"Here are my sleeping quarters," said the prophet as he turned back toward the mountain of rusted cars and pointed to the back of a mid-60s Chevy Van, one that had somehow managed to escape the crusher so that it's body was whole.

Over the two darkened windows were, of all things Ceci thought, hippie-style beaded curtains. San Pablo went to the Van's big chrome door-handle and unlatched the back revealing a Spartan but spacious interior. A lantern sat atop a small crate beside a well-worn mattress at the far end of the van's open interior. Tucked inside the crate were all manner of good books: The Stand by Stephen King, Swan Song by Robert McCammon, The Road by Cormack McCarthy, and dozens of others.

"Apocalypse novels," Ceci said.

"Yes, and I have the actual Apocalypse too," San Pablo answered, as he pointed to the Book of Revelations sitting on the top of the crate.

San Pablo now walked back toward the edge of the ravine. He sat on a large bolder and, to Ceci's shock, began to pet the puma as it nuzzled up beside him.

"You've shown me that you're a holy man," she said. "But I have to warn you that the cat might take your head off."

"I doubt it. We're friends," Paulo answered scratching the puma under its chin. The creature actually began to purr. "Besides, I feed him whenever I can."

"You eat meat?" Esteban asked.

"Not really, eggs... and if I find them I share them with my friend here."

"And the other times?"

"He goes off on his own, great distances away, I think. He spares our little family, maybe just to be nice."

"You're as crazy as I am," Esteban said shaking his head.

"Crazy but holy," Ceci added as she did her famous eye-roll.

"No one here is crazy," answered Paulo. "It's the rest of the world. It's so full of evil. Now, why don't you and the Mrs. stay a week or so? I'd like to try group prayer, a summoning... where we call to the Lord through the moon and the stars... together... late at night. We'll light a great bonfire, let our spirits rise, see if God won't bless us with insights into the ways that we can lead humanity away from all this greed."

"First, I have to tell you," said Esteban, "we're not married, but otherwise I guess we could stick around for a little while. What do you think, Cess?"

Ceci looked around, at the tangle of snakes, at the puma, at the javelina that seemed to be ready to charge her en masse. They were all quite frightening. The cacti didn't seem that friendly either, and poor old Aladdin... might he not be a banquet for the puma, in spite of the Prophet's best warnings?

"Where will I sleep?" she finally asked.

"Same place as me," answered Chucho with a boyish grin that suddenly didn't seem all that innocent to Ceci either.

"I think we'd better go," she said as she got to her feet.

Chucho began to giggle then, so did San Pablo. And Ceci grew more and more alarmed. A single woman alone with three men, who, in spite of their claims of holiness and some tricks with the animals, maybe were all clearly out of their minds.

"Don't get me wrong," Chucho said quickly. "I didn't mean we'd sleep in the same bed... or even the same room."

"Absolutely not," added Paulo. "Forgive us."

"I meant we'd stay in the same kind of place, in one of the guest rooms."

"Guest rooms?"

Chucho smiled and then he immediately stood and went running toward Car Mountain.

He jumped up onto it, and then–with the aid of some neatly placed bumpers and door handles, which made a very convenient ladder–he reached another van that had not been crushed. He flipped open its back doors to reveal another simple but immaculate sleeping quarters. Then he hiked up even higher until he found and opened the doors to another van and another.

"Guest rooms," said Chucho, and Paulo nodded. "There's a fresh pitcher of water, some fruit, and even a chamber pot in each of them. You can even lock them from the inside if you want to."

Ceci felt immediately relieved and even smiled. But then she thought of Aladdin. "And who cares for our camel?" she asked.

"He can pretty much take care of himself, the Prophet answered. "He's a big desert beast, and I doubt that anything would dare to attack him. But if you'd like, I have no problem moving my cot out here and sleeping beside him under the stars. These animals are all my friends, the desert nights are peaceful, and I can guarantee that Aladdin will be safe."

"I guess it could work," Ceci finally admitted, and she saw the appreciation in Esteban's eyes.

"I think we can learn a lot here," he said. "Things that will help us on our quest."

And so they sat there late into the afternoon, talking about ways that the world could be changed and saved, and of the wonderful life that could be possible if greed were just eradicated from men's minds.

"And women's too," added Ceci. "It's not just the male of our species who is cursed with the love of material possessions and wealth."

No indeed.

Chapter 30
Jessica's Big Day

"God, how I love this car," thought Jessica Amado as she pulled her candy colored Corvette into her personal parking space at the Blackmore Mining Company. It was only a week later while Ceci and Esteban were praying that men and women would abandon their greed and seek a less materialistic lifestyle.

Jessica pushed open the car door and spun her legs out onto the lacquered area around her spot. Then she got up from the deep bucket seat, slammed the door shut, and strode proudly into the executive offices. She was wearing an exceptionally short stretch leather skirt today, and a rather tight white cotton blouse too… the kind of clothing that Principal Mortimer had told her not to wear. But then Mortimer was still in the hospital after an entire week, just out of intensive care, still having problems with head trauma. Just what the bastard deserved, Jessica thought. Imagine, telling her that she gave her students impure thoughts. Now Mortimer could barely have any thoughts at all… impure or otherwise. Jessica liked the idea, and then she wondered what her current co-workers would think of her outfit… as she fired their asses.

"Good morning Ms. Amado," said Clark, her very cute, very buffed, very efficient, and very gay private secretary.

"Can I get you some coffee?"

"That'd be great."

She marched into the gigantic executive suite that Lucero had provided for her, slid into the two thousand dollar office chair, tapped the keyboard of her new iMac computer, and called up her daily schedule.

This is really going to be fun, she told herself as she pushed her glasses up onto the bridge of her nose.

Jessica had spent her first day on the job getting to know her executive co-workers as well as she could, and spent the next two days in intense management training sessions in which she paid special attention to the process of firing people. She found that she had a special affinity for it and seemed to enjoy the feeling of power it gave her, even when the interviewees broke into tears or threatened her physically when she terminated them. She loved calling in security and seeing the cursing, hateful bastards literally dragged from the room.

"Terminate!" She liked the word and the strength it seemed to give her: the power to decide on "job or no job" (almost as good as "life or death").

Clark brought a steaming cup of coffee up to Jessica's massive mahogany desk and set it on the Coyote Fetish Coaster he had provided. He *was* fastidious.

Jessica lifted the cup gratefully and sipped. "Mmmmm…

"Now, Clark," she said. "Could you ask Gabriel Romo to step into my office, please?"

Clark smiled and the way his nostrils flared made her think that he must have the hots for Gabe. That was okay, though, she realized. So did she.

"Hi," Gabe said as he entered her office.

"Hi, yourself," she answered. "Get a good night's sleep?"

"Not really. But I guess I'm as ready as I'll ever be."

Jessica handed Gabe a list of one hundred names… the hundred managers who would be laying off their employees today. Each only had to deal with five or six employees... no more.

They would all be delivering the same message:

1. It's become necessary to downsize the mining operations.
2. The number of people doing the job that you've been doing had to be greatly reduced.
3. The mine had arranged for a generous severance package for each employee who is laid off... two full week's severance pay and on-going medical care for another month... IF (and it is a very important "if") you sign a statement saying that you will not speak out against the mine or take action against its owners or the remaining workers.
4. You and all the other employees who are being laid off will be eligible to apply for new jobs at The Clean Sweep Car Wash Chain... the new business that former mine owner, Charlie Blackmore, is starting up.

"It's a pretty fair package," Jessica said.

Gabe shifted uneasily in his seat. "Not really," he said. "It's the minimum we're allowed to give them."

"I think it's very generous when you add in the job offer you were able to negotiate on their behalf."

Gabe hunched over in his chair, studied those big hands of his for a moment, and said nothing.

Jessica looked at the handsome Foreman, former Chief Operating Officer of the mine. His eyes were so damn penetrating, so dark and so brooding. They seemed to look into her very soul and what they were saying to her wasn't really that nice, was it?

Jessica sighed, then took a deep breath, and the top button popped right off her blouse. It flew high into the air.

Gabe reached up and caught the button, apparently without even knowing he was doing it. He looked down at it for a moment, then up at Jessica.

"Guess this is yours," He said as he stood to place in on her desk, and, as he did so, he leaned closer to her.

"Mmmmm," she thought; he smells nice too.

"When's this circus begin?" Gabe asked.

"Soon as the extra security gets here... maybe in another half an hour."

"How many do we have to do?"

"You don't have to do any, Gabe, I told you that."

"No, I want to. These are good people, some of them are my close friends, even relatives like my cousin Rich."

"Richard Romo," Jessica clarified.

"He and I were two of the mine's first employees. Now we're going to fire him. I have to be here to make sure it's all explained as well as it can be... so he'll understand."

Jessica stood too. "Want to rehearse or something?" she asked as she tried to give Gabe an understanding smile. "Role playing the interview can help us get ready."

"That's okay. I'm good. I'll be back in twenty minutes."

"Where are you going?"

"Just down to the church. I thought I'd say a prayer that we get this right. I want it to cause as little pain as possible; I want them to understand."

"So you're praying for...."

Gabe shrugged, "I don't know, maybe just the right words."

Jessica smiled. He was a very good man, she thought. She'd like to get to know him better.

"Be back in twenty," Gabe said. And then he was gone.

There was an armed security guard stationed outside of each of the offices as the hundred second-level managers called in their first candidates. At the same moment, Gabe's cousin Richard smiled broadly as he made his way into the conference room where Jessica and Gabe sat at a wide table. There was a single manila folder sitting in front of the mine's new Director of Human Resources.

"Rich," Gabe said as he got to his feet and walked around the table to greet his cousin and friend.

"Gabe," Rich answered. Then he turned to Jessica and nodded. "Ms. Amado."

Jessica stood, reached across the table and shook Rich's hand.

"Boy things are wild out there," Rich said with a slight grimace. "The place is so full of rumors. From the time old man Blackmore showed up last month everyone's been sayin' that the mine's in trouble, that just about everyone's going to get laid off."

Gabe shrugged almost in affirmation of the rumors.

"So, it's true then?"

Gabe nodded.

"Sorry to hear that. Well, okay, how can I help? Want me to get out there and keep things calm?"

"That would be nice," Jessica answered.

"Sure, what else. I really feel for my fellow workers. You know, so many of them are living from paycheck to paycheck... let's face it; the mine hasn't been that generous with a lot of them. Doubt that they have any savings at all. Still, I think I can help you keep the peace, at least a little."

Gabe sighed audibly, and that stopped Rich's rambling. He turned to his cousin with a sudden look of concern.

"Mr. Romo," Jessica said, as she pushed her glasses up onto the bridge of her nose yet again, "You are one of those guys."

"Who doesn't have any savings? Nah, I've got a little nest egg."

"No," Jessica answered. "I mean you are one of the people who's going to be laid off."

"Laid off?" Richard's face fell. "That can't be right, can it, Gabe? I mean you and I, hey we're family; we go back to the very beginning of the mine."

Gabe recognized Rich's look... it was as though he were pleading with him.

"It's not that we don't value your service," Gabe began.

Rich's expression turned almost at once from concern to hostility. "We value my service? We? That 'we' doesn't mean you and me does it, Cuz? It means 'we,' the mine, 'we,' the guys who get to keep our jobs. 'We,' the ones who have sold out... and part of that is selling out your friends and family too... isn't it?"

"Rich, please, don't make this any harder than it is," Gabe said, and he felt like a jerk as soon as he said it; he felt embarrassed and stupid. When he had been in the church praying just a few minutes earlier, Gabe had begun to feel so inadequate. Now he knew why.

"Don't make it harder?" Rich repeated sarcastically. "Gabe, we're family, and you're firing me. Okay, then listen, cousin, I'm going to make it as hard for you as I possibly can."

"We have an offer for you," Jessica said evenly. "Would you like to hear it?"

Rich's look was now defiant. "You bet I want to hear it. I want to hear every fuckin' word of it. So explain it to me, Ms. Amado, please, in the minutest detail."

"The mine has not been profitable for quite some time," Jessica began, "I'm sure you must have known that."

Rich's look of defiance continued, but he said nothing.

"In a sense, the mine has been carrying all of its employees for at least a year. Unfortunately, that has finally become economically impossible."

Rich eyed Gabe, who nodded, as much as to say, 'she's telling the truth.' Rich's expression softened a little.

"That's why it's now necessary for the mine to shut down. Completely."

"You're shutting down the mine?"

"That's what I said, Mr. Romo. In two weeks the mine will no longer exist."

"Is that true, Gabe?"

Gabe shrugged as though perhaps Jessica's statement wasn't entirely true.

"Well is it true, or isn't it?"

Jessica repeated herself more forcefully, "the Blackmore Copper Mine is shutting down, Mr. Romo."

"But..."

"That's all! It's shutting down."

Anger grew in Rich's eyes. "Gabe, for Christ's sake, what are you guys not telling me? There's something. I know there is."

Gabe looked down at his hands.

"Gabe? Goddamn it."

"There'll be a new company formed," Gabe began as Jessica turned to him angrily.

"It's none of his business, Gabe," she growled.

"Gabe, damn it! I'm your fucking cousin. We've been here forever. You and I worked together to keep the unions out of this mine. Remember? What are you guys not telling me?"

"Gabe!" Jessica commanded.

Gabe lowered his eyes and said nothing. Jessica smiled as she turned back to Rich and then, cleverly, she picked up on Gabe's words and put a new spin on them.

"There *will* be a new company formed to absorb as many laid-off mine workers as we can. It will be a whole new business."

Rich stared hard at Gabe, but he directed his question to Jessica. "What kind of new business?"

"Car wash."

"You want these mine workers to start working in a car wash?"

"It's cleaner," Jessica tried to joke. No one laughed.

"Is the pay the same?"

"Sometimes."

"Is that the business you were talking about, Gabe?"

Gabe lowered his eyes, expecting and getting a harsh prompt from Jessica. "Answer your friend, Gabe."

Gabe raised those big hands of his and studied them for a moment. Finally, he nodded.

In the end, Rich took the package, took the meager severance that the mine offered though his was no better than the ones offered to the other employees. Rich left the office regretting the day that he and Gabe had talked the other workers out of unionizing, wondering if unions could have made any difference in a company that was going out of business. But then there was that nagging question. Were they really going out of business after all... or what?

Chapter 31
Mario's Jukebox

Ten hours later, Gabe drove up to Tres Flores and made his way into the little restaurant. Directly or indirectly, he had presided over the dismissal of several thousand mine workers that day and hoped that the word hadn't yet reached Luís and Carmen.

He was surprised to find the restaurant empty and no sign of any of the wait staff. Still, he slid into a table at the front of the restaurant and waited for someone to take his order. Before anyone could get there, he felt a tug on his sleeve. He looked down. It was Sophia.

"Don't look so sad, sir," she said. "You were only doing your job."

Gabe pulled the little girl to him and hugged her. "Unfortunately," he said, "so were the Roman soldiers who nailed Jesus to the cross."

"You were just following orders," Sophia added.

"That's what the Nazis said when they were tried for killing millions of people in gas chambers."

"But you, at least, came up with something to help the workers."

"Yeah, minimum wage jobs at a car wash. Do you know how many car washes we'll have to open to accommodate everyone who gets laid off?"

175

Sophia gave the tired man a questioning stare.

"A whole lot," he said

"More than is possible?"

"More car washes than *thi*s town needs... this one and the next town over... and the town beyond that... and the one beyond that."

Sophia sighed and a tear formed in the corner of her eye. "I understand."

"Hey, cousin," it was Mario who came out from behind the glass partition that led into the kitchen. "Can I get you anything?"

"You're a waiter now?"

"Whatever it takes."

"Beer then?" Gabe suggested.

"Can't serve it legally," said Mario. "But hold on a second. I'll see what I can do." And he ducked back into the kitchen and came out with a bottle of Coors and a tall glass. "You'd better open it, though," the kid said.

Gabe twisted off the cap and watched the foam rise through the neck of the bottle.

"Where are your grandmother and granddad?"

"Cousin Rich came by, and they all went off somewhere."

Gabe grimaced. So everyone did know that he had participated in the firing of all those mineworkers.

"Please, sir," Sophia said. "Don't look so sad."

"How do you know what happened at the mine?" Gabe asked the little girl.

"I overheard."

"And is everyone mad at me?"

"You're still in the family," Mario answered.

"You think so?"

"That's what Papa Luís said."

"Did everyone agree?"

"No one agreed."

"I did," said Sophia.

"And I agree too," added Mario.

"Agree about what?" asked Papa Luís as he burst into the restaurant. Mama Carmen trundled along behind him. She gave Gabe a harsh look and then turned her eyes away.

"No one agreed that I'm still part of the family," Gabe said.

"Well, I..." Papa Luís began, but before he could finish, Cousin Rich came through the doorway. He saw that his cousin was there and charged him.

"You bastard," Rich called as he grabbed Gabe by both his lapels and yanked him out of his chair.

"You're doin' that bitch, aren't you?" Rich cursed. "That Jessica bitch, you're doin' her. She's more important to you than your own family."

Gabe grabbed Rich by the wrists, pulled his hands from his coat, and pushed the smaller man up against the wall.

"I'm not touching her; I don't even like her, man."

"Don't kid me. I see the way you look at her when you think no one's paying attention. You're fucking her, you son of a bitch."

Little Sophia heard the "F" word and quietly took Mario by the hand and led him to the back of the restaurant where they sat together in a corner. Sophia put her hands over her ears and looked down at the floor.

"You've betrayed your family," Rich shouted. "And after I helped you keep the union from organizing our mine." Rich paused and then laughed bitterly. "Our mine, what a joke that is."

Rich suddenly grabbed a steak knife from the silverware cart and attacked. He took a swipe at Gabe and opened a deep gash in the larger man's shoulder. Gabe groaned and fell backward.

"No wonder Ceci ran out on you, man," Rich jeered as Gabe struggled to his feet. "No wonder she's roaming the desert with crazy-guy-Stevie."

Holding his shoulder, Gabe moved toward his cousin; his expression was guilty as though he wanted to catch him and hold him and ask for forgiveness. The others could do nothing but watch...all except Sophia, who wasn't watching at all. Rich backed away: jeering, taunting, almost begging Gabe to strike out at him.

"Stop it! Both of you," Carmen called. But Rich continued to jeer, to mock, to remind Gabe that he lost his girl to a crazy man.

"And now you've fallen for the most evil, greedy, selfish bitch I've ever seen in my life," Rich continued. "She's a real tease too, man. Everyone knows she got-off on flirting with the teenage boys at the high school!"

Now shaking his head, Gabe reached out toward Rich, who took another swipe at him and caught him in the forearm. Blood spurted out immediately, and Carmen screamed.

Luís tried to rush between the two cousins, but Rich pushed him away.

"Stay out of this, Old Man," Rich said. Then, turning to Gabe, he called out to Papa Luís, "Let's find out just how tough your favorite nephew really is, shall we?"

Gabe moved on Rich in an attempt to disarm him. But his younger cousin spun quickly away and in the process pushed Gabe into the edge of the front counter. Then he swung around behind his larger cousin, pulled the knife back as though he were going to plunge it into his cousin's back, and then...

YOU DON'T HAVE TO FIGHT NOW

The words of the classic song by Donny Gee and the Gee-Men screamed through the little restaurant. Everything stopped.

I SAID YOU DON'T HAVE TO FIGHT NOW

Everyone turned toward the jukebox. It had come to life and was now blaring out the famous rock and roll anthem. Sophia stepped forward hesitatingly and then began to sing along.

THERE'S JUST NO NEED TO FIGHT
BECAUSE WE CAN GET IT RIGHT

Gabe's lips twisted into a half smile as he lunged forward and grabbed the knife out of his cousin's hand. Rich stared at him in anger for a moment and then slid into the relative safety at the back of the counter, where he stood studying the little girl as she and the jukebox sang together.

I SAID YOU DON'T HAVE TO FIGHT NOW

Without even moving, Luís suddenly joined in:

INSTEAD LET'S TAKE A CHANCE
LET'S JUST GIVE IT UP AND DANCE

Sophia started twirling around in the center of the restaurant. Mario joined her and did his best to follow her steps.

I SAID YOU DON'T HAVE TO FIGHT NOW

"Goodness," sighed Carmen as she pulled Gabe onto a seat at the counter, took the knife from his hand, and began working on his bloodied shoulder and forearm. Even though Gabe grimaced as she cleaned his wound, his half-smile remained, and all the while Carmen did her best to sing along too.

I SAID YOU DON'T HAVE TO FIGHT NOW

"After this, it's the Beatles," Luís said as he came up to Rich, pushed all the knives out of the young man's reach, and led him to the front of the counter. The adults all sat there, watching the children dancing. Carmen considered joining them and doing a little shuffle of her own, but she was afraid to leave the two cousins together.

Meanwhile, the jukebox sang on:

THERE'S JUST NO NEED TO FIGHT
BECAUSE WE CAN GET IT RIGHT

Suddenly, Mario's mother burst into the restaurant, carrying a huge bag of groceries. Without looking at either Rich or Gabriel, she smiled at the kids, put down her shopping bag, and started singing.

INSTEAD LET'S TAKE A CHANCE
LET'S JUST GIVE IT UP AND DANCE

"Yes, you don't have to fight now," Vanessa sang as she came up to Gabe and kissed him tenderly on the cheek.

Soon Luís and Carmen were out on the floor too, dancing, enjoying themselves, and forgetting the deadly evils of only a few minutes earlier. In fact, they were so caught up in their dancing and singing that they forgot all about Cousin Rich, and that was too bad. Because when the song finally ended and the dancers all returned to the front of the restaurant... Rich was gone.

Chapter 32
Our Lady of Ominous Foreboding

Esteban sat on top of Car Mountain meditating. He was at last at peace with himself, with the desert, and with the universe.

San Pablo had already descended the mountain and had begun preparing the evening meal. Ceci was with the old prophet, helping him.

Esteban's eyes were closed. He had grown comfortable atop the mound of rusty cars. He was in the center of the hood of that great Cadillac Eldorado. There seemed to be acres of heavy metal all around him. That's why he didn't topple to his death when a voice suddenly broke through his meditation.

"So, are you feeling very comfortable now, Grandson?" It was Estebanico.

"As a matter of fact I am, Great Grandfather."

The ghost of the old man moved up beside him still sporting that benevolent smile.

"Comfort can be good," he said. "It can replenish the body, but it can also weaken on the soul."

"But we're praying for an end to the greed of the world,"

"Well, prayer can be done in comfort, I guess," said Estebanico. "While you're visiting with a hermit in his wild animal park, letting him feed you, sleeping in very pleasant quarters, life can be very sweet and that can be conducive to prayer. But it might also tempt you, distract you, and make you forget about your quest."

Esteban straightened himself and looked at the spirit of his great, great grandfather. "Cíbola has been hidden away for centuries, Grandfather, frozen in time. It can wait a few weeks while we attend to holy things."

"Perhaps. But you don't know what's waiting for you there. You don't know if there are doorways that open for just a moment and then close again forever. You don't know if there are fierce guardians of the place who might just decide to take a day off so you can sneak by them."

Esteban shrugged. "Never thought of that."

"Course not."

"Still...."

Estebanico stepped toward his great, great grandson, clasped his hands together as though in prayer and then opened them cupping his hands palms up and looked into them. So did Esteban. And for just a moment there was a flash of golden glittering towers, a beautiful young woman who smiled seductively, palaces, bridges across a wide river, barges full of expensive goods, a benevolent emperor dressed in royal raiment, then swirling, tangling, hideous monsters that lunged out at the young man.

Esteban jumped away, fell backwards, and this time only saved himself from falling off the edge of Car Mountain at the very last minute by catching onto the windshield wiper of an ancient, rusting Buick Invicta.

Estebanico grabbed his grandson's hand and pulled him back to safety.

"Want me to try that trick on Ceci?" He asked.

"God no."

"Afraid she might run away?"

"I'm not sure I could make it on my own," said Esteban.

"And why would you want to?" answered Estebanico.

An hour later, Esteban was up on Aladdin riding smoothly across the desert. "He looks pretty good," Ceci whispered to herself as she rode along beside him in Chuck's old truck. "Not bad at all... kinda cute." It was a fact only slightly diminished by his obsessions, which everyone else thought were symptoms of madness.

They had left San Pablo of the Cars far behind... had prayed with him for almost two weeks, had eaten his desert foods, had gotten used to walking untouched between rattlesnakes, mountain lions, tarantulas, scorpions, and javelina pigs. And then Esteban had come rushing down from the top of Car Mountain, shouting that he had had a visit from his great, great grandfather, and that they must be on their way, immediately.

And just like that, they were gathering their gear, packing up their possessions, and loading them onto Aladdin.

San Pablo had taken the camel aside and talked to him, soothed him; because the fact was Aladdin didn't seem to want to leave the prophet. San Pablo must have convinced the camel to go on. Then he spoke to Esteban, and Ceci saw him put his hand on the shoulder of her companion and whisper words of encouragement. Finally, the short, wiry prophet came up to her, blessed her, and told her to take care of Esteban and protect his vision because it was real, it was true, and, in the end, it would benefit everyone.

Ceci thanked the prophet for putting up with her initial doubts, and then she kissed him demurely on the cheek. By then Chuck was already in his pickup, revving the engine, ready to take everyone to a Mission that he said was just a short distance away. He wanted them to meet the old priest who worked there. And, considering the prospects of their uncertain future, it seemed like a pretty good idea to Ceci. And so she hopped into the passenger side of the truck while Esteban got up on the camel, and they were off following a road that barely existed at all, heading toward the church known as Our Lady of Ominous Foreboding.

#

Father Samson was a big ugly brute with massive shoulders and arms, a nose grown bulbous from far too much sacred wine, and bushy eyebrows that looked as though owls could nest in them. He was out hoeing the garden that surrounded his little church.

Chuck let out a great cowboy whoop as his truck roared up to the priest and the old man smiled and began to dance up and down transforming his appearance from that of an ogre to something closer to a big, clumsy chimpanzee.

"Chuck, my boy," the priest called, "Welcome, welcome, so glad to see you." And then he took a step backward and looked into the distance as, through the dirt devils and shifting sun patterns, the image of Esteban and the camel materialized.

"You brought friends," he said to Chuck.

"Devoted followers."

"Of... San Pablo of the rusty cars?"

Chuck flinched at the priest's derogatory name for his mentor, but Esteban was more direct. "You must mean The Prophet," he said as Aladdin stopped and kneeled in front of the old man so that his rider could dismount. By that time Ceci had climbed out of the truck and walked around in front of the priest.

"And a beautiful lady too," added Father Samson.

The compliment was so unexpected, coming from such a monster of a man, that Ceci took a nervous step backward before finally offering a shy smile.

"Lovely," he responded; then he cleared his throat and turned to Esteban. "So you've been with the crazy old hermit?"

"Praying for a world without greed."

"Good luck with that," answered the priest, "might as well ask your camel to pass through the eye of a needle."

Esteban laughed. "Where have I heard that one before?"

His comment made the priest laugh, and once again he danced around as though it were the required accompaniment to his laughter.

"I brought you big bags of rice and beans," Chuck said.

"Wonderful. Let's unload, and then you can come in and share a little of my morning's brew."

"Coffee?" asked Ceci, hopefully.

"Of course, plus a good healthy shot of tequila, which I make myself, in the church kitchen."

#

By the time they had unloaded the provisions and were seated around a big oaken table in the old church kitchen, they each had a steaming mug of coffee in front of them. And Ceci found herself expounding on just how impressed she was with San Pablo and his ability to talk to animals.

"Nonsense," answered the priest. "The man is a charlatan, a trickster; it's all an act. Now, if you want to see a real saint who talked to animals, grab your mugs and follow me."

The huge man stood at once and led them through a narrow hall, down a stairway, and into the church's basement storeroom. He flipped a switch as they entered and turned on a single bright light bulb that hung from a raw electrical cord at the very center of the room.

The place was a mess; boxes with hand-lettered labels were stacked against the walls and spread haphazardly across the open floor. There was a dusty pool table with a torn felt cover and a single cue ball tucked against one rail. Also, on the table was a small diorama: an Italian mountainside with hand carved statues of Saint Francis of Assisi and many animals surrounding him. His hands were raised in prayer, and the animals were all looking at him attentively. Part of the display was a delicately carved tree that had many birds nesting in its branches. The birds too seemed to be listening to the great saint.

"Now there was a man who could talk to the animals," said Father Samson as he picked up the little figure of the saint. "He founded an order of priests to do God's work, not to hide in rusty minivans."

He turned to Ceci. "If you would do God's work, Miss, go out and walk with men and women, don't hide away in a mountain of discarded scrap iron."

Ceci tried to smile, but now that she had finally learned to respect San Pablo, she found it hard to hear him insulted.

Suddenly, Esteban spoke up. "And who's this?" he asked as he pulled a dusty painting from a low-slung rack built into the back wall. When he had carried the picture forward into the light, he and everyone else could see that it was a portrait of a coyote. The animal was dancing on his hind legs as though they were human feet. He played a flute, wore Indian garb with feathers in his hair and bracelets around his arms and ankles.

"Where'd that come from?" Chucho asked.

"Old Samuel gave it to me," answered the priest, "traded it for a batch of tequila. I didn't want to give it to him, of course, but selfless Christian charity has a way of taking hold of you and making you follow God's will whether you want to or not."

"It must have been an exceptional batch of tequila," said Chucho.

"It was sludge. I just don't like coyotes."

Ceci gave him a questioning look as she used her fingers to trace the animal's shape.

"Look at the face of that critter," said Samson. "Do you think you can trust one of his kind?"

Ceci studied the animal for a moment, and she did get a sense of the trickster, a creature that liked to joke, make fools of men and women, and sometimes do much worse.

"Steer clear of coyotes," said the old man. "If you run into one out in the desert, don't talk to it."

"We're not like Saint Francis," said Esteban, "or even San Pablo. We can't talk to animals, and they sure won't talk to us."

"Don't be so sure," said Father Samson with a knowing smile, and then he reached up high on the nearby bookshelf and took down a great hand-lettered volume with a thick leather cover.

"So, tell me," he asked Esteban, "just where do you think it is?"

"Our destination?"

"Of course. I assume it's Cíbola?"

The comment made Ceci feel creepy. "Why would you think that?"

The priest smiled. "A man named Esteban traveling through the desert with a beautiful woman and a camel... where else would they be going?"

"Disneyland?" Ceci surprised herself by answering with a straight face. The priest gave her a little chuckle and then cracked open the book.

"Let me just point something out to you." And he quickly flipped to a map that was so detailed that neither Esteban nor Ceci nor even Chucho could make out exactly what it showed.

"We're approximately here," said Father Samson. "Cíbola, if it exists at all, is somewhere out there." He gestured in great sweeping motions to non-specific areas of the map. "But here," and now he pointed to what was clearly a mountain range with a pass running through it, "here lies Charybdis!"

"Named for the ancient whirlpool in the Odyssey and Aeneid?" asked Ceci.

"Maybe," said the priest. "But it's something much worse than that. This New World Charybdis is not so much a whirlpool as a whirlwind over a vast canyon... and do you know what lives there?"

"I get it," answered Esteban definitely not looking for any more discouragement. "We'll stay clear of it."

"You'd better because it's the home of thunderbirds. The beating of their wings and their vile dispositions cause the cyclones and whirlwinds and great dust storms that surround the chasm."

"I've heard thunderbirds are beautiful, all turquoise and orange and white," said Ceci, "if they exist, that is."

"Oh, they exist," answered Father Samson. "And you'd better avoid their pass; you'd better not go anywhere near it if you ever hope to find the Seven Cities of Gold."

Evening came, and Ceci and Esteban took advantage of an offer from the old priest to spend the night in two of the humble guest rooms at the church of Our Lady of Ominous Foreboding.

Esteban said good night to his traveling companion, and in less than five minutes Ceci could hear him snoring so intensely that she was sure the sound would keep her awake all night. She was not that lucky... neither was Esteban.

He dreamed. And in that dream, he was riding a beat up, old train, a small one, the kind that carried few passengers on seldom-used tracks across high mountain passes.

Esteban felt himself clinging desperately to the window ledge beside his seat, looking out over a drop that fell thousands of feet directly down from the outside of the car. He couldn't see the train tracks or even an inch of land beyond them. All that was there was the edge of the car and then nothing. It was his worst nightmare. And even in that dream he remembered how, as a small boy, his father had urged him to hike down into the Grand Canyon on an old abandoned trail, how terrified he was, and how somehow the laces on one of his hiking boots had hooked on the grommets of the other causing the two to lock together tripping him, sending his head and shoulders lunging out over the edge of a great precipice. He remembered watching the little pair of binoculars in his hand jar loose from his fingers and fly off into the nothingness beyond the rim of the trail before his father grabbed him by his shirt and pulled him safely back.

"Vertigo," his father later explained when Esteban refused to even walk up a flight of stairs on the outside of an old warehouse. "You've had it all along. It makes you dizzy, terrified of heights. I'm so sorry."

"Vertigo," Esteban repeated now as he dreamed that the mountain train was approaching a rickety old bridge that spanned a vast chasm. Esteban broke out in a cold sweat, felt the clamminess of the covers around him and realized that he wasn't really on a mountain railroad, but in a dream. Still, it all seemed too real as they approached a bridge that looked like it was held together with nothing more than staples and duct tape. The bridge swayed and tottered as the little train came chugging onto it, and then the span began to groan and creak as the cars moved slowly across it.

Esteban looked directly down as he had when he was a boy and tripped that day at the Grand Canyon. His head was swimming now. He felt his stomach surging into his mouth. In the distance he saw the figure of a young woman, Ceci! She was lashed to a huge slab of rock that jutted up out of the chasm but was still dozens of feet below the train. Only her arms were free, waving to him, "Save me, Stevie," she called again and again as lightning crackled all around her, and her gestures became more desperate and more violent.

"It's only a dream!" called Esteban, and then he felt himself shouting aloud: "No it's not! It's NOT A DREAM!" The words crashed like thunder around him as he rushed forward through the cars of the train always seeing Ceci through the windows, always trying to scream back that he would save her.

He reached the engine compartment. There was no one at the controls. He could look directly down at Ceci now; her look was so hopeful. And then the train veered sharply to the left, turning away from her, cutting her off from his sight. He reached forward, grabbed some unknown lever, and slammed on the brakes. They screamed. The train skidded wildly, and in that instant the bridge cracked apart, spilling the entire train into the canyon. It tossed Esteban through the open train window, and he fell screaming toward Ceci, toward the rock slab, into the boiling mass of clouds where lightning flashed into him like knives and spears that tore at his clothing, at his flesh, shooting into his heart.

Esteban woke up screaming. He jumped up in bed sweating, shaking. "Oh my God! Oh no!" he heard, and then he realized that he wasn't the only one screaming! It was Ceci, from the room next to his. She too was shouting, "Oh, no! Oh, no! Oh God, NO!"

He pulled himself free from the tangle of sweaty sheets and went running into her bedroom. Ceci was twisting back and forth, throwing her arms from side to side, sweating almost as much as he was.

"Cess! Ceci! Cecilia! It's all right!"

The young woman jumped up in bed and opened her wild eyes. "Stevie?"

"I'm here! Everything's okay."

"No, it's not; it's not okay; it was so awful."

Ceci was trembling all over.

"It was just a nightmare," said Esteban.

"Or maybe a vision of what's to come."

"Not a vision, Cess, don't say that."

"But, my God!"

"What was it? What happened?"

Ceci gathered herself, looked into the deep blue eyes of her partner. In spite of the sweat that stood out on his forehead that told her he had been having nightmares too, his eyes looked so calm and so concerned. She waited for a moment to stop shaking and then she took a deep breath and began, "We were on this ride in Disneyland."

Esteban nodded for a moment, then he smiled and suddenly broke out laughing.

"What?" she called. "It's not funny?"

"Of course not... but it is crazy."

Ceci nodded, "I know it is. I was on this ride in Disneyland, going through a haunted house or something. And there were horrible talking coyotes, monstrous thunderbirds, tangles of giant snakes, and Cibola, which was a terrible place. Everyone there was so greedy: a beautiful girl there (a young woman dressed like an Indian) kept stealing things from me: my purse, my watch, my scarf... you!

"And then we were on this train going up this steep hill, and suddenly all these warriors crashed into our car and began chasing me, and I ran out onto this wide highway, and the runners were now on horseback and were gaining on me, and then their leader–the most hideous of them all–kept reaching down to grab me, and I turned to see that his face was a death mask, and he was about to pull me up onto his horse when suddenly... you woke me up."

"My God!" said Esteban.

They stared at each other for a moment, and then Ceci broke into bitter tears: the result of their ordeal so far and the promise of so much more danger to come.

"Hey, it's okay," Esteban said after a moment. "Don't worry. I'm here. We're together. I'll be with you. I'll take care of you." And suddenly he pulled her to him and held her tightly.

"Please don't leave me," Ceci murmured as she wrapped her arms around him.

"I'm not going anywhere," he said. "Honest. And those dreams don't mean anything at all."

"They mean I'll never go to Disneyland again," Ceci said, and they both broke into nervous laughter.

Esteban looked into her eyes and kissed her innocently on the cheek. "Guess I can go back to bed, then."

Ceci looked at him longingly. She didn't want him to leave, but she was just too damn proper to know what to say to keep him there. So finally, she simply nodded and whispered, "Yes. Of course."

And he left. But when he was gone Ceci slid under the covers and felt so alone, so sad. "Would Gabe have done that?" she asked herself out loud.

Would he have left her here with all her fears, or would he have stayed, would he have climbed into bed with her... and loved her and made her feel safe all night long?

"Of course, he would have."

Part Three
The Dangers

Chapter 33
Kenny

"I'm sorry your brothers aren't interested in cooperating," Devlin Lucero said to Kenny McLaughlin. They were sitting across from each other in a booth at Tres Flores. Mario's mother, Vanessa, had just taken their orders. She brought the two men water, chips, and "the hottest salsa west of the Pecos."

"Your entrées will be ready in just a moment," she said.

Lucero gave her his usual crooked smile and nodded. The look sent shivers up the spine of little Sophia, who sat watching the two men from a small booth near the jukebox. She didn't know why, but Sophia didn't like the older man at all. There was something about him. He looked cruel, she thought, and evil. She knew Kenny of course. He was around all the time, chasing Lorena, wanting to marry her even though they weren't even through high school. Sophia liked Kenny and was worried about what this conversation might lead to.

"The way I see it," said Lucero, "your brother's stupidity has just created a terrific opportunity for you, my friend."

Sophia wanted to run up to Kenny and warn him to stay away from the man with the crooked smile and the evil eyes. "And don't be fooled when he calls you 'friend,'" she whispered to herself. She was sure Kenny didn't hear her. Lucero very well might have.

"Watch out now, the plates are very hot," said Vanessa as she delivered two large platters of enchiladas verde. Lucero nodded and held his hands back to make sure she knew that he understood.

"Don't worry, pretty lady," Lucero said. "But I would like another margarita and one for my friend here too."

"Of course, Señor," Vanessa said with a big smile.

"Uugghh," moaned Sophia as she buried her face in her hands. Wasn't there anyone around who understood just how evil this guy was?

"So what's the deal?" Kenny asked.

"You come on board and help us manage our new string of car washes. We'll agree not to threaten your brothers or their operations. Of course, we expect to be far more competitive, and in the end, they may lose all their customers anyway."

"You'll put McCarwash out of business?"

Lucero smiled crookedly. He took a forkful of the enchilada and raised it to his lips, and then he leaned forward.

"We won't put them out of business, but if we offer lower prices and better service.... I mean, there's only room for so many car washes in a little town like this one."

"They will be so pissed off at me."

"Too bad. You have to live your own life, friend. You've got to think about your woman, Lorena, and your future together. Take our offer and you can marry her this summer. You can both put off college for a year or two; stockpile some savings. Then neither of you will need student loans when the time comes."

"It's tempting." Kenny said as he wolfed down a few quick forkfuls of enchilada.

"Come into the office tomorrow," Lucero coaxed. "Meet Jessica Amado, our Director of HR; she can make you a firm offer."

"Ms. Amado," Kenny's mouth fell open. "The substitute teacher? Man, she is so HOT! I had her for a few periods when I was in middle school, and looking at her almost melted my glasses."

Lucero's smile grew even more crooked.

"Does she still wear those... you know... those outfits?"

"I don't know what you're talking about, Kenny. I never notice things like that," said Lucero and then he broke out laughing. So did Kenny.

"Come on in, and we can check her out together, friend... why not?"

"Why not."

Sophia ran up to the table then and glowered at both men. "Don't you do it, Kenny," she shouted. "Don't you dare check her out... or anyone else out either. You're Lorena's boyfriend!"

"I know, I know," Kenny answered, almost trying to hide his face from the intense little girl.

"And as for you, sir," she said to Lucero. "My uncle works for you and he doesn't even like you. He thinks you're a big...."

Just then Vanessa scooped up the little girl and whisked her to the far side of the restaurant. "Shhhh, Sophia. Shhhh," she said. But the little girl looked past Vanessa, back at Lucero. "He thinks you're a big POOP!"

Lucero doubled over with laughter, so did Kenny, until finally, the men stood. Lucero flipped a hundred-dollar bill onto the table, patted Kenny on the shoulder, and they left the restaurant together.

#

The next morning Kenny pulled his car into one of the visitor spaces just outside the entrance to the Blackmore Copper Mine. He was wearing a suit, a tie, and highly polished shoes. Jessica Amado greeted him as he walked through the front door. She was wearing another version of her usual too-tight business attire.

Unexpectedly, she pulled Kenny to her and gave him a big hug. The boy's lips curled into a grin as he felt how tightly she hugged him. Then she pushed him back to arm's length and stared him in the eyes. Her lips were moist; her smile seemed genuine, even eager. But then Kenny couldn't have recognized a false smile from Jessica if his career depended on it, which, of course, it did.

"You look so good, Kenny," Jessica said. "I always enjoyed having you in my class."

"I never thought you noticed me."

"I always notice the cute ones," Jessica said as Kenny's face turned redder than the reddest red in a box of Crayolas. "Anyway, come into my office and let's talk."

Jessica ushered Kenny into the seating area across from her desk. There, three small couches were positioned around a large coffee table. She gestured for him to sit in one, and then she took a seat directly across from him.

Her assistant, Clark, was there immediately with steaming mugs of coffee, a cream dispenser, and some sugar cubes. He placed a mug in front of Kenny.

"You want yours with everything, I'll bet?"

Kenny nodded.

"Thought so."

Jessica pulled Kenny's cup to her, bent forward revealingly, and added a dash of cream and a single cube of sugar; then she pushed it back toward Kenny. Clark was standing smiling as he watched Jessica "operate." The kid was practically drooling.

When she finished, Clark placed her cup in front of her, and then, without taking his eyes off Kenny, he backed out the door.

"Very professional," said Kenny.

Jessica smiled. "He does offer excellent support. I have several very good candidates in line to be your assistant too, if you accept our offer."

"Would they be like Clark?"

"Actually, the candidates I've selected are all women."

Kenny smiled. Jessica swung over to the couch and sat beside him. "I'm sure you'll find one of them to be just perfect."

Jessica was so close to Kenny now that it felt for a moment as if she was going to kiss him, and he swallowed hard. Jessica didn't pull back, just kept staring into his eyes, batting her own invitingly.

Just then Devlin Lucero walked into the room.

"How do you like our proposed VP of Carwash Operations?" he asked.

Jessica smirked as she pushed her chic, sexy glasses up onto the bridge of her nose. "I loved him when he was one of my students, and I still think he's great."

"So, Kenny," Lucero asked, "what will it take to get you to sign on?"

Kenny stopped for a moment; there was only one thing standing in the way of his taking all the knowledge he'd acquired watching his brothers run their car wash chain and applying it to Lucero's new business.

"It's my family," he sighed. "My brothers say they'll kill me if I go to work for you, and my mom's threatened to call in the minister to have me exorcised."

Jessica laughed, but Lucero shuddered at the words.

"She says they'll stand me up in front of the whole congregation so they can all watch the devils being driven out of me."

Jessica suddenly dropped her hand onto Kenny's thigh and gave it a squeeze. "Hey, who believes in that stuff, anyway?" she said. "Just forget it all, Kenny. Your family will come around."

The boy nodded absently at Ms. Amado, who stood then, marched over to her desk, and gathered up a small stack of papers. She brought them back to Kenny and, leaning forward, spread them out in front of him.

"Here's your employment agreement."

She popped the top off of her Mont Blanc fountain pen and offered it to Kenny. "Sign, please."

Kenny didn't take the pen. "I'm not sure. I don't want to betray my family."

Lucero rolled his eyes.

"You'll be part of our family now," Jessica said.

Kenny pulled back. "But I don't want my mom to...."

Lucero slid onto the couch next to Jessica. He took the fountain pen from her.

"Here, friend."

Kenny remembered Sophia's words, remembered his brothers' warnings. He shook his head. Lucero let go of the pen. It hung there in mid-air anyway. Then it suddenly began to quiver like a hummingbird. It darted forward and hovered directly in front of Kenny's left eye.

Kenny tried to swat it away. It moved closer.

"Please don't disappoint us, Kenny," Jessica whispered. "It might make us very angry."

The pen darted forward almost piercing the kid's eye. He jerked his head back, and stared at the point of the pen, and then it flashed from his left eye to his right, slashing across the bridge of his nose as it went, drawing blood.

Kenny felt the blood drooling down the side of his nose and into his mouth. He brushed the thick red liquid away and saw it smeared onto his hands.

"Jesus! I'm bleeding," he screamed, and he tried to jump to his feet and run out of the placed.

Lucero immediately pushed him back into the couch. Then he snatched the pen out of the air, flipped it around and handed it to Kenny. He fanned out the papers in front of his friend.

"Sorry, that was an unfortunate accident."

"I don't know about any of this now."

"Of course, you do, Kenny," Jessica soothed.

Lucero spun around in front of the kid and looked him in the eye. "You did like the trick with the pen, though, right?"

"Trick?"

"Sure just a little parlor trick to get your attention. Look," and he pointed across the room at the mirror Jessica had hanging on the far wall. Kenny looked. He got up and moved closer. There was no blood on his face. He looked at his hands; there was no blood there either."

"Just a parlor trick, Kenny," Lucero repeated. "I can teach you a few of them if you like. Scare your friends, keep your brothers at bay, and impress your girl."

Kenny was suddenly smiling. "Interesting," he said. "Like wow."

Lucero handed the pen to Kenny.

"Sign here and here and here," he said. And of course, Kenny did. He signed everything while Lucero smiled crookedly and Jessica stood, put her hands on her hips, and radiated triumph.

#

Two weeks later, in spite of endless fights with his brothers and being forced to move out of his mother's house (Lucero picked up the cost of a brand new apartment in the nicest complex in town), Kenny was supervising three new carwashes and "pinching every goddamn penny," as Lorena's cousin Rich liked to say. It wasn't exactly what he would have predicted from the kid. But now Rich was out there working the line, greeting customers, urging former mineworkers to move faster, dry those cars better, don't use so many rags, vacuum better, be more efficient and do it faster and faster and faster.

Workers who couldn't keep up were sent immediately to Kenny, who would give them a harsh pep talk the first time and then (if they came back to him again) would fire them on the spot.

"You would think anything would be better than working in a mine," Rich told his friends. "But not with that stupid kid for a boss."

Lucero, on the other hand, was very pleased. He and Kenny had undercut the prices at McCarwash so drastically that the brother's chain had no business whatsoever. Still, the fallout from CleanSweep Carwashes was taking a terrible toll.

Workers came into the carwash in waves, and within three days most of them were fired... with cause. They had no way to complain and nowhere to turn. If they had unemployment insurance, they lost it by taking the carwash job. Bottom line: There was a growing population of the unemployed staying home in La Sentencia, staying home in houses that they would soon be unable to afford, that they couldn't sell... would have to vacate. Soon there were gatherings on street corners in vacant lots and city parks. There was mounting anger and bitterness.

But Kenny was happy; he had a posh new apartment, a hot new Jetta company car that Lucero had assigned to him... and Lorena, someone to take advantage of his newfound wealth. He'd already taken her on shopping sprees in Tucson and Phoenix and booked a vacation in Hawaii for the whole month of March... just before the next wave of carwashes was scheduled to open in neighboring cities.

For her part, Lorena acted like a newly crowned queen. She had little use for the unemployed mineworkers who sometimes gathered outside their apartment complex or near the malls where she shopped. She didn't believe the threats and the catcalls that they shouted at her as she drove past them.

"Assholes," she'd say to Kenny. "Do you know what the assholes called me today?"

"We'll have to get the police after them pretty soon," Kenny said. But they both knew that the local police were understaffed and underequipped, and they sympathized with the mineworkers.

He was eyeing a crowd of desperate-looking unemployed who were gathering across the street from the car wash one morning when Devlin Lucero drove up.

"Look at those hungry bastards," Kenny said. "They look damn dangerous. Should I call the police?"

'Don't think the police are on our side, friend," the older man answered. "You know what I think we need?"

"Our own police force?"

"Let's just call them our security detail. I'll talk to Jessica about it. Maybe we can bring in a few ringers... tough guys who can handle these kinds of situations."

"I do think we have some homegrown talent," Kenny said.

Lucero's smile got more and more uneven. "Yeah, I like that, brother against brother."

"I know you do," answered Kenny with only a hint of bitterness.

"Yeah, we'll set up a Mine Militia, bring in some of Blackmore's crew from Dallas, rehire some of the toughest mineworkers... those who might otherwise be ringleaders against us. We'll get them on our side. Maybe I'll let you run the whole group, Kenny. I mean, you've turned into a really mean little shit. It should be right up your alley."

"Thanks," Kenny responded. And he smiled his own evil smile.

Meanwhile, Gabe was starting to feel more and more pressure himself. Rich and so many other former friends had begun to blame him even more than Kenny for the plight of the mineworkers. There were threats on his life, unhappy workers standing outside of the mine office and throwing rocks at his little Prius as he drove it into work each day. Moreover, he knew things would eventually get even worse for him when the Blackmore Copper Mine shut down permanently, and in its place the new CleanSweep Mining Company was born... with just a handful of employees. Gabe called it the 'dummy mine' or sometimes even the 'mine scam.'

When that happened, anyone who understood mining law at all or could simply put two and two together would realize just how big a swindle Blackmore, Lucero, Hainer, Gabe, and Jessica were pulling off. But now, thanks to Lucero and Kenny's latest efforts, the mine would soon have a small army of toughs to guarantee its safety.

Somehow Gabe thought that it would only make things worse.

Chapter 34
Cowboys and Indians

Esteban and Ceci were riding Aladdin together. They had stopped on a ridge overlooking a small mining camp populated by half a dozen scrawny, dirty men dressed in torn jeans, ragged cotton shirts, and dilapidated boots. There were a few horses, tents, wagons, a fire pit... even a crudely assembled cookhouse. Esteban had taken out his binoculars and zoomed in on the camp. He followed the action of the men as they gathered their equipment and prepared to head off to a mine that might be a mile or so away.

Then Esteban noticed a small Native American boy; the kid had no shirt and was running around in loose-fitting jeans belted with an old rope. He was barefoot, had dark hair and a round face, didn't look like he wanted to be there helping the light skinned men who ordered him around, telling him to gather up picks and shovels that were almost bigger than he was.

"Kid's probably Apache," Esteban murmured.

"Who is?"

Before Esteban could answer, his field of view was filled with more Apaches, a small band of warriors who entered the camp on horseback. The guy in the lead was big, muscular, carrying a rifle. He began gesturing with it. Several of the miners shuffled the kid back behind them, near the tents.

"The Apaches are after that kid," Esteban said. "He's one of their own. The miners are trying to hide him, but the Indians know he's there. "

"This can't be happening in the twenty-first century," Ceci said.

"Hey, common practice for miners to steal a young boy from a local tribe and use him for menial work," Esteban said. "...And other things too."

"Are you sure that's what's happening?"

Esteban shrugged and turned back to the action.

A tall miner with long golden hair stepped forward. He was right in the midst of the horsemen... challenging them. The discussion became animated and angry. The huge Indian kept pointing with his rifle as several Apaches dismounted and started toward the kid. The miners moved to guard him. There was rough pushing and shoving. One of the miners pulled a pistol and fired it into the air; then the lead Apache lowered his rifle and took aim at the blond guy.

"I'm going down there," said Esteban. "I can't let this happen."

"Are you crazy? They're going to kill each other. They might kill us too. At least, wait until you get a better idea of what's going on."

"It's pretty clear to me! The Apache are trying to rescue one of their kids. The miners don't want to give him up. He needs our help."

Ceci and Esteban had spent nearly a week with Father Samson. They'd gathered provisions for their long trip: supplies of water, and some large sacks of beans, corn, and dried beef. The old priest was not a survivalist like San Pablo of the Cars. So he did not hesitate to help equip the pair for the next leg of their journey, the one he said would be the most dangerous.

Ceci and Esteban had then traveled another four days across the Arizona desert, seeing virtually no one, riding the camel together, realizing that Aladdin did not seem to be bothered by the weight he carried whether it was one person or two, with or without containers of water, sacks of dried food, and other essentials. The trip had been relatively pleasant. They traveled mostly after sunset and early in the morning. There had been no talking coyotes, or angry thunderbirds, at least so far. The snakes and scorpions kept their distance, and Ceci and Esteban were able to build fires at night and sleep quite soundly. In fact, the first disturbing sight they had seen in weeks was this altercation between the Apaches and the miners.

"Please wait," Ceci pleaded as they bumped along on top of Aladdin. "We're too far away to know what's really happening."

Esteban didn't answer her. He simply urged the camel down the slope toward the mining camp. Then, as soon as they reached the flatlands, Esteban gave Aladdin his head, and the camel broke into a run.

"Yee-haw! This guy can move," Esteban shouted.

In fact, the camel rushed right into the center of the camp almost running into the riders and spooking their horses.

Esteban reined the camel around and approached the blond miner who now held a gun pointed directly at the leader of the Apache party.

"Stand down," Esteban shouted.

The blond American looked startled and then annoyed. He brushed back his hair, heaved a heavy sigh, and dropped his gun into the dirt.

"Hey, asshole," he shouted at Esteban. "What do you think you're doing? You fucking ruined the shot."

"Nobody's shot," said Esteban still certain that the young brave was in mortal danger. "And you're not shooting anyone, either."

"So then... we have to do everything over again?" The question came from the huge Apache warrior who suddenly looked very familiar. Esteban urged the camel closer, and then he recognized Dwayne Rowdy, the well-known Native American Movie Star.

Ceci quickly realized what had happened, and she put her fingers to her lips to hide her laughter. "You really did it this time, Stevie," she said.

"Okay, break time," came another voice... this one amplified electronically. "Break for lunch everyone. Be back here at two."

The Apaches began to gather in smaller groups. Four men in jeans and black t-shirts came forward and began wrangling the horses.

"Nice going, shithead," the blond haired guy grumbled at Esteban. "It's gonna be damn hot when we have to reshoot this afternoon."

Ceci seemed awestruck by the sight of Dwayne Rowdy, and that was good. If she hadn't, she surely would have been needling Esteban mercilessly. Fortunately, the movie star proved to be very generous. He came up to the camel, looked up at Ceci and smiled at her.

"So, you some kinda nomad or what?"

Ceci blushed and giggled a little. She couldn't really say anything. Then Rowdy turned to Esteban.

"Thanks, man," I know the rest of the cast wanted to get this over with, but I've got a killer headache. I appreciate the break."

A much smaller man now joined the actor. He wore thick sunglasses and a pith helmet. Rowdy looked up at Ceci again and beamed. Then he turned to the much shorter man. "Would you like to meet an authentic Arabian Princess?" he asked.

"Scheherazade, I presume," the little guy said. Ceci suddenly felt like a teenybopper back in junior high school.

"I'm Don Vito," the short man said.

"The famous director!" Ceci gasped. "I've seen all your films. Bloody Bess is my favorite movie of all times." She patted the side of the camel, clicked her tongue as Sophia had taught her, and Aladdin immediately lowered himself so that she and Esteban could climb down.

Don Vito smiled at Ceci. "Who's your heroic friend? Lawrence of Arabia?"

Esteban stepped away from the camel, turned to the moviemaker, and now he was smiling. "Esteban Dorantes," he said.

"Wow, Esteban," Vito said. "Found the Seven Cities yet?"

"How did you know we were looking for them?" Ceci asked.

"Research," Vito answered. "I'm thinking about using the legend in my next big picture... an epic 'historical' to be told from the point of view of Esteban and the Native Americans, not the Spaniards."

Esteban was entranced. His eyes glowed as he walked up to the little man. He actually towered over the director by maybe as many as four inches.

"You know, you're good looking... in a quirky kind of way," Vito said. "Maybe you could play the lead."

"Play my great, great grandfather?"

"You're a direct descendant?"

"That's right," answered Ceci as she walked up beside Esteban.

"Cute couple don't you think, Don?" asked Dwayne Rowdy.

"Very." Vito's eyes brightened, and Ceci could tell that he was interested in Stevie but even more attracted to her... dangerously attracted.

"Why don't you have lunch with us?" asked Vito. "I'll tell you about my plans for a film about the Seven Cities, introduce you to the rest of the cast, and Dwayne here can give you the grand tour."

"My pleasure," said the movie star as he flashed his million-dollar smile.

Ceci beamed and nodded. But Esteban was now looking out at all the production gear and wondering how he could have missed it as he looked through his binoculars. He decided that the long view wasn't clear enough, and the binoculars were zoomed in too tight on the center of the camp cutting out a wide look at the actual production. Still, there were massive klieg lights, film and video cameras mounted on cranes and dollies, and huge reflector cards to direct sunlight into the shadowy parts of the set. There was an extensive make-up area where artists now packed away their cosmetics so they could join the crew at lunch.

Dressing room trailers were parked out near the far hills, waiting for the principals to come in and take a break from the hot afternoon sun. Beyond the trailers, enormous refrigerated trucks were locked tight, protecting the more delicate production equipment from the ravages of the midday sun.

"This is Christopher Wentworth," said Don Vito as he led them to tables where a big lunch was being served under a huge canopy. The actor who played the blond haired miner stood and shook hands with Esteban, then shook Ceci's hand.

"Didn't mean to be so harsh earlier," said Wentworth.

"No problem," answered Esteban. "I can imagine how it must have looked: This crazy guy comes riding in out of nowhere on a camel, breaking up the shoot."

"I have it all on film," said Vito. "If I can think of a way to use the shot I will... and I'll pay you something for your participation."

"Oh you don't have to do that," giggled Ceci.

"Never turn down money from a movie producer," Rowdy whispered to her. "If you do, you may never get paid at all."

Ceci and Esteban were able to squeeze in between the rest of the cast, many of them local Apaches who had earned some of the key roles in the movie.

Esteban, as usual, made no secret of his quest, and that fascinated many of the Native Americans. Quite a few were skeptical, shaking their heads as he described his heritage and the goal of his mission.

Sunshine Morning Dove, who played the heroine of the story, turned to Ceci, rolled her eyes like a teenager and asked, "How'd you ever hook up with this flake, girl?"

"I just think he's cute."

"Well, duh, he's more than cute, but still…"

"I like the idea of your quest," said Peter Nantan, a strapping Native American actor. "But I have one piece of advice for you, Esteban. It's been passed on among my people from generation to generation."

Esteban was feeling happy, and it wasn't just the quality of the food that Don Vito served to his cast and crew… it was more basic than that. Most of these people really seemed to like him and believe him. He turned to Nantan, but his heart stopped suddenly as he saw the serious look in the kid's eyes.

"Just don't talk to the coyotes," said the young actor. "I mean it."

Chapter 35
Picketing

Gabriel Romo was sorry he'd brought Mario and Sophia to work with him that day. He would never have done it if Sophia hadn't insisted. But now, as his little Prius was just about to enter the mine's nearly vacant parking lot, it was suddenly surrounded by dozens of angry mine workers, (make that ex-mine-workers, probably ex-carwash-employees too). The demonstrators were men and woman of every nationality. The one thing they seemed to have in common was their large size. Mine workers were usually big people, and this group was no exception. They began banging on the windows, rocking the car, tipping it from side to side.

"I got kids in here, damn it," Gabe yelled through the closed window.

"So what?" yelled an angry woman carrying a huge picket sign that read, 'Give Back Our Jobs.'

"I got kids at home too," she shouted. "An I'm havin' a hard time feedin' em without a job."

Gabe tried to edge the car forward, but a dozen heavy-set guys were right in front of him, blocking his way, making it impossible to move forward.

"What the hell brought this on?" Gabe murmured to himself.

As if in response, there was a hard banging on the passenger side door. Gabe looked over and saw his cousin Rich, the same guy who had drawn a knife on him at Tres Flores. He was pounding on the window, yelling, "Let me in, Cuz; let me in."

Gabe looked into his cousin's eyes. He had no idea what Rich was thinking. Gabe popped the remote lock. Rich tried to open the door, squeeze in and slam it shut, but three other ex-mineworkers grabbed the door and almost ripped it off the car. Rich ducked inside, pounded on the fingers of the other miners, somehow getting them to release their grasp, so he could close the door and lock it.

"What the hell, man?" Gabe said to his cousin.

"Yeah, what the hell," Rich repeated. "What the hell are you doing bringing kids to work on a day like this?"

"Like what?"

"Haven't you seen the papers, Cuz?" Rich pulled out a copy of El Milagro and flashed the headline at Gabe.

BLACKMORE MINE CLOSES PERMANENTLY
NEW CLEAN SWEEP MINE BEGINS
OPERATION TODAY

"This is what that bitch Amado was talking about when she fired me, wasn't it?"

Gabe couldn't respond. The demonstrators outside the car had seen the headline. It reminded them of why they were there. They began chanting as they pounded on the windows and the hood of the car.

GIVE BACK OUR JOBS
GIVE BACK OUR JOBS

"Gabe, you prick," Rich shouted. "You tricked us... all of us. That carwash business is a joke. Our pal Kenny has a revolving door. He hires and fires right on schedule."

"I don't know what you mean."

"Oh, don't you?" Rich hissed. "The little prick hires you, then two weeks later you're out the door for committing some candy-ass violation of the rules: using too much car wash fluid, too many towels, not working hard enough, or fast enough. Clocking in five minutes too late, clocking out two minutes too early. No second chances, no warnings, just out the door. It's bullshit, man."

"Are you okay, Rich?"

"No I'm not, Cousin," Rich said the last word bitterly. "Little Kenny fired me early this morning."

"How could he?"

"Apparently damn easily. You got your job; he's got his. That cunt Amado is probably making more money than both of you combined. And she's still working."

"Rich, watch your language. There are kids in the car."

Rich glanced into the back seat and nodded at Sophia and a very grim-faced Mario. Then he turned back to Gabe.

"Think of it as education. They come in to work with big cousin Gabe, and big cousin Rich hops in and teaches them a whole bunch of swear words."

"I already know all the swearwords," said the foghorn voice of Sophia from the back seat.

Rich laughed. "I'll be you do, little girl, I'll be you do."

"What do you want, Rich?" Gabe asked. "I can't give you back your job."

"No, you can't," Rich answered bitterly shaking his head. He pulled a gun from inside his shirt and pointed it at his cousin. At the same moment, he pressed down on the door unlock button. The back doors of the Prius were suddenly ripped open, and Mario and Sophia were pulled kicking and screaming from the car.

213

Chapter 36
The Stolen Kiss

Donald Vito had lured Ceci Moreno to his trailer with talk of a movie role he'd concocted for Esteban. Ceci had decided to help her traveling companion in any way she could, and if that meant spending a little time with this self-centered, little man, then that was okay too.

She had always been a very proper young woman, very prim, but that didn't mean that she wasn't confident. Ceci knew men found her attractive, especially those who liked strong-willed women. She also knew she was bigger and younger than Vito, and could probably take him out if it came to that. However, her confidence began to falter when he opened the door to his trailer, and they stepped inside.

The interior space was vast. Oriental carpets covered most of what was surely a hardwood floor. There was a very modern kitchen, a handsome rosewood table with several matching chairs, and beyond all that, a huge round bed with an ornate coverlet featuring the massive scarlet letter, 'V'. A half-dozen pillows were scattered across the bed.

An enormous, close-up picture of an 18-year-old girl hung above the bed. It was a photograph, a headshot that looked like it had been taken in the early sixties. The image dominated the entire room. The girl wasn't exactly beautiful, Ceci thought. 'Sweet' might have been a better word. But her eyes were incredible: so dark and penetrating and sad. She reminded Ceci of Sophia and knew that the little girl might very well look just like the girl in the photograph when she grew up.

"Who is that?" Ceci asked Vito.

The producer sighed, "Just a girl I used to know. The cleaners were supposed to have taken the picture down."

"Why?"

"Some women find it distracting ... you know, when I bring them here to discuss working in one of my movies."

Ceci nodded but added, "We're not exactly here to discuss a role for me, are we?"

"That depends," Vito answered. "I thought you might like to make a short appearance in my next film."

"What about Esteban?"

"Oh, there'll be a big role for him, maybe even the lead. The guy really looks the part. My question is, do you think he can act?"

"Well, he's always been good at expounding on his vision and his dreams."

"Doesn't he get nervous or self-conscious when he speaks up?"

"Never."

Vito grinned. Ceci couldn't help smiling too.

"By the way," Vito continued, "you know you're very beautiful, don't you?"

Ceci began to giggle... wasn't sure why. Maybe it was because she had never thought of herself as actually beautiful, or more realistically maybe it was because the producer's intentions were becoming rather transparent.

"I imagine your cleaning people were supposed to hang a pair of erotic etchings in place of the girl's photo," she said.

"Just one," Vito answered and gestured to the left of the bed.

There, propped against the far wall, was an engraving from the late seventeen hundreds: a young couple standing in a small anti-room. A handsome young man was kissing a young woman gently on the cheek. She wore an elegant satin gown, but the top of her dress was open, and she clutched at her breast as she smiled blissfully. Behind the girl, a door to a much larger room stood part way open, and in that room several older women were talking with each other... oblivious to the erotic events going on in the little chamber right beside them.

Suddenly Vito's arms were around Ceci, and he was kissing her.

"Hey," Ceci called as she pulled away from the little man. "What are you, some kind of satyr?"

She found herself breathing heavily. "Did you drug me?"

"Of course not."

"But I feel faint."

She sat down on the bed, and the producer immediately sat beside her. He took her hand in his and leaned over to kiss her again. Ceci's head was swimming. She turned toward Vito; he looked so silly and yet so eager that she kissed him quickly anyway. His hand rose to her breast. (Damn!) She pushed the hand away.

"No!" she said firmly. "We're here to talk about Esteban!"

"He's taking the grand tour with Rowdy. He'll be gone for at least half an hour. We have some time."

Vito leaned in to kiss Ceci yet again. She stood at once, and as she did the picture of the teenager girl immediately caught her eye. "How can you try to seduce women while she's watching you?"

Vito looked up at the photo of the girl and smiled.

"I think she'd approve. You're so wonderful."

Ceci didn't know what to say. "Thank you. Of course, I'm flattered. But still...."

Vito stood and smiled. "You're in love with Esteban, aren't you?"

"Why would you say that?"

"Well, you mentioned him when I started to kiss you."

Ceci lowered her eyes. "I'm in love with someone... not Esteban though."

"Really? Interesting," said Vito. "Okay, Relax. Let's talk. I need a little more information on your guy."

"Okay. But focus on Esteban, not on us."

Vito smiled. Somehow Ceci saw something in his eyes... a professionalism suggesting that he was serious. She sat down at the table as he went into the kitchen and came back with a spiral notebook.

"So, you've known him all your life?"

"Since high school."

"Do you date?"

Ceci thought for a moment and smiled as images of her dates with Esteban flashed up from her memory.

"We were a couple in high school. But not since then."

"What happened?"

Ceci's expression turned wistful, "Gabe."

"Gabe?" Vito's eyes sparkled. "Now we have a story."

"I've been with Gabe for the last ten years. At least up until he...."

"Would you like some wine?" Vito interrupted.

Ceci sighed. "All right. But just a little."

Vito walked back into the kitchen. He opened the fridge, pulled out an unopened bottle of Dom Perignon, grabbed two crystal champagne flutes from the counter top, and walked back to her.

"I'm sorry if I came on too strong," he said as he put the glasses on the table and began to wrestle with the cork. "Most women are flattered when I kiss them." He deftly pulled the cork from the bottle and poured the champagne into both glasses. Ceci looked on suspiciously but said nothing.

"So, you were with Gabe until...."

"Until a few weeks ago when he let those guys at the Blackmore Copper Mine start destroying our town."

Vito raised his glass. "Salute," he said.

Ceci touched his glass with hers and then took a sip of champagne. It tasted wonderful and made her feel better.

"Oh that's good," she said with a sigh and took another drink. Vito poured more champagne into her glass immediately.

"So, you were angry with Gabe," Vito prompted, "and then Esteban came along and offered to…."

"To end the town's poverty by finding the Seven Cities of Gold and bringing back treasure for everyone."

"And you believed him?"

"I wouldn't have," Ceci answered taking a much larger drink of champagne, "except he'd been saying it all his life… and he is the direct descendant of the original Esteban Dorantes… and…"

Vito pulled his chair closer to Ceci's and studied her. His eyes suddenly seemed so sad.

"You know you're a very lucky girl."

"Why do you say that?"

"You have had two lovers to choose from."

"No… I… maybe… Are you tearing up?"

Vito nodded.

"Why."

Just thinking about…." he gestured toward the picture, "Elli."

"Is that her name?"

Vito nodded.

"Tell me about her."

"I knew her in college. We went to different schools, but we had planned to marry."

"She died?" Ceci finished her glass and didn't even seem to notice that Vito refilled it immediately.

"She was murdered."

"Oh my God! How old was she?"

"Seventeen. Some crazy guy became obsessed with her, stalked her. On the day we were going to run away and get married, she asked to stop and say a prayer at a little chapel. There was this statue of an angel that she liked."

"The guy was there," Ceci whispered as she pulled her chair closer to Vito's, "and he killed her?"

"Slit her wrists... his too... so that they could make love in front of the altar while they died in each other's arms."

Ceci gulped down the rest of her champagne.

"He thought he had already killed me on the way into the chapel," Vito said. "But he'd only knocked me out. I came to, came up behind him while he was...."

"What?"

Vito lowered his eyes. Tears poured from them. Ceci felt tears in her own eyes.

"You poor man," she said as she reached across the table and took his hand.

"Comfort me," he whispered.

Chapter 37
The Parking Lot Riot

Mario felt himself being forcibly jerked from the car. At the same time, he heard Sophia's scream stifled as a huge hand reached over her mouth and silenced her. In the front seat, yet another pair of hands reached for Rich, grabbed him by the collar and yanked him backward. Rich fired the gun he'd been pointing at Gabe and sent a bullet through the roof of the car.

Within seconds it seemed all four of them, Mario, Sophia, Rich and Gabe were out in the parking lot, standing uncertainly as a wall of security guards formed in front of them. The guards were all enormous men and women. Gabe recognized a few mineworkers, but there were many others he had never seen before. They all sported gray pinstriped jumpsuits with the word CLEANSWEEP SECURITY emblazoned on their backs. Each had a thick black leather belt with a billy club and a holstered gun attached. There were long assault rifles slung over their shoulders.

"Clear out," bellowed the largest of the security force, a massive black man with a bald head, one earring, gloved hands, and a megaphone. "These premises are under the protection of CleanSweep Security."

Through the wall of security guards, Mario could make out several mineworkers they had known: frequent customers at Tres Flores, who often came there with their spouses and children. Theresa Gomes, the daughter of the head chef at his grandfather's restaurant was there too. They were friends he thought. But they didn't look like friends now. Several of them held baseball bats; others carried rocks. They were ready for a fight.

"Desist!" the head of security called. "Get the hell out of here or we'll gas you."

Mario could see that some of the mineworkers had children with them even now. Little kids clutched at their mother or father's knees or tightened their grip around their parent's necks. As the head of security said the words the guards began donning gas masks, maybe as much as for intimidation as for protection. The crowd began to move backward.

"Don't let them scare you," Rich called from beside Gabe, behind the wall of guards.

"They're just...."

One of the bigger guards stepped toward Rich raised his billy club and brought it down hard on the young man's head. Blood spurted out across the concrete of the parking lot as Rich slumped to his knees and then fell on his face.

"Let's get em," one of the mineworkers called... and, almost as one, the crowd surged forward before any of the security force could launch their tear gas. One guard was able to pull his pistol, turn and fire into the crowd. A large woman, who carried a little girl, fell dead immediately. Before the guard could turn and fire again, a mineworker raised his baseball bat and split the guard's head open.

Mario turned from one quarter to another. Everywhere guards and mineworkers were engaged in hand-to-hand combat. The mineworkers seemed to be getting the best of the guards, but that was before a harsh siren sounded and a new wave of CleanSweep Security rushed into the parking lot. These guards had already drawn their guns. Mario watched them coming, ready to shoot, and then something else caught his eye, even more important than the struggle, more important than the guards with their guns, he thought.

It was Sophia. She stood in the center of the parking lot, mayhem all around her. Her arms were crossed, her eyes pressed tightly shut, her mouth formed into a hard, angry line.

And then the Haboob hit. It roared in before another shot could be fired. It engulfed them all, blinded them. Caused most of the mineworkers to drop their bats and fall to the ground. Mothers clutched at their children. Guards dared not shoot into the maelstrom for fear of hurting one of their own. The wind picked up, swept across the floor of the parking lot, stealing away weapons from either side.

Mario could see that most of the participants were down on the ground, hands over their faces, trying merely to protect themselves from the wind and flying dust. He felt someone grab his arm. It was Gabe. His big cousin had Sophia pressed tightly against him and slung over his shoulder was the wounded, unconscious body of Rich.

"Come on, boy," Gabe grunted, and he pulled them all quickly to the Prius. Mario couldn't imagine that Gabe could get the back door open in the midst of all that wind, but he did. Gabe pushed the children inside, slammed their door, pulled open the car's passenger side door and dumped Rich into the car, then he moved carefully to the other side, pressing himself against the Prius for whatever protection he could gain against the wind.

Suddenly, the air was filled with a monstrous cracking sound that rose above the roar of the Haboob. A sheet of iron roofing tore from the nearest building and flew across the parking lot miraculously sparing the mineworkers and security forces who lay flat on the pavement not even daring to look up.

"Oh God," Rich moaned as he began to regain consciousness. He sat up for a moment just as there was a sudden break in the ferocity of the storm.

Guards and mineworkers looked up at him. They had all laid down their weapons, so they could shield themselves from the swirling winds. Gabe threw the car into reverse and backed directly out of the lot and into the street. The little car barely missed several of the combatants who were behind it.

As they roared away, Mario saw that both sides were drawing back from one another. The mineworkers were moving away from the parking lot. The security forces were letting them go.

"Where we going?" Rich managed to ask. Blood had dried in his hair and all over his face and shoulders.

"We're taking you to Tres Flores," Gabe answered, "you son of a bitch."

Chapter 38
Talking to Coyotes

Ceci laughed softly to herself... all the way back to the spot where Esteban and the camel waited. She could still picture Vito on the floor of his expensive trailer, legs stretched out in front of him, a big black eye forming, growing puffy, turning dark and feeling awful. His expression was one of shock and disappointment.

"What did you expect?" Ceci mumbled as though the famous producer could hear her. "Grab at me the way you did and I'll punch you right in the face every time."

Apparently letting him caress her backside was Vito's idea of offering him consolation. But it wasn't Ceci's.

Dwayne Rowdy was standing beside the camel talking to Esteban. As she approached, he smiled sympathetically and shook his head. He seemed to know just what had happened.

"Don't talk to me," Ceci told him as she marched up to the camel and took hold of the reigns. "He's a creep."

"Made a pass at ya, huh?"

Ceci nodded.

"Want me to go back there and kick the shit out of him?" Esteban asked.

Ceci studied her friend; his face was outlined against the sun, giving him a kind of halo. He looked almost like a saint but somehow more vulnerable and foolish.

"I already punched him in the face," Ceci answered. "The letch!"

"Well, yeah," Rowdy said, scratching the back of his head, looking down at the ground, unwilling to meet her eyes or Esteban's. "But you know he is a great director."

"Maybe," Ceci answered. "But that doesn't give him license to go around groping every woman he sees. And that bit about his dead girlfriend... that was all nonsense wasn't it... something he made up to get a little sympathy, so he could catch his victims off guard?"

"Actually, no," Rowdy answered. "He really is obsessed with Elli. Carries pictures of her everywhere he goes. Says he's going to make a feature film out of the scene where the crazy guy kills her."

"Then it actually happened?"

"I've seen the headlines. He's got scrapbooks full of them."

"Oh," Ceci answered. She stared at the ground herself for a moment. "Well anyway, it still doesn't give him permission to grab me."

"It sure doesn't," answered Rowdy.

"Anyway, tell him I'm sorry I gave him a black eye," Ceci said. "But he has to learn to keep his hands to himself."

"He knows that," Rowdy answered. "He hears that from nine out of ten women he takes into that stupid trailer."

"But he does it anyway."

Rowdy shrugged. "Well, there's always that tenth one who wants to use him as much as he wants to use her."

Ceci rolled her eyes and shrugged. "Whatever," she said. Then she and Esteban climbed onto the back of the camel and looked down at the famous movie star.

"Thanks, man," Esteban said.

"Vaya con Dios, amigos," said Rowdy.

"Let's get out of here," Ceci whispered to Esteban.

So they did.

#

Much farther ahead of Esteban, Ceci, and Aladdin (but directly in their path), five coyotes sat having their morning chat about all things family, business, and spiritual. They had their own names for each other, their own language too. But this is who they were and what they said.

Slick, the sharpest, fastest and most dangerous of the group was looking off into the distance, watching the camel and his riders approaching.

"Hey, here he comes now."

"Who, Slick?" asked Rosie, the lone female in the crowd. She was sweet and foxy. They all had a crush on her.

"Yeah, who?" asked quiet, uncomplicated Anthony.

"The Moroccan's kin."

"The Moroccan's kin... who the hell is that?" asked Runner. He was Slick's constant companion... the biggest jokester.

Slick answered, "The kin of the African dude who came here with the Spanish explorers."

"Come on," said Runner. "All I see is a man, a woman, and a damn camel. Probably just some fools lookin' for a circus!"

Anthony let out a loud yip of laughter. Rosie joined in while Winston, another member of their party howled hard and long.

Slick didn't laugh at all. "Hell, all humans are fools, Runner," he said. "But this dude's a distant relative of Estebanico Dorantes, the scout for the Spanish Conquistadors."

"Well, if that's the case," growled Rosie, "then the idiot's gotta be lookin' for Cíbola!"

Everyone stopped for a moment at the mention of the legendary location of the Seven Cities of Gold.

"The spirits told me he was coming," said Slick, "said that he was lookin' for Cíbola. I've been feeling his presence since yesterday."

"Well, may a rattlesnake bite my ass," said Runner. "This shit is not okay."

He moved forward, flashed his bright eyes at Rosie and grinned. "Hey, let me transform into a huge bobcat. I'll scare 'em so bad that the camel'll piss all over em!"

There was another fit of coyote laughter before Rosie moved in beside Runner.

"The Spaniards were gold crazy," she said. "All humans are."

"Not sure about camels, though," said Runner. (Winston and Anthony chuckled.)

"Didn't the Zuni Indians kill Esteban Dorantes?" asked Rosie.

"That's one story," answered Slick. "Another is that he married an Indian woman and lived with the tribe."

"Wild," grinned Runner.

"So what's the plan, then?" asked Rosie. And they all leaned in to listen.

#

Hours later, Slick stood near the dry wash that Aladdin followed as he and his riders made their way through this part of the desert. Slick's companions watched from caves in the nearby hills. They couldn't be seen from the wash.

As Aladdin approached, Slick just sat there, looking cool, as all coyotes do, and when the trio was directly in front of him, he spoke up.

"Howdy."

Esteban reigned in the camel, and they came to a stop.

"You talkin' to me?"

"Course," said the coyote.

"Stevie," whispered Ceci. "How many times have people warned you not to talk to coyotes?"

"Oops," Esteban answered. And he blushed.

"So, where are you heading?" asked Slick as he came down into the wash. "I think the circus is in Albuquerque this month."

"Is that supposed to be funny?" Esteban asked with some annoyance.

"I'm just stating a fact. If you're not taking this camel to the circus, then just where are you heading?"

"Stevie," Ceci said. "Don't talk to the darn coyote."

Esteban nodded and gave Slick a steely-eyed stare. He didn't say a word.

"Okay, be that way," Slick said. "I was just trying to be neighborly, just asking where you were going. Can't believe there's anything wrong with that."

Now Esteban and Ceci were both giving the coyote that steely-eyed stare.

"Okay, hurt my feelings, no problem," said Slick with a sigh. "I just came to warn you about going east."

"We are going east," said Esteban.

"Stevie!" Ceci hissed, trying not to move her lips so that she wasn't technically speaking to anyone.

"Never mind, Cess," Esteban said. "If this critter's got some advice about which way to go, I think we should hear it." And then he winked at her. Of course, the coyote saw the wink and just shook his head.

"Look," said Slick as he loped up to Aladdin and started talking to the camel. "You appear to be the coolest head in the bunch. So, why don't you and I have a talk?"

Aladdin lowered his head as though in agreement.

Slick put his paw to his mouth as if to whisper in the camel's ear. "Your kind is known as the ships of the desert, am I right?"

Aladdin nodded.

"Okay then, I'll state my case in nautical terms."

"Don't listen to him," Ceci hissed.

"It's okay," answered Esteban. "No one said that Aladdin couldn't talk to coyotes."

"If you want smooth sailing, friend," Slick said, "Then, don't go east around the base of those mountains in the distance. There are rough currents that way, whirlpools. Have you heard of Charybdis?"

Esteban eyed Ceci nervously and whispered, "Remember Father Samson's words... about the whirlpools, the whirlwinds, and the thunderbirds?"

"But didn't he say something about a canyon?"

Slick ignored their conversation and focused on Aladdin.

"On the other hand," he said to the camel, "if you want a nice smooth passage, head up north, toward the four corners: Monument Valley, and all. It's a mystical spot. The great spirits will guide you and take care of you from there on. Trust me. You won't be sorry."

Slick looked up at the couple as they sat on top of the camel. Ceci was purposefully staring off into space. She was whistling too. But Esteban was clearly paying close attention.

"Okay, neighbors," Slick said. "That's my advice. Take it for what it's worth. Do what you want, but for heaven's sake don't go due east."

The coyote turned then and loped up out of the wash and into the distance.

"Do you think we should go due east?" Ceci asked Esteban when Slick was gone.

"As a matter of fact, according to the map, it's the best way to go."

"But the coyote just warned us about Charybdis, told us not to go that way."

"Yeah, but I'm smart like a fox," answered Esteban. "Smarter than a coyote, and I say he was conning us."

"So we should go due east... toward the whirlwind and the thunderbirds?"

"It's a con, Cess. The thunderbirds are probably somewhere else. And, yes, I think we should go east."

229

"Maybe the coyote thinks that we'll figure out what he's doing," Ceci suggested, "So he told us not to go east toward the whirlwinds, so we would go north toward Monument Valley, but really that's the wrong direction."

"Or maybe," countered Esteban, "he told us to go up north toward Monument Valley, knowing that we would decide *not* to go the way he recommended, but then we'd decide that he knew we would probably have that idea, and so we should go north toward Monument Valley, after all."

Aladdin lowered himself into the wash and just lay there. He flattened his head into the dust and closed his eyes. If he could have, he would have covered his ears with his hooves. He really didn't want to listen to this.

Esteban and Ceci got down from the camel and continued to consider the possibilities.

"What other way is there?" asked Ceci.

Esteban smiled knowingly. "There's a pass right through the middle of the mountains," he said. "The coyote didn't even mention it. It's north east."

"Then maybe we should go that way," Ceci said. "Is it a canyon?"

Esteban smiled slyly as though recognizing his own genius. "According to the map it's just a pass, not a canyon... certainly no thunderbirds and whirlwinds there, so yes, absolutely, we should go that way."

Chapter 39
Urgent Care

"Shouldn't we be taking Rich to the hospital?" Mario asked as Gabe's little Prius sped toward Tres Flores.

"Don't think so," said Gabe. "CleanSweep Security probably has insiders there. If I know Devlin Lucero, he's already got several doctors and nurses on his payroll, and not for the welfare of his employees. He'll want to get rid of Rich... fast."

"You mean he might have someone try to kill cousin Rich?" Mario asked.

"What better place to dispose of someone than in a hospital?" Gabe answered. Mario's eyes grew wide and frightened.

The little car cruised up to the door of Tres Flores, and Gabe got out, went to the passenger side, and pulled his cousin from the car. This time, he carried Rich in his arms. Mario ran ahead opening doors and then calling on his grandparents for help.

"This way, this way," shouted Luís as he pulled two tables together and motioned for Gabe to lay the wounded man across them.

"Carmen, where are you? The boy needs help."

Mama Carmen was there before Luís even finished the sentence. She carried a bowl of boiling water and a crisp, clean washcloth. She came up to one of her favorite nephews and pressed her hand against his face... stared into his eyes.

"You're always so violent, Ricardo," she sighed. "What's wrong with you?"

She began looking at the wound in the young man's hair. "Oh, so bloody," she murmured.

"Sophia, get more boiling water from the pot on the stove. More washcloths too."

The little girl scurried away leaving the two men and the boy to look on as Carmen began the nasty chore of cleaning off the dried blood in Rich's hair and then swabbing the wound. Within seconds, the bowl and the cloth were filled with dark red blood, but Sophia was right there with another bowl of boiling water and a fresh, clean cloth.

Rich opened his eyes and grimaced as Carmen came into direct contact with the wound.

"Here take this," said Luís, and he held out a shot glass filled with Tequila.

Rich's hand trembled as he reached for the glass, but years of practice downing shots had finally paid off, and he brought the drink to his lips and tossed it down without spilling a drop.

"One more for good measure," said Luís, and he refilled the shot glass and handed it back to the young man. Rich downed it too and was able to smile a little.

"It's okay, darling," Carmen soothed as she took yet another cloth and bowl of water from the little girl, soaked the fabric, and continued to swab Rich's head. "Gotta make sure it's clean," she said. "Now brace yourself; this is gonna hurt."

Rich reached up looking for a hand to grasp and Gabe's was there. Rich looked at his cousin uncertainly.

"Hey, you're family, remember?" Gabe said and offered a slight smile.

Rich returned the look and then grimaced as Carmen pressed a cloth full of hydrogen peroxide against the open wound.

"MOTHER F... GOD!" he screamed somehow managing to correct the obscenity in mid-sentence.

Carmen laughed. "It's a good thing you remember who's taking care of you, Rich."

Carmen had brought a little sewing kit with her. "Lighter, please," she said to her husband, and Luís brought out an old Bic and flipped it on. Carmen stuck the needle into the flame, felt it burn, and shook her hand. Then she took out a short length of thread, threaded the needle, and began sewing the wound closed.

Rich squeezed his eyes shut, locked his jaw, and didn't say a word. The sewing ended. Rich kept his eyes closed and felt something soft against his cheek. He opened his eyes.

Little Sophia was standing beside him. She'd gotten up on tiptoes and placed a gentle kiss on his cheek. "We all love you, Cousin Rich," she said. "Please get better."

Luís smiled tearfully.

"But when you do, don't you dare try to kill Cousin Gabriel again."

The grandparents looked at each other with troubled expressions.

"Is that what happened?"

"I'll explain it all later," Gabe said. "Can you put Rich up in your back bedroom?"

"Of course, we can," answered Luís, but he was now looking at Rich angrily. Carmen read her husband's look, slapped him gently on the arm, and shook her head.

"Gabe, you and Luís carry Rich into the bedroom. The bed's already made up."

"I can do it alone," Gabe answered. "You guys need to be ready for customers." And then he looked around. They were standing in the middle of a popular restaurant at noontime, and there was no one there.

"Yes," said Luís. "We do have to get ready for customers… just in case someone shows up. But in the meantime, I think I'll help carry my nephew into the back bedroom."

"The truth is, Gabe," Mama Carmen said, "We haven't had any customers in over a week."

Gabe and Luís carried Rich into the back bedroom; they pulled back the covers and laid him down carefully to protect the new stitching on his head wound.

Rich opened his eyes for a moment, reached up and grabbed Gabe by the shirt. His fist clenched tight. He pulled Gabe to him, raised his head slightly and managed to whisper out a few syllables.

"VL."

"VL?" Gabe asked. "VL Johnson? The Vet?"

"VL Johnson," Rich moaned in response to his cousin. "The newspaper reporter."

Rich's mouth was dry, he grimaced in pain, but there was something he had to say.

"VL Johnson… he's called a rally for tonight… all the unemployed mineworkers… to meet in the town square."

"Damn," said Gabe as he turned to Luís in panic. "If Devlin and his goons find out about it, someone's gonna get murdered."

Chapter 40
La Llorona

Esteban and Ceci had traveled far beyond their encounter with the coyote. They'd decided not to go north or east but to head for the chasm that cut through the high mountains to the northeast. It was clearly the most direct way to go, but experienced mountain travelers like Ceci knew that the most direct way through the mountains was seldom the easiest or the fastest.

They had pitched their tents on the side of an old dried up wash where the stunted trees provided a little cover for their camp and protection from the nighttime winds. They gathered up some of the plentiful brush nearby and built a fire to keep out the harsh desert cold.

Among the provisions that Father Samson had given them were several tins of meat including a canned chicken, which Esteban decided to prepare for their evening meal. He cut up a few potatoes and carrots, threw them into a big pot with the canned chicken, added a few herbs and spices that he had tucked away into the saddlebags before he had left home, and boiled up a delicious-smelling stew.

Ceci watered the camel, found some nearby vegetation that would suit him, and then came back to share in the evening's dinner.

"Smells good," she said as she dumped some water into a small coffee pot, added coffee to the basket, and placed it on the little metal rack Esteban had laid across the fire.

"I always knew you'd make someone a good wife," she said with a grin as she watched him fussing around the campfire.

Esteban laughed and then turned quite serious. "The offer still stands, you know, Cess."

"What offer is that?"

"Marriage and a family."

"You made someone that offer?"

Esteban sighed and shook his head as he reached over and pulled the big stewpot from the grating, then he swung it into the little patch of open ground a short way back from the fire. His eyes sparkled as he ladled out a big bowl for Ceci. She came, sat beside him, and looked directly at him as he handed her the bowl. Ceci was struck yet again by the power of his eyes: mad, magical, and tonight somehow seductive. Their adventures had buffed him up too, she thought. His shoulders were broader, his waistline slimmer. He was turning into more than a very neat, good-looking guy. He was turning into some kind of a hunk.

"Don't you remember when I asked you to marry me?" he asked her.

"You never did," Ceci giggled.

"Of course. Sixth grade."

"We hardly knew each other then, didn't get to be friends till high school."

"Ah, Cecilia, but I've been dreaming about you ever since kindergarten."

Esteban shoveled some chicken into his own bowl and moved closer. "Dreams of a five-year-old. You were cute then," he said with a broad grin. "But now you're fucking gorgeous."

Ceci blushed nervously. "Fucking?"

Esteban dropped his eyes to his plate (too damn direct, he thought to himself).

"Sorry," he whispered. "That wasn't cool."

Ceci studied her companion. It suddenly reminded her of the times they had made out when they were in high school. He had those demanding hands that became so gentle when they finally reached their goal. The kids may have made fun of his dreams and his ambitions, but he really was hot, and it probably didn't hurt that he was a little bit of a victim. There are a lot of girls, she knew, who like to save troubled, persecuted boys.

Marriage had actually flitted through her mind back then. But that was before she fell in love with Gabriel Romo, and later decided that going to college was more important than anything or anyone.

Still, here they were in the desert together... just the two of them, and the nights were cold.

"You think I'm beautiful?" she asked.

"Oh, yeah..." and then he chuckled. "Way more beautiful than the camel anyway."

Ceci laughed out loud, reached for a handful of dust, and threw it at him.

Esteban pulled his bowl back to protect it from the dust, but he was smiling.

"Better get you some coffee," he said as he moved to the fire.

"Yes! And I've got a little treat to add to it."

"Strawberry shortcake?"

Ceci giggled. "Much better than that." And she ran back into her tent and came out with a small flask.

"Brandy. I've been saving it. I think we're safe enough here tonight."

"Probably from the wolves and the coyotes and the snakes," Esteban said as he held out both cups of coffee and watched as she poured a generous amount of brandy into each of them. "But maybe not from each other."

Ceci looked into his dreamer's eyes and just stared for a very long time.

#

Esteban awoke in the middle of the night to the sound of sobbing.

"Damn," he whispered. "I've broken Ceci's heart."

His head was throbbing. His mouth felt like the inside of a weather-beaten desert shack. He began to sit up slowly realizing in the process that he was fully dressed, so was Ceci, but she was inside her sleeping bag; he was outside. Nothing had happened. But that was good, Esteban thought. Wasn't it?

Every muscle in his body seemed to be cursing now. The empty brandy bottle fell from his chest and clanked against the tent floor. Ceci opened her eyes halfway, gave him a sleepy smile, cuddled up against her pillow, closed her eyes, and whispered one groggy word, "Gabe."

"Damn," Esteban repeated. A sudden knife of jealousy cut through him, made him pull away from Ceci as though she had sliced his fingers.

And then another loud bitter wail cut through the air.

It wasn't coming from Ceci though. She had a smile on her face, as though she couldn't hear the sobbing or the wailing. Was that possible? He wondered.

Esteban got to his feet, picked up his jeans, which as always were folded neatly in the corner. He hobbled into them, shook out his shoes (in case some scorpion had decided to spend the night), and put them on.

Another loud wail… it was coming from outside.

"God help me!" Esteban whispered as he escaped from the steamy tent and out into the moonlight that glistened sliver across the open desert and the river.

"Damn," said Esteban for the third time, the wash was flooded with water. In fact it had turned into a river that swept along just beyond the trees that now were actually protecting their tent from the raging water. But where had the river come from? It hadn't rained.

Another loud banshee wail and Esteban looked down to the edge of the water where he saw a young woman bent down by the river's edge. Her face was buried in her hands and she was sobbing. "Oh, my children," she sobbed. And then she threw her head back and let out a scream of pain that seemed to shatter all the silver of that moonlit night.

"What is it?" Esteban cried as he ran down to her, "What's your name?"

The woman stood, pale, ghostly, but somehow beautiful with wide eyes that seemed at first questioning and then suddenly bright with recognition.

"My boy, my son," she said, "Come to me."

Esteban could see that the woman was younger than he was. What madness made her think that she could be his mother?

"The river is sweet, my son," she said as she began striding out into the middle of the raging waters.

The fast moving current pulled at her long gown and swirled up around her legs as she moved further and further into the depths.

She turned then and opened her arms to Esteban. "Come to me, son, please." And Esteban suddenly felt that this somehow must be his own mother who had died when he was very young. She had come back to be reunited with him.

"Come play," she said and she splashed the water all around her, caught it up in her hands, lifted it above her head and let it cascade down over her body, and then she once again held out her arms as though offering a welcoming embrace.

Esteban was suddenly five years old again, running to his mother across their wide lawn, opening his arms to her.

"Mother," he called as he charged toward the woman, out into the river that immediately grabbed hold of his wide linen slacks, dragged at him, pulled him along. He was about to be swept away when a strong pair of hands grabbed him and jerked him back up onto the shore.

The woman in the middle of the river let out a desperate scream.

"Who are you?" yelled Ceci.

She had caught Esteban and pulled him to safety.

"I'm your mother, Cecilia," answered the woman with a terrifying smile. "You and Esteban are my children. Come to me... both of you."

Esteban was once again trying to head toward the fast moving waters, wanting to drag Ceci with him, except that she stood like some unmovable statue stopping him cold.

"I've heard of you," Ceci said suddenly. "You're La Llorona, the weeping woman."

Even Esteban had heard the legend. And now, realizing what was happening, he called out to her, "You murdered your children!"

"No," the woman answered.

"Yes," Esteban cried. "To get even with your husband when he left you; you drowned them in a river."

"No!"

"And then, when you realized what you had done, you killed yourself too."

"Stop it!" Ceci called. She turned Esteban toward her, away from the river, and she looked at him so intensely.

"What are you doing, Stevie?"

"She murdered her kids, Cess. Now she wants to kill us. It's all part of the legend. She can't move on to the next world until she finds the souls of her dead children, and if she can't find them, she'll murder other children so she can take their souls."

"But we're hardly children," Ceci said.

240

"Maybe she can make us children again. Who the hell knows what ghosts can do?"

"Come here," wailed La Llorona. And she extended her arms to Ceci. And with her words, the river roared and splashed great frothy waves against the riverbank. They reached for Ceci and tried to drag her out into the powerful current.

Now it was Esteban who grabbed his companion and jerked her back farther from the shore.

"Help me," sobbed the ghost. "Come to me."

"How the hell do you help a murderous ghost without getting yourself killed in the process?" Ceci asked Esteban.

"Sometimes being direct is the best solution." He remembered his great, great grandfather telling him that very thing. And where was Estebanico anyway. He was the guy with the advice; he was probably the guy who could help La Llorona.

"Where the hell are you when we need you?" Esteban suddenly called to the sky.

And there, farther down the shore, the lightly robed figure of his great, great grandfather appeared. He nodded at Esteban as much as to say, "See I *am* willing to help you." And then he turned to the woman.

"I'm here, daughter," he said.

"But my children, I need them."

"I can take you to them. I have been watching these deserts for centuries. I know all the hiding places. Come with me."

La Llorona looked at Estebanico questioningly for a long moment.

"Come, I will help you," he said. And so the woman moved slowly toward him, waded up out of the river, reached for Estebanico, took his hand, and allowed him to lead her toward the morning stars that were just now rising over the horizon.

Esteban turned toward Ceci.

"Well done," she said and kissed him on the cheek. She stared into those strange seductive eyes for a long moment and then added, "It's not really morning yet. I'm going to try and go back to sleep."

He nodded. "I'm sure I won't be able to, but go ahead."

Ceci gave Esteban another quick kiss and walked sleepily back to the tent. Esteban made his way to their old campfire then, stirred the embers, and added kindling of dried brush. It was alight in moments.

Deciding to make some new coffee, he added fresh water to the pot, spooned some coffee into the basket, tossed the little metal grill over the fire, and set the pot right on top of it.

He vaguely remembered a question he seemed to be asking himself all last night. What was it? His head hurt so bad that he could probably never remember. And then it came to him. Oh yes. "How many different ways are there to say 'no' to someone, someone you really like, someone you once were in love with?" As he recalled, Ceci in her own prim and proper way had said all of them to him, even as she had gotten almost as drunk as he had.

"What a woman," he thought. No La Llorona... In fact, Ceci had actually saved him from the ghost woman hadn't she?

Above the deepest cleft in the mountain wall, which had to be the entrance to the canyon they hoped to follow, hovered a bright reflective object. It glittered like a small star showing off in the final moments before sunrise.

But then suddenly, it hopped upward into the center of the sky, moved slowly around their camp as though it were studying him, and then, with a quick zoom, it shot across the horizon and out of sight.

"Flying saucer," said Esteban his eyes growing wide and excited. "And we haven't even gotten to New Mexico."

Chapter 41
Town Square Confrontation

Luís Romo's beat up old pickup roared around the corner and plowed toward the town square of La Sentencia. Luís was intense, clutching the steering wheel so tightly that he felt it digging ridges into the palms of his hands. Beside him, little Sophia looked every bit as anxious as he, and next to her sat Mario. His jaw was set, his brow creased, his fists clenched.

The roar of a police siren suddenly began to blare behind them. The cop car's lights flashed a bright, accusing red. Luís cast a nervous glance at Mario and then pulled over to the curb. A tall young cop got slowly out of the car and strolled up to the driver's side. He tapped on the window twice in a staccato rhythm, and Luís slowly rolled it down.

"Goin' pretty fast there, Uncle Luís," said the cop.

"Damn, Carlo," answered Luís. "What are you doing stopping me? We're on an important mission."

"With little kids in the car, doing nearly sixty on a city street? I'd call that irresponsible, Uncle."

"Listen, Carlo," Luís was almost pleading. "Bad shit is about to happen."

"Where?"

"The town square."

Carlo pushed his cop's hat back on his head. He was 24, tall, with a thick black beard and sunglasses that he sometimes even wore at night.

"Better stay away from there, Uncle Luís," he said. "You're right about the bad shit, and it's certainly not a safe place for these little ones."

"We are going to stop the bad things from happening," said Sophia in her foghorn voice.

"You have to let us pass," said Mario.

"How are you going to stop the bad things?" asked Carlo with a half smile.

"Hey! You know the damn jukebox is magical, don't you?" someone called from directly behind him.

Carlo jerked his head to the side and saw Gabe standing there. He studied his older cousin for a moment. Gabe looked as anxious as the rest of them.

"Where the hell were you?" asked the cop.

"Riding in the back of the truck."

"Damn, that's illegal too. I should run you all in," Carlo said.

"Please don't run us, Cousin Carlo," said Sophia. "Just let us get to the town square so we can stop all the trouble."

"The workers are massing in the town square," said Gabe.

"I know that."

"Devlin will have his goons there, anxious to break some heads."

"I know that too."

"We're hoping that a little music will wake everyone up, distract them, and calm them down."

Carlo looked from Gabe to Luís to Mario and at last to Sophia... the most serious of them all.

"Are you sure you know what you're doing?" he asked.

"Absolutely," said Gabe.

"Follow me," said Carlo. "I'll give you a police escort."

#

Dr. V. L. Johnson was more that a veterinarian, guitar virtuoso, newspaper reporter, and photographer. Apparently he was also quite a master of propaganda. Since his long-time friend, Jessica Amado, had gone over to the dark side and taken a job with Devlin Lucero, VL's articles for the El Milagro had become more and more militant. And he was doing more than reporting on the activities over at the CleanSweep Mining Company. He was also writing editorials urging the unemployed to demand jobs at the new mine, not at its carwash subsidiary.

In this morning's piece, VL called on the workers to meet at the town square just after sunset, to bring torches and flashlights, and to march on the new mine offices. He hadn't asked the workers to burn the place down, not in so many words, but there certainly was an undertone suggesting that violence by the former mineworkers was not only within reason but maybe even overdue.

For her part, his wife Melinda supported her husband every step of the way. After all, if he had turned against the mine, he had also turned against his ex-partner at the newspaper. And although V. L. never mentioned her by name, Jessica Amado was clearly the object of much of his anger. Melinda was delighted with that.

VL stood in the center of the town square now. To his right was a throng of ex-mineworkers, maybe as many as five hundred men and women. Some had brought their children with them to help drive home the purpose of the protest.

Many carried signs:
"HELP US FEED OUR FAMILIES"
"GIVE US BACK OUR JOBS"

"I BELONG IN A MINE NOT A CARWASH"
"DOWN WITH BLACKMORE"
"DOWN WITH LUCERO"
"GABRIEL ROMO IS A TRAITOR"

VL pulled a bullhorn from his car and began shouting to the crowd.

"It's time to show those bastards at the copper mine what we think... isn't that right?"

The crowd let go with a raucous, "YES!"

"Are we going to let Blackmore and his bunch destroy our families and our town?"

"NO!"

"Are we going to let his cronies get fat while the rest of us starve?"

"NO!"

"If they don't know how to run a copper mine, let's take it away from them and run it ourselves!"

"HELL YEAH!"

"Take over the mine!" VL shouted into his bullhorn.

"TAKE OVER THE MINE!" echoed the crowd, and it became their chant.

"TAKE OVER THE MINE!"
"TAKE OVER THE MINE!"
"TAKE OVER THE MINE!"

The chant grew louder. People pumped their signs up and down in rhythm with the call. They hoisted their children onto their shoulders and lifted them even higher.

"Let's get 'em," VL cried, and he swung around and started in the direction of the old Blackmore Copper Headquarters.

"TAKE OVER THE MINE!" Chanted the crowd as they marched. But just as they moved onto the boulevard that led to the main entrance, a dozen Cadillac Escalade security vehicles, each with the emblem of CleanSweep Security emblazoned on its side, pulled up and blocked their paths.

About fifty members of Lucero's new security force stepped from the vehicles. They were all armed with assault rifles.

"TAKE OVER THE MINE!" VL called into his bullhorn. And he marched directly toward the roadblock... right up to Lucero, who stood flanked on either side by his security team.

It was Mel Johnson who first understood the magnitude of the threat.

"Jesus, VL, he's got a gun," she cried.

And Lucero raised a pistol and pointed it directly at her husband's face.

"I think you'd better disperse," he croaked in a voice that sounded like Dirty Harry Clint Eastwood, himself.

In response, VL raised his bullhorn and blasted his message back at Lucero.

"GIVE US BACK OUR JOBS," he shouted.

Lucero laughed. "I wouldn't mind blowing your brains out, doctor," he said so that only VL could hear him. "In fact, I'd love it." And he cocked the gun.

VL turned around and glanced over his shoulder. The rest of the protestors were pressing in on him, signs still pumping, children still lifted above their parents' shoulders. The security force raised their rifles and pointed them at the crowd. The crowd hushed. Parents brought their children quickly to the ground and pressed them to the back of the gathering. There was a long terrible silence.

'YOU CAN'T STOP US!" One woman shouted now that the children were safely behind the marchers. And those with signs began to pump them up and down again.

"GIVE US BACK OUR JOBS," someone shouted.

"VL, for God's sake," cried Melinda.

VL looked at his wife, and then out from the first Escalade stepped Jessica Amado. She wore a pair of black slacks, and a tight leather jacket with a raised collar. She smirked at VL, and then she moved beside Lucero and put her hand on his shoulder.

"Shoot the sorry son of a bitch," she told Devlin.

Lucero smiled, raised the gun to the sky for a moment and then brought it down slowly until it pointed right at the doctor/reporter/organizer-of-insurrections.

A dozen police sirens suddenly blared around them. A cop cruiser with its red lights flashing swung into the space between the security force and the crowd. Right behind it came Luís and his raggedy old F150. They screeched to a halt almost rear-ending the cop car.

Mario and Sophia climbed out of the cab and raced around to the back of the truck where the jukebox sat. They climbed onto the flatbed, crawled to the machine, punched in some numbers, and waited for something to happen. Many in the crowd were now watching the two children. But most were still staring at Lucero and his men because they still had not lowered their weapons.

The jukebox sat there silently. No sound came from it.

"Where do we plug it in?" asked Sophia.

Mario slapped his forehead, then raked his hand across his face and sighed. "Duh! There's no power. But we didn't need it out by the crater."

"Get down from there, kids," called Lucero, "or I'll blow this horse doctor's head off. You wouldn't want to be responsible for that now, would you?"

"That man is evil," said Sophia.

"The worst, but still..." Mario took the little girl by her hand and led her to the back of the pickup. Luís ran around and helped each of them down.

"This was a bad idea," he said.

"Bring those kids over here," called Lucero. "I understand that little girl is a bit of a miracle. Let me take a look at her."

Luís lifted Sophia and carried her toward the man with the gun. Mario held on tightly to his arm. As they passed the cop car, cousin Carlo got out and flanked him. He held a rifle that he pointed skyward. Gabe got out from the other side of the car and joined the group.

A buzz spun through the crowd when he appeared.

"Traitor," someone called. One of the protestors threw an empty beer bottle at him, even though he was moving with the children and their grandfather.

"You should be standing with us, Gabe," called Lucero. "Don't forget, you're still an employee of CleanSweep."

Gabe remained with his uncle and the kids as they moved carefully toward the security forces. A rotten tomato struck him on the side of the head. Gabe didn't even flinch; he let the tomato slide down his neck and over the outside of his jacket; he just kept moving.

"Those kids are so cute," Jessica suddenly gushed, and she fell to one knee and held her arms out to the little girl. "Come here, honey, I'll keep you safe."

Sophia stopped in her tracks, stood frozen to the spot.

"Come on up here, kid," Lucero called. "My lady wants to get to know you. She doesn't bite. She likes kittens, for God's sake."

Sophia gave Mario a worried look and stayed put.

"Leave her alone, Jessica," VL called through the bullhorn.

"You shut up, you worm," she shouted back. "I'm working with a real man now," and she gave Lucero a sexy smile.

"Get the little girl up here, Gabe," Lucero called. "You still work for me. Bring her up to Jessica so they can get to be friends."

Gabe and the others did not move, but Sophia shook herself free of her grandfather and began walking toward Jessica and Lucero. The woman made kissy faces at her, but the man's smile was pure evil.

Mario couldn't believe what was happening; his friend was about to give herself up to the bad guys... maybe get taken back to their headquarters, he thought, put in a dungeon, tortured on a rack, disappearing forever. Still the little girl moved toward the bad guys purposefully.

Mario crossed his arms, gritted his teeth, and tightened every muscle in his body.

"Quit it, kid," Lucero called to him. "You're gonna split a gut or something." But Mario didn't quit; he continued to clench his fists, hold his breath, turn redder and redder until suddenly:

IT'S TIME TO BEGIN IT! YEAH! YEAH!

Mario spun around and saw the jukebox blasting light across the whole town square. It was blasting music too... the pounding beat of the old heavy metal classic from The Randy Royals.

The drums pounded loudly. The protestors began stomping their feet and pounding on the cop car and any other vehicles nearby. The melody rocked on. The chorus came around again.

IT'S TIME TO BEGIN IT! YEAH! YEAH!
CAUSE WE'RE GONNA WIN IT! YEAH! YEAH!

The crowd was screaming now, advancing toward Lucero and his men. Just as Jessica was about to run forward and grab Sophia, Gabe rushed up until he was almost staring her in the face. He jerked Sophia up into the air and carried her back toward the cop car. The crowd cheered him. Lucero pointed his gun at the little girl, but Jessica grabbed his arm and pushed it toward the ground before he could squeeze off a shot.

Lucero looked at her for a moment, looked at the kids, looked at the crowd that was now stomping toward his position like zombies in a Michael Jackson video. His men still had their rifles drawn, still could have fired into the crowd.

And that's when a half dozen more cop cars roared into the square. Within seconds the cops were out, using open doors for shields. They had drawn their rifles and aimed them at the security forces whose weapons still pointed into the crowd.

"Stand down," Lucero called suddenly to his troops. "Let's leave these idiots."

He grabbed Jessica and rushed her to his Escalade. His security forces ducked into their own vehicles and wheeled away. The police ran toward them, but they were too late to catch the bad guys.

And still, the music rose. The crowd cheered.

WE'RE GONNA WIN IT! YEAH! YEAH!
YES. WE'RE GONNA WIN IT! YEAH! YEAH!

Gabe jumped inside the cop car still holding Sophia. The little girl was crying bitterly. "She wanted to own me," she said. "That bad woman wanted to own me."

"It's okay," Gabe told her. "They've gone."

"But that man hates everyone, even you, even his own friends."

252

"I know, honey, I know. But it's all right now. You're safe."

"He would have killed you."

"I know, but he didn't."

Gabe comforted the little girl for a long moment and then got out of the car. Now the crowd cheered him. He waved. Cousin Carlo ran up to him. "Jeeze, he said. "From zero to hero."

Gabe smiled and waved to the crowd again. They continued cheering. The cops, seeing that they couldn't catch the security team on foot, decided not to initiate a vehicle chase.

"What about the crowd?" the commander asked Gabe. He had a megaphone in his hand and looked like he wanted the crowd to disperse.

"Let them be... unless they start breaking things," said Gabe. But the people didn't want to break anything. All they wanted to do was dance and sing. And just then the jukebox blasted out another tune, just as raucous and crowd-pleasing as the first... but maybe not as violent.

BRING ON THE BRIGHTNESS...
OH BABY WON'T YOU
BRING ON THE BRIGHTNESS...

It was The Randy Royals' second biggest hit, a hard rock riff on the old Negro spiritual. The crowd started hand clapping, foot stomping and singing out with all they had:

DONTCHA KNOW WE NEED A LITTLE MORE
    LIGHTNESS
BRING ON THE BRIGHTNESS
BRING ON THE BRIGHTNESS
NOW.

Chapter 42
The Passage

Esteban and Ceci had ridden Aladdin for three days to get to the passage through the mountains... the one Slick had not even mentioned. Ceci had immediately labeled it a trick on the coyote's part, of course.

During that period, Esteban thought Ceci's behavior was a bit unusual. During the day, she'd be very cheerful... businesslike, much as she must have been as the successful head of HR at the mine. She explained everything that needed to be done in great, proper detail. That was just fine with Esteban, of course. He liked details. And there was always a smile on her lips, joy in her eyes, and even an occasional very clever joke to be told. Then, every night her personality changed. She was no longer joyful Ceci, but a wistful romantic, perhaps softly flirting with him but not really. She seemed to be more in love with the concept of romance than with the man she traveled with. And she also seemed a little sad.

Esteban prepared delicious meals for her. He was beginning to enjoy stretching the capabilities of their food supply in very original ways. He called it creative cuisinery. But when the food was consumed and the dishes put away, and the camel fed and bedded down for the night, Ceci would turn melancholy and stare into the fire with a lonely expression.

Esteban tried for pleasant conversation. He got charming, sweet, but unenthusiastic responses and became rather melancholy himself.

On the last night before they entered the chasm, when Esteban was sleeping soundly, he began to feel that something was scratching at the outsides of the tent, something with long nails that might, in fact, be claws, something almost but not quite human. Esteban's hair bristled, a litany of prayers tumbled from his lips, and then something ripped open the side of the tent and came straight in. It was Estebanico, his great, great grandfather.

"Why didn't you just show up inside the tent?" Esteban asked. "Why come in like some wild animal? You scared the shit out of me!"

Grandfather Estebanico smiled. "I wanted to get your full attention. This is very important."

The ghost looked down at Esteban as he lay in his bag and at Ceci sleeping in hers a short distance away. He smiled.

"Splendid," he said aloud, and Esteban heard the word, and began to relax.

"It's not what it seems," he whispered to his great, great grandfather. "We're only friends... at best."

Estebanico laughed. "Of course, you are. And that's fine. Friendship will unite you through the trials you are about to face."

"Trials?"

Estebanico nodded. "Fierce trials: the Unceglia. You must pass by them to reach Cíbola, and you must use great care. Try not to anger them, try not to draw them down on you. If you can do that, you may very well reach the Golden Cities without incident."

"I've never heard of the Unceglia," Esteban said. "What are they?"

"Their legends are from The North," Estebanico answered. "They've been brought here to guard this passageway... to prevent entrance by anyone. There are times when they become exhausted and you can sneak by them. But it is very rare. Let's hope you arrive at such a time, but it's unlikely."

"But what are they? And how can you help us escape them?"

"I won't be able to help you," Estebanico shook his head. "I have other realms to visit. I can't be with you any longer. I can't even come to you in dreams."

"But, grandfather," said Esteban. There was a moment of dead silence as he began to feel more and more like the little boy who first heard of Estebanico from his father. "Why can't you..." and then he merely broke down and sobbed.

The ghost went to him and put his arms around him.

"I'm not sure we can make it without you,' Esteban sighed. "Why didn't you tell me all this before you brought us on this...."

"Quest," said the grandfather. "If you complete the journey it will be more than worth it, I promise you... even with all the dangers."

Esteban looked into the shimmering eyes of his ghost grandfather. "There must be something you can tell me to help me get past the ugly, whatever they are."

"Unceglia," said Estebanico. "If things get really bad, try calling for help."

"And someone from the city will come and save us?"

"Hardly, but there are other creatures who might like to know that the Unceglia have exposed themselves. They do have natural enemies."

"You've got to explain this all to me, great grandfather," said Esteban. "Before we enter that passage, we need to know what we're up against."

"Better that you don't know, son," said Estebanico.
And then he vanished.

It was practical, sensible Ceci who listened to Esteban's retelling of his dream. He had allowed her to continue to sleep while he lay awake trying to figure out exactly what his great, great grandfather had told him.

"Unceglia?" she repeated. "I've never heard the name before. If only there were wifi out here, we could check it out on the Internet. "I'm sure someone has posted something... some northern Indian tribe, maybe... someone... on Wikipedia or somewhere."

"It's mythology, Cess. I doubt that anyone has posted anything on how to escape from them." Esteban gathered up the camping gear and carted it over to the camel as he continued to talk.

"Try to sneak by them when they are exhausted; that's the advice my great grandfather gave me. Let them sleep, whatever they are, and maybe we'll be all right."

"And if that doesn't work?" Ceci asked as she toted her own gear over to the camel.

"Scream for help."

#

Four hours later, as Ceci rode Aladdin and Esteban led the camel on foot, they entered a cleft in the mountains and soon found themselves in the depths of a great chasm. They were on an ancient, dusty pathway. It was shadowy, shady-cool. Rivulets cascaded through the moss-covered rocks that rose high above them. That was great, Ceci thought and was amazed to see that, within half an hour of entering the shade, a broad river began to flow beside them, separating them from the steep granite wall on the other side of the chasm.

The camel strode out, Ceci's ride became pleasant, and the song of the river seemed reassuring. Little birds that lived in the shadows hopped among the small yellow-green bushes and warbled comforting songs.

"We have to keep moving," Esteban whispered back to Ceci. "The faster we get through this, the less chance we have of awakening whatever those creatures are."

The pathway descended then. Less vegetation grew along its sides. The river dropped, first five then twenty then a hundred feet below them. The cliffs that jutted above were now cracked and scarred with black lichen, but there was no greenery of any kind.

At last, the pathway brought them down to an open area on the edge of the river once again. And that's when they heard it: a loud crashing in the sky above that made Ceci think of boat sails slammed by the winds on some distant lake. She had once visited the great reservoirs of Lake Powell with her father. He had taken her sailing, just that once. But the wind came up, the sky became very dark, and little Ceci was terrified as their boat, with its wind-whipped sails, was tossed about so violently. That was the sound she heard now: a loud, vicious slapping of something taut and cloth-like against the wind.

Slap! It was high above the walls of the chasm. And then the winds around them picked up and grew more intense.

Whirlwinds spun down through the crevices, gathering up the dust of the trail and throwing it harshly against them. Ceci pressed herself against the rocks on the side opposite the river. She crept along, head down, hoping that the whirlwinds would cease. But they did not.

Something great and dark and looming passed across the top of the chasm then, blotting out the sun, driving them into total darkness by its massive size. Was it an airplane? No, it was silent... a glider... a glider the size of a jumbo jet... or a thunderbird.

"Is this the Charybdis that father Samson warned us about?" she asked Esteban.

"I'm afraid it must be… maybe we should have listened to the coyote after all." Esteban answered. And as the whirlwind howled, he pulled a kerchief from his pocket and wrapped it around his head giving himself just enough of a slit to see through. The camel trudged on somehow impervious to the gale. And then, after they had moved through long deep passages of dark and shadow, when they had reached a verdant spot where small trees were growing, the opening at the very top of the chasm widened, and sunlight streamed in.

Whatever massive forms had circled in the sky above the mountains seemed to have moved on. The air was now fresh and peaceful.

"I think we'd better stop for a moment and rest," Ceci said.

"We're not supposed to stop."

"But we made it through Charybdis, didn't we? Or was that the Unceglia that your great, great grandfather warned us about?"

"Not sure," answered Esteban. "I was never able to sort out all that damn mythology."

"Well, whatever we were supposed to be so afraid of," said Ceci, "it hasn't come down into the passage. We're okay. But I'm exhausted. I need to rest. Please."

Esteban surveyed the whole area. The river now split, dividing the mountain walls in three so that the place where they stood seemed to be the base of an enormous letter "Y" that could only be seen when God was looking down on it. The overall effect was to create a large open space where they stood: a place for trees to grow, for the river to calm and become a broad, smooth waterway. The pathway only followed one tributary, however, and, at least for Esteban, that was clearly the direction in which to head.

"Hey, I want to swim," said Ceci. "I'm covered with grit and my clothes are caked with dust. I need to get clean."

Esteban shrugged. "Looks safe enough, I guess."

"Good," answered, Ceci. "And I'm going to give Aladdin a drink; the poor guy deserves it." But when she grabbed the camel's reins and tried to draw it to the water the camel was having none of it. He dug in his hooves and pulled back against her.

Ceci looked at Aladdin curiously. "Okay, be that way," she said. "I'm going in."

She turned back to the calm of the river... was no more than ten feet from its shore when a monstrous serpent reared up and towered above her. A great reptilian water monster! Its black, scaly body seemed almost as long as the river... hundreds of feet long. It opened its jaws, and double rows of shatter-glass-sharp teeth rimmed the terrifying cavern of its mouth. A great plumed crest shot up above its head with an electric crackle and spread open like some deadly wizard's fan.

The serpent's tongue, long and forked and wet with a harsh green slime, flickered out at Ceci. Sticky yellow ooze began to spread from under its scales and brought with it a stench that nearly overpowered her. Ceci fell on her backside and then crawled backward through the dust still looking at the monster.

Esteban stepped into the path of Aladdin as the camel moved away from the serpent. He grabbed the reins and pulled the camel closer; then he reached into the saddlebag and took out a pistol.

The monster had now lowered its head onto the bank of the river and was gliding toward Ceci. Esteban held the pistol with both hands and fired into the eye of the serpent... two, three, four times.

The bullets hit their mark. The serpent jerked back as black blood oozed from the wound. The creature's thick scales made a harsh metallic scraping sound as it retreated.

"Thank you, Stevie, God, thank you," Ceci screamed.

And then a second serpent, twice as big as the first rose up and towered above the clearing. This beast was deep green. A ridge of scales ran down its back and then rose behind its head to form that same kind of fan that had been so terrifying on its mate. Esteban fired the gun, and the monstrous snake recoiled. Then it rose up above them all and hung there poised to strike as the black serpent again began gliding toward the shore and toward Ceci.

Esteban tried to fire again, but the revolver was empty. He threw it at the black monster, and it struck the beast in its bloodied eye, causing it to rear up beside its mate.

Esteban rushed for Ceci, lifted her to him, spun, and ran to the far wall of the clearing. They were as far as they could get from the bank of the river, but they were still well within striking distance of the twin serpents. Esteban stood with Ceci, facing the monsters that now pulled themselves up even higher, drawing back in anticipation of a deadly attack.

And then the monsters slammed forward, scooping up their victims into their hideous jaws, tossing one into the air, devouring the other. But it was not Ceci and Esteban who were attacked. It was Dido and her retinue of warriors, as many as a hundred of them, who had trailed behind Esteban and Ceci hoping to follow them into the Golden Cities, only to be led instead into death.

The great bulk of one serpent slammed down on an entire platoon crushing thirty men into bloody pulp. Four men including Joseph, whom Ceci remembered from their pleasant conversation in the casino, pulled farther back from the shore, set up a machine gun and trained it on the black serpent. But before they could fire, the green monster fell on them from the other direction. It was snatching up the soldiers and the gun and flinging all of them against the far wall of the passage where the impact finally did set off a barrage of bullets that riddled a dozen men who were frantically rushing from the onslaught.

An entire battalion of soldiers joined the fray, but with their arrival seven more monster snakes rose up out of the water and began gulping down the warriors. Some of the men used hand grenades, which did fly up and explode the heads and bodies of two of the serpents, but other serpents rose up in their place, lunging at the scrambling survivors on the shoreline, swallowing them whole, crushing them with their massive bodies, or, in some terrible cases, catching soldiers between two of them and tearing them apart as they fought among themselves for the remaining morsels of human flesh, until at last the whole bank of the river was swarming with monstrous serpents.

Dido, at last, somehow unscathed, rushed from the middle of the slaughter, spotted Esteban and Ceci against the far wall, and made her way to them. But a great indigo serpent suddenly reared up behind her.

"You bastard," she screamed at Esteban, "You fucking ba...." But before she could finish her words the monster swooped down, grabbed her raised arm in its drooling mouth, flipped her high in the air, and caught her as she fell kicking and screaming down its throat.

Now Ceci and Esteban pulled back even farther against the wall, watching a writhing knot of serpents attacking each other as they fought for the few remaining men in Dido's retinue. Then, one by one, as the last scraps of human flesh were devoured, they hissed their satisfaction and gradually slid back into the river until there were only the two original black and green monsters left on the shoreline. And now these beasts trained their still hungry eyes on Esteban and Ceci.

"Help! Help us!" Esteban shouted, and Ceci closed her eyes in terrified anticipation. That's why she only heard the swift whoosh, the loud cackle, and the horrific, slamming, blood-churning clash. And then she opened her eyes again to see two enormous birds lifting up toward the top of the canyon, each carrying one of the writhing, hissing serpents in their talons. The birds were turquoise-blue, flecked with red. White horns jutted from their heads. Frosty white feathers lit the tips of their wings, which seemed long enough to span the entire opening above them.

The snakes twisted in agony; black blood flowed from where they were held. The blood drenched the pathway and the river. The serpent's violent thrashing caused the birds to slam hard against the chasm walls dislodging huge sheets of rock that plunged into the earth all around Esteban and Ceci. But somehow the falling rocks missed the pair.

The twin snakes almost pulled free once, only to be gripped even tighter in the talons of the monster birds. "Let's get out of here!" yelled Esteban, and he grabbed Ceci by the arm and took off down the pathway. She did her best to keep up with him, as did the camel, which – without being urged by anything other than fear – chased after the pair nearly running them down.

It seemed as though they were running endlessly, but at last, Esteban pulled back into a hollow in the wall of the chasm. He swung Ceci around and jerked her into his body. "We're all right; we are all right."

Ceci pressed herself against him. "Oh, my God... if I had known..." she gasped.

"We're going to be okay now," said Esteban. "I know it."

Ceci was crying, burying her face in Esteban's shoulder, sobbing uncontrollably. "I want to go home."

"But we're here, Cess," he said.

Ceci pulled back and looked at Esteban's face through her tears. He was smiling, and his features were so bright, so happy, so golden, that for a long time Ceci didn't realize that he was looking beyond her... off into the distance at the far end of the trail, through an opening in the rocks, at the golden glow of cities in the distance.

Part Four
Beyond

Chapter 43
The Maidens

They were in the river, nearly up to their waists, giggling, splashing each other, and having fun... bathing in the brightness of the sunshine that poured in through the skylight of the translucent mountain wall.

Their skin was almond colored, not as dark as Esteban's, who still showed the traces of his Moorish ancestry, but very much like that of Ceci Moreno, who peered at the girls now in wonder.

Two of them (much younger than the third) swam farther out into the current, circled, and came back nearer the shore. The third girl stood alone, sunning herself, head and shoulders thrown back, lifting her naked breasts into the sunlight. Esteban could not stop looking at her.

The girl was gorgeous; even Ceci had to agree. She had long black hair pulled back tightly and woven into a single long braid that ran down her back and disappeared into the water. Her lips were full, her nose sharp, angular. Her eyelashes were real of course, but so long that they almost seemed store-bought. Her eyebrows were thick and expressive, now arching with delight at the ripples in the crystal clear water she bathed in.

Ceci set the girl's age at about seventeen, maybe a little older, maybe as old even as nineteen. The only thing she wore was an ornate necklace that seemed to be pure gold, and it told Ceci and Esteban that they were indeed on the outskirts of Cíbola.

The girl appeared to have entered the river from some spectacular Disney musical cartoon, and Ceci half expected to see hummingbirds dart up to her and try to kiss her, sparrows and cardinals, raccoons and chipmunks along the shoreline break into some ridiculous rhymy song.

Ceci glanced at Esteban and saw that the girl had captivated him completely.

"Want to use the binoculars?" Ceci asked sarcastically.

"No, Cess, you don't understand," Esteban said.

"I think I do."

"No, you don't." And then he blushed. "I know her."

Ceci rolled her eyes. "In your dreams."

"Exactly. She was the girl in the vision that my great, great grandfather held in his hand."

The girl in the river must have heard them. She immediately crossed her arms across her breasts in embarrassment. She turned away and then looked back over her shoulder.

She was looking at Ceci, and then she smiled. Ceci couldn't help but smile in return.

"Hey now," said Esteban, who held out his hand to the girl and began wading into the water to shake hers.

The girl giggled for a moment and shook her head. Instead, she danced away, out of the water and into a stand of tall grass a short distance from where Ceci and Esteban were standing. The younger girls must have watched the encounter because, when the older girl splashed her way to the shore, so did they.

"You met her in a vision," asked Ceci, "really?" and she smirked at Esteban.

"I know her, I really do."

"Well, she doesn't seem to know you," Ceci said and at those words, the three girls walked up behind Ceci and

Esteban who heard them coming and turned. The three were now fully dressed. Each wore a long robe and an ornate sash around her waist. The oldest had placed the golden necklace over her robe so that it rested proudly on her chest.

"¿Le puedo ayudar?"(Can I help you?) asked the girl. Her expression and posture were almost regal.

"She speaks Spanish," thought Ceci and wasn't exactly sure how she felt about the fact... or the young woman herself.

"¿Donde estamos? (Where are we?)," asked Esteban.

The girl cocked her head and a glint of recognition did flit for a moment in her eyes. Then she giggled again and offered a smile so glowing that Esteban's eyes brightened in response.

"Cíbola," she answered.

"This really is incredible," thought Ceci. "We've nearly completed the quest and have been greeted by who, Princess Tiger Lilly?" As soon as she had the thought she felt guilty. The fact was that a beautiful and (more importantly) a peaceful person from the fabled city had greeted them... so much for her own ominous dream of being chased by warriors in death masks.

"Can you take us to the city?" Esteban asked in Spanish.

"Of course," the girl answered.

The other girls were not as stunning as their friend. And they were a few years younger, maybe ages twelve and fourteen. Still, in their own youthful way, they were very pretty. They talked among themselves, sometimes in Spanish, more often in some native language that Ceci could not understand at all.

"Follow me," said the youngest and smallest of the girls. She climbed from the shore and disappeared. The other girls followed. Esteban stepped back like the gentleman he often was. He was smiling happily at Ceci, and let her precede him.

Then came the scream.

Esteban charged through the tall grass and there, standing in a clearing, eyes cold with fear, were the girls who had come face to face with the terrifying, never-before-seen shape of Aladdin.

"What is it?" the smallest of them asked.

"Our camel," Esteban answered. "He's a good animal, a friend; he carried us here."

"Like a horse," the second girl suggested.

"Very much," said Ceci. "He won't hurt you."

But Aladdin was indeed curious about these new humans, and he had begun to sniff around the smallest of them who stood the closest. She was making a terrified and somewhat disgusted face at the animal.

Esteban rushed forward, took Aladdin by his head and turned him away. He walked Aladdin a few paces up the beach to where some delicious-looking grass was growing. When Esteban turned back again, Ceci was engaged in conversation with the three young women.

"What are your names?" she asked.

"Liliana," said the beauty.

"Reyna," said the middle girl.

"Lola," whispered the youngest.

"And are you married?"

"The girls all giggled at the question.

"Not yet, of course," little Lola answered.

"We're not of the age," added Reyna.

"And what is the marriageable age?" asked Ceci.

Liliana just shrugged as though the answer was as big a mystery to her as to anyone.

"Liliana's day is close," said Lola. "But my marriage is far in the future."

Ceci nodded. Esteban had come back to them. He smiled.

"So, shall we take you to the citadel?" asked Liliana, "We'd love to."

"The citadel of Cíbola," murmured Esteban in wonder. It was hard to believe that they were almost there, that his quest was nearly complete. Ceci could see his excitement and felt it herself.

"That would be very kind of you," she said.

"Then come this way," said Liliana, again flashing the brief look of recognition, and she led them inland from the river.

Chapter 44
The Highway

They marched on toward the city with its skyline gleaming golden in the distance. The path they followed soon widened into a broad highway. The two younger girls led the way, gossiping as they went. Ceci rode on Aladdin while Esteban held the reigns and led the camel along. Liliana walked beside him, offering a few comments on the sights they were passing. She seemed so refined to Ceci.

The river that flowed through the passage they had traveled was much wider now. Boats sailed upon it, and Esteban found himself focusing on a long transport that, for the moment, at least, came up along beside them. On board, facing them, a couple stood enjoying each other's company. The young man on board waved at Esteban, and he returned the wave.

Soon, smaller vessels sailed around the long transport... personal boats that scooted through the water at twice its speed. Farther out, in the deepest parts of the river, barges carried baskets of trade goods and wooden cages full of animals.

Large docks came into view along the waterfront. They had stone stairways that led down to the river's edge, and – from her high vantage point on the camel – Ceci was the first to see workers unloading the crates of produce, while, on wider piers farther down the river, passengers stood by, queuing up to board the transports.

On the side of the road opposite the river, green hills rolled into the distance. Much of the land was cultivated and Esteban at once recognized corn and rice and broad fields of beans. The economy seemed to be booming, and everyone they saw appeared happy to share in the prosperity.

Now there were others on the road. Many were on foot, but some traveled on horseback.

"Horses," Esteban called to Ceci as they both realized that these imports of the Conquistadors had somehow, like the Spanish language, found their way into this vast hidden empire.

The roads were lined with palm trees and with gardens bright with flowering trees in varieties Esteban had never seen before. Large, colorful birds darted between the trees or soared joyfully above them.

The dress of those who passed them was Native American but with an unexpected influence of Aztec design and images, and everyone who passed turned to stare. It wasn't Ceci and Esteban's clothing that interested them, however; it was Aladdin. The people of the seven cities may have been familiar with horses, but none of them had ever seen a camel before. There were expressions of wonder, Oooohs and Aaahhhs that became so common that the small group soon began to ignore them.

The carved stone faces of warriors, coyotes, kings, and hawks stared down at the group as they passed under the first of a series of bridges and aqueducts that crisscrossed the river. And all of the stone faces, all of people and places, the whole scene glowed a bright golden color in the light reflected from the towers of the vast city ahead of them.

But before they got to the citadel, Ceci, Esteban, and the girls passed through an area that held markets, shops, and the homes of the poorer residents. Lola ran up to a small open-air market and picked up a large pear. Then, bringing it back to the group, she offered it to Aladdin. The camel slurped it up greedily, and then, to the amusement of the girls, he belched loudly without missing a stride as they traveled along.

They passed a small troop of children playing some unrecognizable game with sticks and rocks. When they saw the camel, the children began to run along beside Esteban and the others, hooting and trying every way they could to catch the camel's attention. It annoyed Ceci who kept shouting to the children, "Get! Get out of here." But of course the kids didn't; they kept chanting until Aladdin, who apparently was as tired of the jeers as Ceci, turned and spit at the children splattering one in the face. It was a big tough looking boy who stopped in his tracks and grunted unhappily while his companions now made him the object of their jeers.

As the little band moved into the central plaza of the city, Liliana turned and gestured to a railing where several horses had been tied. "Leave your animal here," she said. "It will be safe. Reyna will watch it. Won't you, cousin?"

The mid-teen made an unhappy face. But Liliana came up to her and whispered something in her ear that made Reyna stop and smile, her eyes widening as she put a hand over her mouth as though she had been told an important little secret.

"Come along now," said Liliana, and she led Esteban and Ceci on foot through a great wide gate while little Lola followed a few steps behind.

They entered a great central plaza. The floor was made of polished white stone that reflected the grandeur of the surroundings: large open areas where Esteban saw people clustered together or walking apart in groups of two or three. On the outer edges of the plaza were ball fields, with tiered seating and play areas made of rich red clay. A game was in progress and cheering erupted as one team scored. Esteban stopped in his tracks and said, "I'd love to see that."

Later," answered Liliana. "We can go to the next match if you want... I'll tell you all about the game and who to cheer for."

Esteban nodded, and they continued, past the ornate residences of the wealthy and the posh palaces of rulers and priests, to the towering multi-level pyramids in the center of the plaza that were built in a classic Aztec design.

There were three pyramids there: two shorter ones flanking a gigantic, steep-sided, central temple that must have been seven or eight hundred feet high. Up the center of the great pyramid ascended a stairway that allowed access to each level, but which also led directly to the top.

"Come," Liliana said, and she began the great ascent... hundreds of stairs constructed, Esteban decided, of sparkling sandstone. He turned back to Ceci.

"Doing okay, Cess?"

"Just fine," she answered. "That endless hike through the desert makes this climb seem easy."

When they reached the third platform of the great Pyramid. Liliana stopped and gave them a moment to rest. Esteban and Ceci were able to take in the vast panoramic view.

Esteban pulled Ceci to him for just a minute and whispered to her, "We made it, we make it, Cess."

But Ceci couldn't take her eyes off the overwhelming site.

"My God," she said after a long moment. "There really are seven cities."

"Can't count that high, Cess. But I'll take your word for it."

Vast fields of well-tended farmland separated the cities, each of which appeared to be a carbon copy of the others. Some cities had been built on hills so that their temples seemed to be higher and more majestic. But the largest, grandest city of them all was the one in which they now stood. It sat at the forward edge of the domain, as though it were the first to be built, and all the other cities had been copied from it.

"Cíbola," shouted little Lola as she gestured to the fabulous place, and then she threw her arms around herself and spun in a giddiness of pride and excitement. "Come see," she called to Esteban. "Come see." And she began running up the steps toward the very top of the pyramid.

Esteban started after her, not running but walking slowly so that Ceci could catch up with him. Instead, she passed him on her ascent, grinning broadly, challenging him to catch her as she charged on ahead. But Liliana caught up to Esteban and then walked along beside him.

Ceci might have waited for them, but it was then that she rose over the edge of the final platform and gasped at what she saw. The edifice at the very top of the pyramid, the crown jewel of each city, was a temple. With its peaked roof and multiple columns, it looked remarkably like a classic Greek structure except that it had been covered entirely with sheets of pure gold.

"Dear Jesus, is it a church?" she asked as she noted that there was no cross sitting atop the structure.

"A temple for a great gift," answered Liliana, "from the star people."

"The star people?" Esteban asked, and at that moment, rough guards moved on them.

The guards pulled Ceci and Esteban away from the young girls and then a harsh looking man walked proudly up to the couple. He wore brightly colored robes, a neckband of brightly colored feathers, and a headdress of the same plumage.

"Who are you, and what are you doing here?" he demanded.

Esteban was too shocked to answer, but Liliana spoke up quickly. "They are visitors, Coyotl. And they are my guests."

"We have no visitors, he answered. "We have no guests."

Then he turned to the other guards.

"Take them!"

Chapter 45
The Dungeon

Ceci sat on a straw bed in the corner of a dank and dingy cell. The place smelled of ancient mold and dead rats. Her spirits couldn't be much lower. She felt let down by Liliana, by Esteban, and by herself. Why hadn't she stayed with Gabe? At that moment, she missed him more than ever. Oh, he wasn't any more confrontational than Esteban, she thought. But he always tried to work things out, and most of the time that turned out to be the best thing to do. He had worked out a plan to get jobs for the workers, hadn't he? She wondered for a second if it had succeeded as well as he had hoped. Then she smiled. Even if it hadn't, Gabe would have found a way to keep things moving in a positive direction.

"Gabe," she sighed out loud.

She wanted his arms around her now, and his comforting words that would tell her that he would find a way to save them from all of this, no matter what. Why wasn't he here? If he really loved her, he would have come along. Esteban probably would have welcomed his company.

She looked over at her companion. How could she have been crazy enough to follow him? He'd been right about the existence of Cíbola, of course. But so what? Monster serpents had almost devoured them, the guards had handled them very roughly, and they could be no more than a few hours away from their own execution... probably in some primitive and hideous way.

And as far as Liliana who had so captivated her friend, she could have been some siren sent to lure them into the city, to deliver them to the guards so that they could be sacrificed like every other person who had crossed into Cíbola in the last four hundred years. That's how they'd kept their existence secret, she decided. Simply by murdering anyone who managed to get past the serpents.

Did any of this make any sense? Ceci wondered. She didn't care. She felt that the cumulative events of the last several days had "pushed her to the wall," as her father used to say. And when she was pushed to the wall, she tended to change personalities... to use one of those "back-up styles" that she had read about in her Psychology textbooks. Push me to the wall and I'm no longer sweet, prim Cecilia Moreno, she realized. I turn into a whole different person, someone Stevie had discovered years ago and decided to call *Celia the Bitch*.

She felt that change happening to her at that very moment, and she knew that the longer she held in her anger, the worse she would behave when she finally blew. Then she looked over and saw that Esteban was smiling at her... stupidly she thought, and that did it.

"You have to admit this is a pretty nice dungeon, Cess," Esteban said, gesturing around the room.

"You would say that," Ceci snapped. "You're so hot for that girl that you'd put up with anything just to be around her. How do we know these people aren't into human sacrifice?"

Esteban jumped. Whoa! *Celia the Bitch* had arrived? He'd forgotten all about this part of Ceci's personality. It had been years, after all. He remembered encountering Ceci's back-up style when they were dating. The first time he had ever tried to touch her breast, *Celia the Bitch* had nearly taken his head off.

"You're so infatuated that you don't even see what's going on." "Ceci growled. "I didn't trust that Liliana the moment she started batting those long eyelashes at you."

Esteban wished he could remember how to handle the bitchy side of Ceci's personality. Maybe there was no way.

"Hey, calm down, Cess," he said at last. "Liliana's just a sweet kid."

"Yeah right. It was probably her plan to lead us into captivity all along. She's some local siren or sorceress or something." She smiled cruelly. "Probably a dancer at a local Cíbola strip club."

"Ceci!"

Electric tension sizzled between them. Then Esteban grinned. "Know what I think? I think she'll get us out of here."

Ceci shook her head and mumbled bitterly. "You dreamer."

#

Twenty-four hours later, Ceci and Esteban were still in the dungeon, quite a bit scruffier, he starting to feel more and more let down, she more angry than ever. They hadn't spoken to each other since Esteban tried to put his arm around her to console her a few hours earlier, and *Celia the Bitch* had punched him right in the stomach.

"Keep away from me, you little shit!" she had said, and they hadn't exchanged another word since then.

About four hours after that, a guard, one of the same spearmen who had initially captured them, came down to their cell and slid two bowls of thick bean soup through the cell bars. It smelled to Ceci like it was made from whatever dead things were rotting in the walls.

"Eat it. It may be your very last meal," he cursed at them, then turned and left.

Esteban went to the door of the cell and took both of the thick clay bowls. He gave one to Ceci, then brought the other back to the corner of the cell and began to eat.

"Hey, you know," he said. "This is delicious."

"Will you just shut up," Ceci said. "Don't you realize what's going on?"

"Yes, I think I do."

"And what's that?"

"These people don't know how to handle prisoners. They probably haven't had a prisoner in decades."

"I sure feel like a prisoner."

"The cell is too clean," he said. "No one cleans dungeons. And this food is too good. It tastes like it came from Tres Flores."

Ceci couldn't believe what he was saying. Did he smell the same glop that she smelled? Still, she closed her eyes, ignored what to her was a terrible aroma, and took a sip.

She had to admit that it tasted good.

"Maybe I'm just damn hungry," she said.

"Or maybe these guys don't know that they're supposed to feed prisoners garbage and put them in a place that's an actual dungeon. "

Ceci rolled her eyes. "Are you even in the same room that I am?" she asked. And then she immediately gulped down the rest of the soup. "You know, it doesn't matter that they feed us well if they end up sacrificing us to their gods."

"The Star People?"

"Yes, and who the hell are they?"

"You know, the old belief that Native Americans are so tuned into nature that they just accept interstellar beings as part of their universal existence."

Ceci looked at her partner in disbelief. "Where'd you hear that?"

"Saw it in Wikipedia," he answered, and then he grinned, "or maybe the Syfy channel."

Ceci burst out laughing. She rocked back on the bed and gave out a howl that echoed down the hallways. She had been under such stress, had been so angry that she couldn't help herself. "You are such a god damn idiot," she said.

"A cute idiot, though," Esteban answered, and he held out his arms to her once again.

She iced him with a cold, hard stare. "Not on your life, Stevie, not anymore," said *Celia the Bitch*.

"But I really think we'll be okay."

"How can you say that? We're in a fucking dungeon!"

"My great, great grandfather wouldn't have urged me to come here if it wasn't going to be okay."

More bullshit, Ceci thought.

"The thunderbirds wouldn't have saved us from those serpents if we were just going to be executed when we got here."

"I hope you're right," she whispered. But she felt more and more certain that he wasn't.

And just then heavy footsteps approached from the end of the hallway.

Chapter 46
Acalon

An hour later, Ceci and Esteban sat on a wooden bench in a high-ceilinged room with a polished stone floor and walls richly painted with murals. The immense pieces of artwork on the forward walls depicted the building of the great pyramid. The fourth wall (behind them) presented a swirl of colors, an abstract interpretation of the energy and the power of the other images. Across from them, four people sat on high-backed leather chairs. They were probably judges, Esteban decided. There was an elderly man whom Esteban felt must be some kind of diplomat (maybe a representative of some council of elders) and a high priest (somewhat younger, whose rich robes suggested that he was more than just a medicine man, probably a healer, a Curandero). Beside them, staring intently at Esteban, was Coyotl, the warrior who had initially captured and imprisoned them, and then there was Liliana. The girl now wore ornate ceremonial robes fringed with leopard skin. She too must be someone important, Esteban decided with a bit of embarrassment. Then she smiled and waved at him like a schoolgirl.

After no more than a minute's wait, they all heard the sound of a great door slamming, and a tall man dressed in brightly colored robes decorated with gold and other gems entered the room. On his head, he wore a headdress of turquoise blue, red, and purple feathers. In spite of the man's regal bearing and ostentatious clothing, the openness of his expression suggested that he was looking forward to meeting them.

The four judges immediately stood and bowed their heads as he approached, and Ceci was grateful at least for that cue. She knelt. Esteban did too.

"This is Acalon the Great," the diplomat announced. "Our Emperor."

Acalon came directly to Ceci and Esteban. He took Esteban by the hands and pulled him to his feet. Then he did the same for Ceci. He smiled gently at her, and he reminded Ceci at once of the Dalai Lama, a man of peace. In spite of his bright and regal clothing, this man looked peaceful as well.

"These visitors came through the passage," said the diplomat. "Thunderbirds pulled the guardian serpents from their paths and allowed them to find our world."

"And what do you make of that, Talaloc?" asked the Emperor.

"Talaloc, the diplomat, thought for a moment. "Of course, it means that they were destined to come here and live with us."

Esteban eyed Ceci and saw her flinch at the words. The Emperor saw it too.

"Wasn't it your intention to stay with us?" he asked them both.

"Actually," answered Esteban, deciding that he probably should not yet announce that their goal was to steal some valuable artifact and return with it to their homes in La Sentencia, "we just hoped to find you as my great, great grandfather Estebanico did. He came to me in my dreams and urged me to visit you."

"Estebanico, yes," the Emperor said. "I understand that he was a fine man who lived with us for many centuries. He was a little before my time, of course." Then the Emperor chuckled.

"But you should visit his descendants … your uncles and cousins. I'm sure you'd enjoy getting to know them."

"Can I ask you something, your highness?" Esteban said.

The Emperor grinned. "Remember my name is Acalon," he said. "Please. You must call me by my name."

"Thank you, Acalon," Esteban answered, and then he turned to Ceci, and seeing some actual encouragement in her eyes and a possible return of the gentler Ceci that he liked so well, he continued. "We know you've made it difficult to find your land and are aware of the obstacles you have put in place to keep it hidden."

Everyone nodded at these words, and the Emperor smiled.

"So I was just wondering if anyone has ever, you know, left this beautiful spot and gone back to their homes."

"Why would anyone want to do that?" asked Acalon.

Again Esteban eyed Ceci cautiously. "Because they got homesick maybe," he suggested. Ceci nodded.

Before the Emperor could answer, the warrior jumped up and moved toward them.

"Apparently you've forgotten the history of your own people, boy," Coyotl said as he came right up to Esteban and faced him. "The Spanish found gold in the Aztec capital and that brought a never-ending stream of conquerors to our lands.

"Anyone who leaves here will bring tales of what they have found. They'll probably steal something too, bring it back to their people, show it to them, sell it, raise money, draw maps on how to get here, bring a whole convoy of outsiders to discover our cities and descend upon us."

Ceci felt a terrible chill as she listened to the warrior. She understood his logic and began to feel certain that these people would never allow them to leave Cíbola.

Esteban eyed her warily. He turned to Liliana, who smiled at him and mouthed the words, "stay with me."

"Those who try to leave us should be put to death," said the warrior.

"Death," said the diplomat, "especially if we find they have stolen something."

"Death," repeated the warrior more forcefully.

"Death," echoed the healer.

As much as she tried to hide her feelings, Ceci's eyes were filled with fear.

Acalon read her expression. ""Don't upset yourself, child," he said. "Others have come to our cities, not many lately thanks to the protections we have erected... but a few have. The last couple came our way over forty years ago. They have aged very slowly, as we all do, and they are still here. You should spend some time with them... hear how much they love being with us."

Esteban nodded. He looked at Liliana, who gave him an encouraging smile.

"Might be a good idea; what do you say, Cess?" he asked.

"Like I have any choice," she whispered to him. But she gave the Emperor as sincere a smile as she could.

"Please," said the Emperor, "Talk to them."

"But know this," added the warrior, "our laws declare that any outsiders who decide to run from us will die." And then he turned to Liliana, easily able to recognize her budding affection for Esteban. "And it is also written that anyone who tries to aid the escape of outsiders must die as well... no matter who she is."

Liliana looked stunned for a moment. Ceci turned to the Emperor and saw that even he was shaken by the words.

#

Ceci awoke in one of the most comfortable beds she had ever slept in. But where was she? She could hear whispers coming from the room next door, and then she heard giggling... a girl's giggling.

Gradually her memories returned. They'd been taken to the imperial palace, had been given an apartment in the royal quarters, had been required to stay in separate rooms... and she remembered thinking that was tragic. She was sure that a few hours alone with Esteban after the trial would have allowed her to remind him of his goals in coming here (to help La Sentencia) and their need to escape no matter what threats were leveled against them.

She heard more giggling, first a woman's and then a man's. Esteban was in the adjoining room joking with Liliana. Ceci closed her eyes and listened.

"Well, yes. I am the Emperor's daughter... so I guess you could call me a princess. But we live freely here in Cíbola. I can go anywhere I want... alone or with my friends, and I can marry whomever I choose."

"And will you rule as Empress or will your husband become Emperor?" Esteban asked.

"Our lifespan is long," she said. "My father will be with us for many more years... he'll have more children. One of my brothers or sisters will rule in my father's place when he moves on. That will allow me to do what I choose."

"And what do you choose?" asked Esteban with that drippy infatuated tone that was bringing out *the Bitch* in Ceci all over again.

Liliana responded softly. "I've been studying with the healer, what your people might call a Curandero. I'm trying to learn his craft. Did you know that much of the medicine we practice came to us from Estebanico."

"That's right," Esteban remembered. "He was a great healer."

"Yes, you need to stay here with me, help me learn his art, become part of my life, my..."

"Career?" Esteban suggested.

Ceci sighed. Just what she didn't need... something to encourage Esteban to want to stay in Cíbola forever.

Esteban said something that Ceci couldn't hear, but it certainly sounded as though Liliana liked it because there was more giggling, followed by a long silence and finally the princess said rather breathlessly, "Come... let's go out and look at the stars."

There was a scuffling in the outer room, and Ceci decided that she'd better see what was going on. She didn't trust Liliana, didn't want her making plans with Esteban out in the moonlight. So Ceci gathered up her robes and made her way into the adjoining space.

Esteban and Liliana were about to go out into the night.

"Wait," she called. "Let me come with you."

They turned. The girl frowned, but Esteban's smile seemed welcoming.

What the hell was he thinking?

Chapter 47
VL and the Kittens

That very same night, a powerful Haboob came smashing through La Sentencia. It slammed down trees all across the parking lot of Tres Flores. It ripped apart the metal sheds at the Blackmore Copper Mine. It obliterated the only remaining station of McCarwash and sandblasted the corrals, pens, and cages on the outside of the veterinary clinic.

VL had done his best to calm the camels and horses and bring in as many small animals as he possibly could. But it just wasn't enough. Mel was out of town, visiting her mother in Minneapolis, where it was much quieter and cooler than in broiling, wind-whipped Southwest Arizona.

Cursing through the whole process, VL dragged the cages into the operating rooms, turned out the lights, and headed to the shower to soak off the grime that seemed to be embedded in his face, arms, and legs.

An hour later, he was alone in his study. He looked into the computer and re-read the new article he was writing for El Milagro. It was an expose on his one time reporter-pal, Jessica Amado, and her new boss, Devlin Lucero.

VL had a thick decaf cappuccino going, one he had made himself, one he sipped with sweet satisfaction now that he was out of the wind and able to proofread his piece for maybe the twentieth time. "This ought to put those assholes in their place," he murmured to himself as he saved the draft and decided to give it one more read in the morning before sending it off to the publisher.

The record was clear. Jessica had been the hatchet woman. No matter how bad old Blackmore had been, Amado and her boss, Lucero, were worse. Things hadn't heated up until Devlin had jerked her out of that job at the junior high school and sent her to all those classes on firing people. She might have always had a bit of a sadistic streak, VL thought, but she'd come back a killer.

Jessica had engineered that massive layoff that skated around all the laws on fair employment without ever breaking one of them. She'd managed to keep Gabriel Romo, the last humanizing force at the place, and not lay him off until she didn't need him anymore. Then Lucero and Amado had summarily fired Gabe for his role in the downtown dance of hope (as VL liked to call it).

VL drained the last of his decaf cappuccino, stood to turn out the overhead and then saw car headlights heading through the raging wind and into his parking lot. Moments later he ran to the door and jerked it open letting in a maelstrom of wind and dust and the sandblasted form of Jessica Amado. She carried a big box as she pushed her way past him and into the peace of the office interior.

"Okay," she said breathlessly as she jerked off her trench coat to reveal her classic tight white blouse - black skirt uniform. "Okay, I know you hate me." She waved her hand at him dismissively. "But I also know you're a good vet, and you care about animals. So help these little guys."

VL stared at the woman he was about to roast in the next day's editorial and wondered how she dared come to him.

"Jessica, you have no business being here," he began. But she cut him off by screaming at him.

"You're the only fucking vet in town, okay? My kittens need help! They've gone catatonic on me."

VL looked in the box. The two kittens cowered in one corner.

"They're just afraid of the storm," he said.

"No, baby," Jessica answered, and she turned her big eyes to him pleadingly. "They're going to die; I know they are. Remember your Hippocratic oath or whatever the fuck it is you veterinarians take. Save them."

"I guess I could give them a sedative to calm them down," he said.

"Yes, that would be good." She said. "I'll pay you whatever you need to help them."

"I don't want your money," he answered. He wanted to throw her out and her kittens with her, and then he looked in the box, and the pitiable look of the little cats made him remember all the reasons why he had chosen to become a vet.

"Just leave them here overnight, okay? I'll give them a shot and keep an eye on them."

"Sounds good."

Jessica gathered up her things, her coat, her purse, and she made her way to the door. "Please don't be too hard on us... on Devlin and me. We're only doing what has to be done."

VL just shook his head and turned his back on her. As soon as he heard the door close, he reached into the box to grab the first cat, and it lashed out with its claws.

"Ouch!" he said as the cat stared at him in anger.

"Jesus, okay."

He turned back to the door in time to see Jessica's car swerving through the parking lot, turning and heading out onto the windswept highway.

An hour later, his damning article still unsent, VL lay dead on the floor of his operating room. His hand was swollen to twice its normal size. The cat's scratches were raised into ugly welts that still festered and hissed as though they had taken on a life of their own.

Once he was dead, the cats began to grow. Their purring turned into growls. They stepped from the box and prowled toward the door. When a blast of harsh wind blew through the nearby window, they leaped up and through it, no longer kittens or for that matter even housecats. They were now full grown panthers that slunk out into the wicked Haboob.

Chapter 48
Willem & Robin

When Liliana led Ceci and Esteban into the area where Robin and Willem Dickenson were working, they found the pair engrossed in the creation of an enormous mural. The last people to make it through the defenses of Cíbola, these two had gone on to establish themselves as successful artists in their new home, and today they were applying great swatches of color to a wall in what seemed to be a neighborhood plaza. Willem brushed on foreground tones the color of the pale desert earth while Robin was up on a large ladder just starting to add the deep blue of the Sonoran sky.

Liliana waited a few moments so that Ceci and Esteban could watch the two at work, and then she called out, "Robin! Willem!" and the two turned at once accidentally smearing paint on themselves and each other in the process.

Will was tall, thick-necked, and hairy. He looked more like a linebacker to Esteban than an artist. He wore ragged bib overalls over a thinning black t-shirt. Paint-encrusted Jesus sandals covered his feet, and his well-developed biceps and forearms bulged even with the simple act of holding a paintbrush.

Robin was short and round-faced with cropped blond hair and big eyes that sparkled when she saw the visitors. She wore bib overalls too and apparently nothing else, because the side-swell of her breasts were visible around the edges of her clothing. Her simple flip-flop sandals were somehow immaculate.

The one thing Ceci found most remarkable about the couple was that, in spite of the fact that they had arrived in Cíbola some time in the 1960s (which would have made their ages over seventy), they looked relatively young, perhaps still in their forties. Yes, people did age more slowly in Cíbola, Ceci realized.

Robin descended the ladder as Will grabbed a rag and was wiping the paint from his hands as he approached them.

"'Low," he said, his thick British accent coming through in that single word.

Robin padded up beside him and raised her hand in a friendly gesture. "Hi."

Even that sounded British.

"This is the couple that has just arrived in Cíbola," said Liliana as she gestured to Ceci and Esteban.

"Right," said Will. "So, how'd you get past the serpents then?"

Esteban laughed at the man's directness.

"These two great birds swooped down," he answered, "and carried them off."

"Amazing. Must have been thunderbirds," said Robin, her eyes growing wider than ever.

"Did they help *you* escape from the serpents?" asked Ceci.

"Nope," Will answered. "There weren't any big snakes there when we came through."

"Guess the council put them in after we made the trip," added Robin, "Probably didn't like the fact that we were able to find the place so easily."

"That's right," said Will. "See, we'd come to the states from Oxford, to do a bit of desert touring, looking at the various dwellings and works of the indigenous peoples. And the next thing we knew, we were exploring this chasm and the passageway through it, getting deeper and deeper in, until Voila... we're in Cíbola. "

"So, who do you think decided to put the serpents there after you arrived?" asked Ceci.

"Why, that warrior guy, of course," answered Will. "What's his name?"

"Coyotl," said Liliana. "But let's not talk about him. Acalon would like you to tell our guests how much you enjoy living here."

She led the group over to a shady area against the far wall and gestured for them all to sit on the ground. They did, and Ceci was amazed how easy it was after all the stretching and straining she'd experienced on their journey.

"'Living here's been just great," said Will as he leaned against the wall.

"Really great," continued Robin. "When we arrived we were taken before the council and Acalon asked us who we were and what we did.

"I said that we were students, but Will told them we were artists. He took a pad and pencil from his kit and drew a quick likeness of the Emperor right there."

"That's right," said Will. "And then he asked us if we would like to a make a painting right inside his Imperial home... so we did that too. You know, simple stuff, snowy mountains, animals running around... that sort of thing. He liked it and after that, he just turned us loose."

"The best thing about living here is that they like our paintings," said Robin. "One's hanging in the great hall. Did you see it?"

"The construction of the great pyramid?" asked Esteban.

"Yeah, that's it... the abstract one. We tried to show the spirit of the effort, the energy and all."

Ceci studied the pair for a moment. They certainly seemed happy enough, and that was encouraging. She turned to

Esteban and smiled at him, but his eyes were fixed on Liliana, who kept casting inviting glances back his way.

"I see," whispered Ceci, and she began to feel more and more anger growing inside her once again. He was infatuated that was certain, and as that feeling grew her chances of leaving Cíbola and seeing Gabe again diminished more and more.

"Do you think the council would welcome us and give us the freedom to do what we want to do?" Esteban finally asked.

"As long as you don't want to run away," said Will with a sad smile.

"We thought of doing that ourselves," added Robin. "But that Coyotl, he'd have none of it, made it clear that if we ever tried, we'd end up being boiled in oil or something."

"We don't boil people in oil," said Liliana quickly. "We're not barbarians."

"No, guess you're right," said Will. "You'd just feed us to those monster snakes."

"My advice to you," said Robin before Liliana could respond, (she was now speaking directly to Ceci) "is just make up your mind that you're going to like it here... then find yerself a handsome native guy and settle down."

She leaned forward and patted Ceci's hand suggesting indirectly that she knew that Esteban belonged to the princess.

"Okay, enough a this," said Willem suddenly jumping to his feet and making his way back to the painting. "Come on... help us get some work done here." And he reached over to a table near the mural and picked up a palette and several freshly cleaned paintbrushes.

This was the first time the newcomers had really looked at the painting, and they were amazed. The plaza where they stood was clearly intended to be a children's play area because the mural reflected that theme. The scene was layered with bright pink and purple hills beneath a baby blue sky. Across the base of the hills ranged a herd of mule deer. On an outcropping of rock that framed one foreground corner, three coyotes had gathered by a campfire. They all wore bright red bandanas and appeared to howl, bark and yip wildly. In the foreground of the painting, lizards, snakes, jackrabbits, and roadrunners watched as javelina pigs danced on their hind legs. Meanwhile, vultures and hawks circled overhead looking not like predators but as interested observers of all the fun.

"Help me add a few flowers in the foreground," said Will as Ceci approached him. He gestured to the empty lower left edge of the painting. To her surprise, Ceci found herself grabbing a palette loaded with various shades of red and black paint. Without even waiting for the others, she began dabbing black thorny branches onto the wall. It was an image not at all in keeping with the theme of the work, but she didn't care. She added red roses, but the vines were harsh and tangled; the roses were dark, violent smudges. Esteban stood back and eyed his partner's work with a look of great concern. Clearly, what she thought she was creating was a flower garden, but what she made, really, was a statement of personal rage.

He and Liliana went over to Will and selected palettes and paintbrushes of their own; the colors they chose were pastels. On the side of the canvas away from Ceci's harsh stabbings, they created a stand of cottonwood and cacti that stood in sharp contrast to Ceci's work.

With a great splat, Ceci's slapped one final misshapen rose onto the canvas, and in the process used up the last of her red paint. "I need more," she called and hurried back to Willem who started to add more shades of red onto her palette. But as he did so, Ceci turned and looked at the images Esteban and Liliana were creating: soft strands of pastel greens on pathways that entwined as though the paths themselves were in love.

Willem touched Ceci's arm and held up the palette and brushes suggesting that she should take them and add to her creation, but she turned away instead, moved back to the corner, and just sat cross-legged on the floor watching the display being created by the lovers... because at this moment, that's what they were becoming. Liliana was falling in love with Esteban and he with her. Ceci was in love with Gabe, of course.

"But it's starting to be damn clear that I'm never going to see him again," *Celia the Bitch* growled inside her.

NICK IUPPA & JOHN PESQUEIRA

Chapter 49
In Grandpa's Garage

The aftermath of the latest killer Haboob was still in evidence as Mario climbed down from the school bus, kicked his way through the mounds of debris that still littered the Tres Flores parking lot, and went around to the back of the wind-ravaged restaurant. He wanted to sneak in the back door, run up to his room, and hide his report card under his mattress. For the first time in his life he had gotten bad grades: a "Needs Improvement" mark in "Avoids Needless Talking" and "Listens Attentively." Mario was a smart kid, no doubt about it. It's just that, since Sophia arrived anyway, he had become so outgoing. He couldn't stop talking in class, telling jokes to his friends, laughing and having a good time, even when the teachers told him not to. He was just happy, right? So, why should that count against him?

Maybe, he thought, he could find Sophia and ask her to forge his mother's signature... not that she would do it even if she knew how. On the other hand, Mario knew that Sophia could do just about anything. There was something magical about her. She might help him, but first, he had to make her understand how important it was not to have any bad feelings in the house right now...about anything... even bad grades.

The little boy made his way past the old garage where Papa Luís kept his old pickup truck. As he passed the door, he heard something inside, a loud scrambling that sounded like a raccoon might have been caught in there when Papa closed the door.

Mario grinned, feeling that at last something interesting might happen on this boring, disappointing day. (Why did kids have to avoid needless talking and listen attentively anyway?)

"Hey boy," he called as he pushed back the side door to the garage and looked into the darkness… not even sure what kind of creature he was addressing. "I'll let you out."

Scrambling sounds!

"Hey, what are you? What are you doing in my grandpa's garage?"

Silence.

"Strange," whispered Mario, and he dropped his backpack outside the door and gradually moved into the narrow space between the old truck and the wall of the garage.

"Hello," he called into the darkness. In answer the door to the garage slammed shut.

Only a sliver of light from the small window on the far side of the building now lit the truck. In front of the beat-up old machine, Papa's workbench bowed down under the weight of Luís's enormous cast iron vise, a mound of nails, two handsaws, four or five hammers, an assortment of chisels, and a big, yellow, battery-powered electric screwdriver.

Mario remembered how Papa Luís had always said he needed to put the garage in order. Right now, Mario wished more than ever that he had.

"SNARL!"

Mario froze. On the other side of the workbench, just off to the left, was a big, shiny, black mound of something, half the size of a full-grown man.

Maybe it's a leather jacket slung over the old stool in the corner; Mario thought as he moved cautiously toward it. At the back of the workbench was a light switch that controlled the fluorescent overheads. If he could get to it, if he could turn it on, the lamp would brighten the whole place... chase away whatever demons were hiding there.

"SNARL!"

The scary sound came from the black shape just ahead of him. And then the form shifted somehow, and Mario could see wide yellow eyes staring back at him.

Mario backtracked, shuffled toward the door, reaching up sliding his hands over the side of the old truck as he went. He felt sweat releasing under his arms and across his forehead... everywhere really. And then there was a pounding sound in the bed of the old pickup and the head of a full-grown panther rose up in front of him. Mario turned and looked at it and, for a horrible moment, the boy and the big cat stared into each other's eyes.

Then the cat bounded down behind Mario and blocked his path to the door. Mario glanced in panic up to the front of the garage, to the workbench, to the light switch, and he saw to his horror that that black thing beside the workbench was a second panther, and it was now climbing across the work surface and then jumping smoothly onto the hood of the old truck. It stood perched there staring at him with interest.

Mario glanced backward to see (thankfully) that the other panther hadn't moved. And then the cat on the hood of the truck glided down onto the floor in front of little Mario, and the boy found himself trapped between two giant cats that now began advancing slowly toward him.

Chapter 50
The Original Goal

Ceci walked from the partially completed mural back toward the imperial palace where the Emperor had given them temporary quarters. Tears blinded her eyes. What was the point of this quest anyway, she asked herself. What was the original goal? They were supposed to discover some prize, some treasure, and bring it back to La Sentencia, sell it to raise enough money to begin the revitalization of the city. But that wasn't going to work, was it? There was no way that either she or Esteban could escape Cíbola. And, even if they could, there was no way they could steal a priceless artifact and bring it with them, even if such an artifact existed.

Ceci now entered the great plaza that surrounded the pyramids. Her eyes were drawn to the very top of the central edifice, the one with the temple atop it. The building was covered with gold... pure gold... enough to save La Sentencia certainly. But how could she cart all that gold back to her city?

She thought of Aladdin. Liliana had left their camel in the imperial stables where Ceci knew that it was being well cared for. Maybe Aladdin could carry the treasure they needed. Maybe she could go to the temple each night, chip off a little gold until she had enough to do some real good for her hometown.

No way, she realized. It was impossible.

Almost without thinking she began to trudge up the central stairway to the temple. She should, at least, check it out, see if there wasn't something there that would be valuable enough to help finance the restoration of La Sentencia.

She wore a loose fitting tunic with deep side pockets, and in one of them was the most magical thing she owned, she thought: her iPhone. She hadn't used it at all on the trip since there was almost no reception. It was probably still fully charged. If she could find a prize that would do everything she hoped it would do, if she could take a picture of it and show it to Stevie, he might actually remember his quest; he might get excited enough to decide to do what they had set out to do so many weeks ago. He might even forget Liliana and return to La Sentencia with her.

Chapter 51
More Panthers

Mario glanced at the panther that blocked his way to the door on the side of the garage. It moved toward him on silent paws that nevertheless hinted of huge claws that the little boy couldn't help but picture ripping his head off. Mario turned in the other direction and saw that the second panther, just as big as the first and emitting a threatening growl, had moved very close to him. The big cat stopped, licked its lips and almost seemed to smile at the prospects of having a plump little schoolboy for dinner.

These might be the last seconds of his short life, Mario decided, and he knew that he had to do something to save himself... but what? A block and tackle hung from a beam in the center of the ceiling. It consisted of pulleys and a heavy counterweight that, if let loose, could slam down hard and flatten one of the panthers with one horrific blow... then scare the other one off. The thought made Mario smile. The cat twisted its head in curiosity at this.

"But how would I get out of the way?" Mario wondered almost aloud. "And how would I get up there to let the tackle loose in the first place?"

The panther growled angrily, as though it understood the fledgling plan and didn't like it.

"Easy, Mr. Panther," Mario said snatching another quick look over his shoulder at the panther by the door. For some reason, the cat was frozen in place. But that was good.

"You really don't want to eat me," Mario said as he turned back to the first panther. "I had a big bean burrito for lunch, and it's the kind of thing that would make you really, really sick... make you throw up all over the place. Ewww, panther barf."

The cat growled hungrily. Apparently bean burritos were very much to its liking.

Then the cat behind Mario growled again, and the boy jerked his head backward to see that it was now baring its fangs.

Mario turned back to the cat by the workbench, and out of the corner of his eye, he spotted a bit of a blur; something or someone was climbing out of the truck bed, over the back window and onto the top of the cab.

Mario glanced back at the cat by the door. It was looking at the figure on the truck. So was the second cat. As surprising as Mario found it, he was sure they both seemed worried.

"Hey there cats!" came a cry loud enough to cause the panthers and Mario to step backward.

There, on top of the truck cab, bedecked in sparkly little tennis shoes, tights, and a pink tutu, was Sophia. She had her hands on her hips as though she thought she was Wonder Woman.

"Lucero!" she called as she pointed to the panther by the doorway, and invisible energy from her fingertips (or something like that, Mario wasn't sure exactly what) sent the big cat flipping backward. It scrambled under the truck.

"Lucero!" the little girl repeated as she swiveled and did the same trick with the panther at the front of the garage. It had the same effect. The big cat dropped down and disappeared under the truck.

"Don't just stand there, Mario," Sophia shouted, "Help me get 'em," and she bounded down onto the truck bed and then vaulted over the side and dropped to the floor of the garage. She scrambled under the truck yelling, "You can't get away from me, you ugly cats."

Mario heard wild scrambling around down there then. For the first time in months, Sophia started prattling in Italian. The cats were spitting and hissing and putting up some kind of a fight.

"Here, hold this," said the little girl as she emerged from under the truck with a dirty black kitten in one hand. "Hold it away from your body. Don't let it scratch you. I'll get the other one."

Mario held the cat by the scruff of the neck and kept it well away from his body. The cat flailed away for a moment and then finally settled and just hung there.

Sophia dove under the old truck again, scrambled around down below while the other cat hissed and spit and rumbled around. But at last, the little girl reemerged with the second cat, now a kitten, well in her grasp.

"Holy…." Began Mario.

"Don't say it," said Sophia holding up her hand against him. She was covered with grime from the undercarriage of the truck and the dirty garage floor. Jerking the cats away from Mario, she held both animals out in front of her. She was out of breath and shaking with anger.

"You tell him," she shouted at the cats, her voice quavering, and her eyes looking as though they were filling with tears. "You tell him that he can't have my friends, do you understand? He can't kill them; he can't hurt them at all, AT ALL."

Then she turned to the boy and yelled, "Open the door, Mario."

Mario ran forward and pushed the side door wide open. He ran through it and out into the windswept desert afternoon.

Sophia followed holding the wilted kittens away from her body.

"You tell your master that he's not welcome in this town either," she added. "He never was... he never will be!"

And with that, she pitched the kittens out into the rubble on the edge of the parking lot.

"You tell him to keep away from us... or else!" And then she started sobbing.

Mario walked up to the little girl and put his arm around her. He pulled her to him and smelled her sweat and the grease and grim from the truck's undercarriage.

"I think you need a bath," he said.

"Yeah," she brushed her grimy nose with the back of her hand and left a big smudge there. "Do you think you can get some clothes for me and help me sneak upstairs?" she asked. "I don't want anyone to see me like this."

Mario studied the little girl for a moment. Her eyes were fierce, the muscles on her arms and shoulders tense, and her greasy pink tutu was ridiculous.

"Do you know how to forge my mom's name on a report card?" he asked in return.

Sophia studied the boy. And then she smiled.

"Yeah, sure," she said. And they walked to the back of the restaurant together.

Chapter 52
Capturing Lightning

Ceci walked into the golden temple of Cíbola feeling as though she were entering the Parthenon in Greece. Massive columns supported a pediment that gleamed in the sunlight. Beyond the columns, a door to the inner temple stood open revealing wooden floors, gilded walls, windows that angled all the light onto a round pedestal in the center of the room. And that's where it was; Ceci realized... the artifact she and Esteban had come here to find.

She looked carefully around. No one was there, any-where... no guards, no visitors, no pilgrims, no vestal virgins or whatever the Native American equivalent of such priest-esses might be, no medicine men either.

She glided up to the pedestal and studied the object resting on it. It was silvery, shaped like a shallow bowl. It had a wide rim etched with strange runic figures, and, inside it, a helicoid pattern spiraled hypnotically into a point that tried to draw Ceci into it if she stared for more than a brief moment.

Ceci took another look around the temple. No one was in sight, and so she pulled her iPhone from her shirt picket, selected the camera app, and aimed the phone at the artifact.

Flash! The camera clicked; the iPhone grabbed an image of the object, and a hand closed around Ceci's arm. She turned and stared into the eyes of Coyotl, the warrior.

"So, you've captured a little lightening and brought it into our temple," he said with a stony expression.

"No," said Ceci. "Just taking a picture of this beautiful place, and...."

"The Helicoid."

"Helicoid?"

"Our most sacred treasure," said Coyotl. "A symbol of our covenant with the star people. May I have your light catcher, please?"

"My what?"

"You captured lightning," Coyotl said, "and with it the face of our treasure."

Ceci looked at the warrior, looked down at her iPhone and then back into his eyes. She recognized all of the dangerous possibilities whether she gave him her phone or not. Chances are he had no idea how to use it. Better to give it up and escape with her life.

"Of course," she said and handed the phone to the warrior. He smiled proudly. "Captured lightning," he murmured again, and he turned and walked away from her to study this newfound miracle.

Ceci watched him go; within minutes, the temple was once again deserted. It was just she, alone with the artifact. It would be difficult to describe to Esteban without the picture, she thought. Of course, Liliana might help.

Ceci shook her head; she didn't want to be beholden to the princess in any way. She'd have to convince Stevie to help her steal the artifact. He'd probably want to consult with Liliana about it. She would disagree; there'd be a scene. Stevie really didn't want to go home anymore, anyway, she realized. He wanted to stay here in Cíbola in spite of all his earlier talk about saving La Sentencia.

Why bother, Ceci wondered. Why bother with him... she could do it alone; she and the camel could save La Sentencia all by themselves.

Ceci turned slowly while she studied every entryway, every corner of the temple. The warrior had gone. There was no one anywhere. The place was dead silent... deserted.

She could do it!

Minutes later Ceci rushed into the Imperial stables, past corrals full of horses and up to the single pen where Aladdin was being cared for. He bellowed when he saw her.

"So, I suppose you want to stay here too," she called as she rushed up to the camel. "Well, I don't care, you're with me, and we're getting the hell out of here even if we have to take on those damn serpents again ourselves."

She grabbed the bridle and reins and began trying to put them on Aladdin. She was nervous now... terrified really, even though she was sure that she had made her way to the stables unobserved.

The camel didn't want to cooperate. He kept turning his head away, rejecting the bridle as if he had indeed decided that he wanted to stay.

"Come on, damn you," she called. "Don't you realize that I have it... what we came here for... a valuable relic that can save our city?"

She pulled The Helicoid from deep in her tunic and held it up for just a moment. The sight of it stopped the camel cold. She set it down at the edge of the corral, used both hands to put on the bridle, and then – while the camel knelt down – she added the saddle. It was an ungainly task but one she'd learned well as they had traveled through the desert.

Ceci put the artifact into one of the saddlebags. Then she jumped onto the camel and urged him out of the pen. Minutes later she had him at a full gallop just as Coyotl and his warriors came into sight far behind her. They were on horseback, moving swiftly... gaining on her. For just a moment she considered the possibility that Coyotl might have *let* her take The Helicoid... given her the chance so that she could be caught in the act. Whatever the case, it was too late now.

Ceci turned Aladdin onto the great highway that ran all across Cíbola and urged the camel on... she'd had quite a head start on Coyotl and his warriors, and the road was made for fast travel. They charged through the outskirts of the city, on past the spot where she and Esteban had first seen Liliana and her friends, to the very edge of the chasm from which she and Esteban had emerged only a few days earlier. And then she stopped. Where exactly was the entrance? She and Aladdin turned in one direction and then another, but no entrance was visible, no cleft in the rocks, nothing... and then Coyotl and his men were upon her.

The warrior seized the reins of her mount, jerked the camel forward to him, and stared at Ceci.

"Where are you going?" he asked.

"Home," she said.

"No one leaves. No one even tries to leave!" His men had caught up with him now. They took control of Ceci's mount and led the camel and his rider back toward the golden city.

#

That evening Liliana walked into the apartment in the Imperial palace that Ceci and Esteban had shared. Ceci's trial had been immediate and hopeless. Liliana was required to attend, and now she reported back to Esteban on what had occurred.

"It's no use,' she told him. "I talked to my father; I talked to Coyotl and many of the others. Nothing can be done."

"What's the charge?" Esteban asked though he had already heard. Everyone in Cíbola was talking about it.

"Trying to escape from our cities," said Liliana.

"So then we really are prisoners?" Esteban asked.

Liliana didn't like the implication of the question. "No one has ever really wanted to leave before," she said.

"But if they do… if they even try to leave?"

"Justice will be done," Liliana said, and Esteban noticed that she was trembling.

"What the hell does that mean?"

"The Star Ceremony," she answered. "The warriors take her onto a mountaintop at midnight, chain her to a great rock and offer her into the night."

Esteban shook his head. "I still don't understand."

"Her life is over."

"And then what?"

Liliana moved close to Esteban. She put her arms around him, and pulled him close. "I'm so sorry."

"They execute her?" he asked.

"I think so. I've never seen it… we're not allowed."

"Can I speak to your father?" Esteban asked.

"I already have," Liliana answered. "He's a kind man, but he tells me that there's nothing even he can do when someone steals anything, let alone something as valuable as The Helicoid."

Esteban walked across the floor and into the room where Ceci had slept. The place was as immaculate, as he knew it would be. He sat on the bed, buried his face in his hands and began to sob.

Liliana walked in beside him, sat next to him and just stared down at the floor, after a moment she turned to Esteban and asked, "What was she thinking?"

"Of our home," he answered. "She was thinking of my great grandfather and the dreams and the promises and the plans we made."

"What plans?"

Esteban smiled at the irony of it all. "Everything she did we had planned to do."

"You planned to steal from us?" Liliana's eyes pleaded for the right answer.

"To save our city, yes. We planned to steal something."

Liliana opened her arms and took Esteban into them. They sobbed together. "Oh Esteban," she said. "Oh no."

Chapter 53
Evil in the Air

"A horrible judgment has fallen on our town," said Luís Romo. He sat in the center of a long row of tables that had been pulled together so that he and his family could all be together and share an important meal.

If you ignored the row of guests sitting on the opposite side of the table and just looked at the family and friends beside Luís, it looked very much like Da Vinci's mural of The Last Supper. Luís sat in the center.

"I smell evil in the air," he continued. "It's everywhere. First came the terrible dust storms that brought sickness, death, and mysterious events. Then came incredible poverty. Family turned against family. We can only fight with our prayers and our hope. We need a miracle."

Carmen, who sat beside her husband, reached over and squeezed his forearm. There were tears in her eyes. Gabriel and his brother Ricardo sat side-by-side looking on grimly. The children, Mario and Sophia, sat across from Luís.

"That's why I've called you all here together," Luís continued, "to make a very sad announcement...."

Suddenly the door to the restaurant opened and in crept Lorena and Kenny, still teenagers, still literally part of the family, though Rich gave them an unforgiving stare. Kenny's work at the CleanSweep Carwash had made him the enemy of everyone in town. No one yet knew that Jessica had fired him that morning as La Sentencia had become so impoverished that no one was left who could afford to pay for a car wash.

Luís glowered at the couple for a moment. "Are you sure you want to come slumming with the unemployed?" he finally asked them.

"We're unemployed too," said Lorena. "Kenny was fired today."

"Serves him right," said Rich and then looked down at his place setting and began to re-arrange his knives, spoons, and forks. No one else said anything. But, after a moment, Sophia ran over to Lorena and hugged her. The two had always been close, and now Lorena pulled the little girl even closer.

"As I was saying," Luís continued, "I have a very sad announcement to make. Tres Flores must shut its doors. We can't afford to stock food any longer; we can't afford the electrical bills or the water. We can't afford to pay anyone." His words were interrupted by a sudden sob from Carmen, who was able to express what all of them were feeling.

"I'd be happy to work for free," said Kenny, suddenly. Everyone turned to him in surprise. "So would I," said Lorena.

"Me too." It was Rich who looked up with resolve. Then, one by one, the others around the table joined in.

"That's very kind of you," answered Luís now sadder than ever. "But we have no money. We can't afford to buy the ingredients we need to prepare our food."

Gabe suddenly spoke up. "I have a little money saved," he said. "I could contribute."

"So could we," added Lorena as she cast a quick glance at Kenny, "We have savings."

"It's the least we can do," Kenny added. And when he did, Lorena leaned over and kissed him.

Again there was silence. Tears now began to stream down Luís's face. "I'm so sorry," he began. "But it won't work. You could all put your money into our restaurant, but what good will it do. No one in our town can afford to come here and pay for their meals."

There was a very long silence then. Rich rearranged his forks and spoons once again and almost tipped over a glass of water in the process. Gabe caught it, righted it, and patted his cousin on the back. Then he smiled.

"So we'll give the food away," he said, "What if we became like a mission... feeding the hungry people of La Sentencia."

"But what good will it do?" asked Luís, and he shook his head. "The town is dying. What happens when the money runs out?" And he sat down as they all lowered their heads.

"I have hope," Sophia whispered to Mario. "I think something good will happen to us."

The crowd had become so silent that everyone heard her words. The little girl looked up and blushed.

"I have hope too," said Mario more loudly.

"So do I," said Rich. "We can be a mission; we can feed anyone in La Sentencia who can't afford food."

"Until the town gets back on its feet again," said Luís.

"We can get Father Riley down here every evening to say mass," said Vanessa. "And we can follow it with a big dinner, free for anyone who will come."

"I'll work out the meal plans... I'll make it work," said Gabe.

At this point, everyone started talking at once. The tone, which had once been so glum, was now enthusiastic and cheerful. Meanwhile, Mario snuck over to the Jukebox and pushed in a few numbers. He watched as the machine's mechanism moved the record into place, and then the song began.

"LOVE IS HERE AND IS THE WAY..."
The voice of the jukebox sang.
"TIME HAS TAUGHT US EVERY DAY ..."

One by one the attendees stopped talking and turned to the glittering machine.

"OPEN MINDS CAN FEEL ITS FLOW....
"FEEL IT GROW, YES, FEEL – IT – GROW!!"

"LOVE IS HERE JUST FEEL IT," Mama Carmen sang to her husband as the words now blasted from the jukebox.

"LOVE IS HERE JUST FEEL IT," Luís sang back to her.

"LOVE IS HERE JUST FEEL IT... JUST FEEL IT," Lorena and Kenny sang to each other.

"FEEL THE LOVE THAT'S HERE," sang little Sophia as she ran up to Mario and hugged him.

The little boy pulled away from her and raced to the back of the machine. He turned up the volume so that the words of the song blasted out across the restaurant and out onto the highway.

Kenny and Lorena burst from the building and began dancing in the parking lot.

LOVE IS HERE JUST FEEL IT!

Cars roaring by on the road stopped and pulled into the lot. Occupants jumped from their vehicles and started to dance. More and more people came. Songs sang out across the evening sky. Soon there were dozens, then nearly a hundred dancers, not even sure why they were dancing, or what they were doing, except they could see hope in the faces of the Romo family. There was Gabe, who had done so much to fight for the rights of the mineworkers. Hope was shining in his eyes and in the eyes of Kenny McLaughlin, who so many people in the town had hated. But there was no hate vibrating from those around him now. That gave Kenny and Lorena new hope.

More and more people pulled into the parking lot, got out, and began dancing. Some, having heard the music from a distance, had hopped into their cars and sped over to Tres Flores drawn by the music and the dancing... and the HOPE.

When Father Riley finally got to Tres Flores to find out what as going on, Luís pulled the priest aside and asked him, "Can you say mass in our parking lot every evening next week, Father?"

The old man seemed to know exactly what Luís was talking about and why.

"You want to say prayers and then serve dinner to those who come, my son?"

Luís smiled. He hadn't been called anything like Son, in dozens of years, but why not?

"Exactly, Father," Luís said. "People will come, eat, and pray for hope."

The priest smiled. "Of course, Luís," said Father Riley, "of course."

Chapter 54
At the Mountain Top

That very night, the night of Ceci's crime against the people of Cíbola, Liliana led Esteban along unknown passageways, up hidden staircases, across windswept fields to a great jumble of rocks on a mountainside that looked out over a broad meadow. A great stone slab jutted up from the center of the open area that now sparkled blue-silver in the moonlight.

Liliana had never met anyone like Esteban. It wasn't just his unusual features, or the fact that he was so clever and intelligent. She herself was as intelligent as anyone she knew, had no trouble keeping up with any conversation or any idea that the tribal council discussed.

Yet, Esteban was more than intelligent; he was fastidious, organized, qualities she admired. And with all that came a sense of humor, a playfulness that made her fall in love with him. In the short time she had known him, her life had been so much more fun, so much more enjoyable than it had ever been before. She didn't want to let that go... didn't want to go back to what could only be seen as a very routine life, even here in these Golden Cities of Cíbola.

So now the princess decided that she would risk almost anything for her new love... almost, but not try to save the life of his companion. That was utterly impossible.

317

When her father, the Emperor, said that he could not stay the execution, Liliana had offered Esteban the only thing she could... the privilege of being present at Ceci's passing, witnessing it all... if only from afar.

Now, minutes away from that dreaded event, Liliana and Esteban rested atop the great jumble of rocks and watched as her father and the elders made their way across the silvery meadow. Thunderheads gathered in the sky above them. Lightning crackled within the menacing clouds.

Esteban had brought his binoculars and now he used them to focus on the council. All were grim-faced. The Emperor looked sorrowful, as though he didn't want to be there, didn't want to participate in this horrific but necessary act. Still his jaw was set. The Emperor would do what had to be done.

Beside the Emperor, Coyotl, the warrior, looked almost gleeful. He was getting what he wanted, the execution of a woman who tried to steal an ancient artifact and run away with it. She must be made an example of so that her fate could be cited for others who came after her. Was there more to his delight in Ceci's execution, Esteban wondered. Is that why the warrior smiled?

Beside the warrior, the other council members looked deliberate but also rather miserable. There had not been an execution within their lifetimes. They really wanted no part of it. And yet here they were.

The wind kicked up. Four young warriors, naked except for their loincloths, now made their way through the meadow leading Aladdin by the reins. The beast followed obediently... so did Ceci. Esteban could see her now, chains on each arm, being led by much older more experienced warriors. They were prepared to execute a beautiful young woman though each of them hated themselves for agreeing to play a role in such an event, and hated Ceci for making it necessary that they do it.

He saw Ceci turning, peering across the distance toward him. He could read her expression, terrified, barely able to move and yet hoping against hope that someone would come at the last moment and save her.

Esteban stood. He wasn't sure, but he thought Ceci could see him in the distance; she was looking right at him. She suddenly gave a hopeful smile. Her guards saw, followed her gaze, and motioned to Coyotl who came forward and peered directly at Esteban.

Through the binoculars Esteban could tell that Coyotl might not be able to recognize him, but still, he gestured to other guards standing on the periphery, pointed at Esteban's position, apparently asking them if they too saw any would-be rescuers. The group stared for a long moment, then shaking their heads they turned away, turned back to Ceci who now began to struggle desperately.

"I have to save her," Esteban said as he turned toward Liliana.

"If we go down there, we'll be captured and sacrificed along with your friend," Liliana said. "And look at what it will take to get there."

Esteban now turned his attention to the distance between their position and the place of execution. There was a mountainous ridge between them. A short, narrow path cut through the ridge, but the path led up along a high, dangerous cliff and ended at a bridge that looked like most of it had rotted and fallen away. The drop was immense, the path no wider than a footstep. Esteban swallowed a moment of harsh panic, remembering for a second the dream he had at the mission: a narrow passage, a rickety bridge, Ceci chained to a massive rock, fears of falling, and then he thought of his vertigo as a young boy on the edge of the Grand Canyon.

"We have to try," Esteban screamed and bounded away from the princess. She dove at him, caught him by the legs, threw him to the ground, climbed onto his back, and rolled him over. Esteban reached up to throw her off, but Liliana slapped him hard across his face.

"We can't go anywhere," she insisted. "Now... I can hold you here and you won't see anything, or you can give in and watch the events unfold."

Esteban tried to sit up. She pushed him down. He struggled to escape. Liliana was too strong. And so he just gave up, stopped fighting, and felt so inadequate and helpless.

Now thunderheads rolled across the mountaintop. Bolt after lightning bolt crackled down onto the meadow offering a horrific light show. The guards led Ceci to the great rock slab; others brought Aladdin and anchored the camel beside her.

One of the men bound Ceci's hands into the bridle of the camel. Then they chained her arms to great hooks mounted into the slab. She looked on uncertainly... not knowing what would happen next. But she was oh so terrified. She kept glancing back in Esteban's direction with a look of fading hope. Still, she said nothing as the wind grew violent and the others hurried away, leaving Ceci and Aladdin standing there chained to the slab that was now besieged by wind and bombarded with lightning.

"NO!" cried Esteban, and he got to his feet and bolted down from amid the boulders and ran as fast as he could toward the execution site.

Liliana called to him. But it was no use. He plunged into the chasm running full out along a path so narrow that there was barely enough room for each footfall. His speed propelled him. There was no time to sway or to fall.

He got to the bridge. The whole center portion of it had fallen away. The other boards were rotting, and the entire structure was twisting and curling in the high wind. Esteban bounded far across the bridge in one long stride and landed on a slat that gave way at once. He fell, caught the rope sides of the bridge in each hand and vaulted upward, landing at last on perhaps the only slat that was intact. He lunged forward, dove across the bridge, hit the other side on his belly, jumped to his feet, and raced out of the canyon, to the top of another rise ready to charge into the meadow that separated him from Ceci. But, just as he did, lightning crackled across the face of the execution site. Monster clouds swept in and swallowed it up. Yet somehow he saw Ceci's long black hair blown wildly in the swirling madness of the storm, her figure standing upright and strong against it. And suddenly a great metallic disk appeared to hover amid the turbulent, lightning-infested clouds. It and Aladdin and Ceci, in fact, the whole rock slab to which she was chained, everything was electrified with a sudden blinding flash. The storm clouds screamed and sizzled, building in a great crescendo to a sky-splitting explosion!

And then everything was hidden in blackness.

Moments later, the storm clouds seemed to pull back on themselves. The lightening bolts drew away. The disk had vanished without a sound. But so had Ceci and the camel.

They were gone.

Chapter 55
Lucero's Last Day

Back in La Sentencia, Jessica Amado was preparing to leave her office for the evening. There were only two employees left at the CleanSweep Mining Company now... she and Devlin Lucero. Lucero had fired Donny Hainer and Kenny McLaughlin earlier that week.

Jessica was surprised to see that Lucero's office was now filled with banker boxes. They were the containers that executives often use when preparing to move on to another position or even another company.

"What's this all about?" asked Jessica as she walked up to Lucero, who was busy pulling books down from a high bookcase and shuffling them into the box on his desktop.

"My work's done here, don't you think?" he said turning toward Jessica.

"But I thought we'd be able to sit back and enjoy what we've accomplished... for a little while at least."

Lucero gave his protégée a rye smile. "And just what have we accomplished, Ms. Amado?"

Jessica twisted her face into a thoughtful but somewhat confused expression, and then she lowered her eyes. She didn't know quite what to say... they hadn't really accomplished anything, had they? All they'd really done was tear things apart.

"So where are you going," she asked him at last, "back to work for Blackmore?"

"YES… He's got something new lined up for me."

"In Texas?"

"Saudi Arabia."

Lucero moved around in front of his desk, lifted the carton of books, carried it out to the large stack of boxes that was sitting outside his door, and added it to the stack. Then he turned back to the office. There was only one box left. It was on the floor in the corner; the rest of the large room had been stripped of every book, every sheet of paper, every pen, pencil, stapler, and all the pictures that had been hanging on the walls.

Jessica tottered over to the box in the corner and peered down into it. Her kittens were there. They looked as sweet and cuddly as ever. She picked one up and pressed it to her cheek. The kitten gave a cute meow, but for some reason, the touch sent a surge of fear through her.

"What's going to happen to me?" she asked suddenly.

"What do you mean?"

"When the mine closes, where will I go?"

"You've certainly made enough money here to retire for a while," said Lucero, "and you have a brand new car."

"Will I be able to keep it?"

"Don't see why not." Lucero's smile was hollow and frightening.

Jessica dropped the kitten back into the box and stood very tall. She reached down, took the hem of her un-tucked white blouse, and yanked down on it, pulling the top tight against her curvy figure. Then she walked over to Lucero.

"I'm sure I could help you in your new position, Devlin," she said. "Don't you think so?"

Lucero looked at the sexy young woman. He put his arms around her and pulled her to him. He kissed her greedily, and she used every moment of that kiss to remind him what a good partner she had been.

"Want to come to Saudi Arabia with me?" he asked with a smirk.

"Is there a role for me?"

"There's always a role for a woman of your obvious talents, Ms. Amado."

"I'd like that," she said.

"Great." Lucero smiled. And his expression did not even waver when he added. "One last thing."

"Sure."

"Would you go into the office and bring that box out here."

Jessica nodded breathlessly. She turned and ran into the room, picked up the kittens and their box. Suddenly, the cats seemed bigger than they had only a few minutes earlier, she thought. She turned back to the door.

That's when she saw it closing on her and heard Lucero slam home a deadbolt on the outside.

She was locked in.

Chapter 56
Power Failure

Ceci Moreno's eyes popped open. She was staring into an overwhelmingly bright light. (At the end of a long tunnel?)

"Is this heaven?" she asked not at all sure where she was or how she had gotten there. It was almost as though every thought, every event from the last week had been erased from her memory.

She turned her head to the side then and saw familiar creosote bushes, cacti, and mountains.

"This isn't heaven," she murmured. "It's Arizona."

Ceci felt a little weak; still she staggered to her feet and looked around. There, not too far from where she stood, Aladdin the camel lay resting, looking none the worse for the ordeal that had brought them there… whatever it was.

Ceci's brow furrowed. Could she remember anything, where she had been, how long she'd been gone? No, nothing.

Ceci began walking toward the camel, and as she did she spotted something else, something that lay just beyond Aladdin, some object that looked like it came from an archeological dig. . It was a silvery object shaped like a shallow bowl. It had a wide rim etched with strange runic figures, and inside it, a helicoid pattern spiraled hypnotically to a central point.

Sparks of electricity crackled around its edges. Ceci reached forward to touch it and then jerked her hand away as the sparks shot up her arm and she felt a shock.

Aladdin bellowed softly, and Ceci looked at the animal, then back at the artifact. Somehow, in some trace memory from earlier, she thought she had a memory of it… but from where?

Ceci trudged over to Aladdin, who was still wearing his saddlebags. She reached into the bag and took out her old sleeping bag that she somehow knew would be there. She went to the artifact, wrapped the sleeping bag around it and smothered the crackling arcs of electricity.

"Okay now," she said as she lifted the artifact (The Helicoid) and found it to be surprisingly light, "Let's go home, Aladdin," she said, and she suddenly realized that she knew exactly where home was from where she stood. Then another image came to her, a tall, handsome man who had been in love with her for a very long time, loved her in spite of everything, loved her still, she was certain of it: Gabe.

Ceci climbed onto the camel, gave his flanks a little kick and felt him rise under her. She didn't even touch the reins; she just let the camel go where it wanted to; at this point, everything seemed preordained.

#

At Tres Flores, the glow of the jukebox stood against the oncoming darkness. People were already gathering outside the little restaurant, sampling the food that the restaurant had put out for anyone who wanted it. But mostly they had come to dance; a dance of prayer Father Riley had called it.

As the night grew darker more and more people would come. They would eat, drink, and dance for hope and for the recovery of La Sentencia. The jukebox blasted out one hopeful tune after another, and the later it got, the heavier the beat, the wilder the dancing.

Luís gave a squeeze to Carmen and whispered to her, "Are you having fun yet?"

"Oh, yes," Carmen answered with a blushing smile. "Lotsa fun."

"Me too," he said, and then he went behind the bar and flipped on the lights that would illuminate the outdoor parking lot and the restaurant interior.

No lights came on.

Luís flipped the switch several more times, up and down. No light.

"Gabe," he called to his nephew who was carrying a tray of taquitos out to the dancers, "No light."

"I'll check the breakers," Gabe said as he passed the tray to Carmen. "Take it out for me, please," he said.

Gabe went around to the back of the restaurant and pulled the cover off the electrical box. He studied the panel of breakers. He shrugged and flipped them all off and on again. No light.

He moved over to the generator that Luís used to power the restaurant and parking lot during emergencies. He started it up and waited. No light.

By this time Luís and Mario had joined him, looking on curiously, wondering why they had no source of electrical power no matter what they did.

No lights anywhere," Mario said as he scanned the horizon and saw that no homes in any of the nearby neighborhoods had any light either.

Darkness began to press down upon them then. In fact, the only source of light from anywhere came from Mario's jukebox. The glowing machine continued to play loudly and to flash its kaleidoscope of colors out across the evening.

"Guess we could roll it outside," said Gabe.

"The power cord won't reach," answered Luís.

"Doesn't matter, though does it... seems to be generating its own power."

Gabe went into the restaurant, unplugged the jukebox, rolled it across the floor, and out the front door. The box never stopped playing, never stopped inspiring the dancers to call down hope from the heavens.

Cars that roared along the highway still had interior lights, still had headlights, weren't in any real danger. But the drivers did notice a dimming of their lights as they passed Tres Flores, where perhaps as many as a hundred people now danced to the heavy beat.

Gabe was once again carrying trays of food from the kitchen to the tables in front of the restaurant, dumping great tins full of refried beans and rice and chunks of shredded chicken into pots that were warmed with burners below them. As he scraped out the last remnants of a giant tray of guacamole, he happened to glance to his left, across the horizon, and saw a dark shape moving toward the restaurant. It was unmistakable, though, the silhouette of a rider on a camel.

As the rider moved through the neighborhoods the houses it passed became illuminated, as though they were lighting up in celebration of some long expected return. Slowly, gradually, one home after another brightened as the rider passed and then they stayed lit after the passing. When the rider reached Tres Flores, all the lights in the restaurant, all the lights in the parking lot, streetlights out on the highway, lights everywhere came on.

It was in this illumination that Gabe recognized the sweet face of Ceci Moreno. She was up on the camel, holding something that was wrapped in an old worn out sleeping bag, and her eyes were fixed on his.

"Cess," he said as he ran to his girl, grabbed the reins of the camel and led it out into the parking lot. The dancers stopped immediately and formed a circle around her.

Ceci got down, looked at Gabe for a moment, then turned to the closest person to her, handed him the quilt and its contents, and then threw her arms around Gabe.

"I've missed you so," she sighed.

Gabe hugged her back.

"God, where have you been, Cess?" he said as he looked at her and saw the strain and sorrow in her eyes.

"I don't know." Ceci's forehead creased as she tried to form a picture of the events of the last months. "Maybe in a few days, I'll be able to remember some of it... something."

"But what happened to Esteban?"

Ceci's expression was blank. "I can't remember very much," she said. "I think he's okay, though. I think he's happy."

"Whoa," called Mario, the person to whom Ceci had handed the artifact. "Look at this thing."

"What is it?" asked Gabe as he took Ceci by the hand and led her to the little boy.

"I don't know," Mario answered.

"It runs things," said Sophia who now walked through the crowd and up to Mario. Her eyes were fixed on the artifact. "It's The Helicoid... it makes electricity."

"How do you know that," asked Gabe.

"My father and mother spent their lives looking for it," she said. "It's only given to civilizations who are ready for it... who can use it without becoming too greedy."

"Given?" asked Gabe.

"Given," Sophia answered, "that's what my father always said." The little girl's expression moved into sadness for a long moment, tears formed in her eyes, then she shook her head, reached up, and tugged Mario by the arm.

"Come on," she said to him. "I want to dance."

Mario shrugged, handed the artifact to Gabe, and followed the little girl out into the parking lot where the people of La Sentencia had begun to dance once again.

THE END

Available NOW
The Carlos Mann Trilogy

Love, Obsession, Murder, Mexico, Mannequins,
Rattlesnakes, Drug Lords, Chinatown, Ghosts...
And the World's Most Haunting Heroine

Book One
Alicia's Ghost

The astoundingly beautiful Alicia has ended her modeling career in Mexico City, married the love of her life, helped pay his way through college, settled into a comfortable existence in Los Altos California, and now she's dead... MURDERED. Her husband, Professor Carlos Mann, has wrapped himself in an obsessive-compulsive disorder to hide from that fact. But when Amy Joy, one of Carlos's students, is sold into slavery by a Chinese mob that traffics in Asian girls, Alicia returns with a vengeance.

Can Alicia save her man, foil the human traffickers, and destroy her murderer? Overwhelming supernatural forces stand against her. But that just makes her stronger!

Told in the voices of Carlos and Alicia Mann, Alicia's Ghost is a funny, imaginative and thrilling ride through the human and spirit worlds of Mexico and the American Southwest.

Read on for a preview of the adventures of Carlos and Alicia.

Chapter 1
Carlos Mann

Alicia and I are walking along the beach in San Lucero, Mexico. Endless sand, endless condos, endless kids running up to us trying to sell toys and tacos and woodcarvings of turtles and starfish.

Alicia is wearing a bikini so skimpy I'm embarrassed. I'm also proud and excited. She looks lovingly at me, blessing me with the brightness of her smile and those eyes that won't stop sparkling.

Two old women approach us from the other direction. They are dressed in flowing summer wraps. They hobble through the wet sand and stare at us in disapproval. Alicia is hanging on me, kissing me, and giggling. One arm is around my neck; she's bending forward. Her breasts struggle to jump out of her bikini. Her legs step across mine as though we're dancing.

To the old women we're naughty children. And sometimes Alicia looks like she's about fifteen. To me, she's the little girl I grew up with, my best bud, my lover, and my fiancée. She's actually making it possible for me to attend graduate school at Leland University in the United States.

She flashes her engagement ring at the old women, but they still sneer and call her "Puta!"

334

She sticks her tongue out at them and crosses her eyes. Then she missteps, trips over my legs, and falls pulling me down on top of her. She rolls us both over and straddles me. The old women are disgusted. They snap their heads in the other direction and struggle on up the beach toward a bright orange taqueria whose canopy promises margaritas and shade from the Mexican sun.

"Take me with you tomorrow, mi amor," Alicia says, "… to the University. Take me."

I smile. I can't say no. But I have to.

"We're just not ready to move to the United States together." I say.

She scrunches up her face like a spoiled five-year-old.

"You know I'll send for you as soon as I have things set up."

"That won't be soon enough," she sighs. Suddenly her voice starts fading, becoming very distant.

"It's just a few months away."

"NO!" She sounds desperate.

"Why?" I ask.

"BECAUSE I'M ALREADY *DEAD!*"

Gashes suddenly cut across Alicia's chest and arms; a deep wound opens on her throat. Her legs are shredded. She rolls from me … a wretched corpse!

"Alicia!" I jump to my feet and go to her, looking down at her in the sand. Her hand reaches up to me as blood pours down her arm. It fills her eyes, pools in her hair, spills over her lips. "Mi amor!" Her words are little more than a whisper.

The sand now fades into the soft carpet of our apartment in Los Altos, California. But Alicia is still dead, more dead *here* because this is where I found her, the way I found her, slashed and murdered.

"I love you," she moans as her image begins to fade. "I will always love you. Love me forever."

I jump bolt upright in bed, awakening from another terrible dream. My t-shirt is soaked front and back. The sheets are dripping with perspiration. The pillows look like a swamp. But the ghostly moans still ring in the air: "Love me forever."

I turn to Alicia's side of the bed. No one is there. No one has been there for three years. Alicia is really dead, really murdered. But I've been true to her. I still love her.

Too bad she doesn't believe me.

http://www.amazon.com/Alicias-Ghost-Nick-Iuppa-ebook/dp/B00CU4RZMK?ie=UTF8&keywords=alicia%27s%20ghost&qid=1462126136&ref_=sr_1_1&sr=8-1

About the Authors

Nick Iuppa began his career as an apprentice writer with famed Bugs Bunny/Road Runner animator Chuck Jones and children's author Dr. Seuss. He later became a staff writer for the Wonderful World of Disney. *As VP Creative Director for Paramount Pictures, Nick did experimental work in interactive television and story-based simulations. He is the author of* seven novels, Management by Guilt *(Fawcett Books 1984—a Fortune Book Club selection) and eight technical books on interactive media. He lives in Northern California with his wife, Ginny. For more about Nick, visit www.nickiuppa.com.*

John P. Pesqueira's studies at the University of Arizona, Columbia, and Stanford prepared him for an impressive career in media design and development. His passion for the visual arts and popular culture continue to inform his creative efforts and still inspire his writing and photography. John grew up in the Sonoran desert and his love of the history, legends, and people of the American Southwest and Mexico remain a major focus of his work. John lives with his wife in Northern California.

Proof

Made in the USA
Charleston, SC
19 August 2016